# PROSPERA PASS

## PHOENIX SERIES | BOOK 3

## KIMBERLY PACKARD

abalos
publishing

Abalos Publishing
P.O. Box 333
Colleyville, TX  76034

Book cover designed by okay creations.
Edited by C.A. Szarek
The text in this book is set in Baskerville.
Library of Congress Cataloging-in-Publication Data
Available Upon Request

ISBN-13 Print: 978-0-9992015-5-8

ISBN-13 Ebook: 978-0-9992015-4-1

*For Colby*
*There's no one I'd rather be on this journey with than you.*

# ALSO BY KIMBERLY PACKARD

# 1

The exhale of her door opening jolted Amanda awake. The Mexican desert faded in her mind, taking David and Josh with it.

Cruel reality confronted her with white-washed walls, air conditioning and the constant beep of a machine that told her, unfortunately, she was still alive.

The slow click of heels announced her guest. Doctors and nurses rushed in with short steps, the sound of their footfalls smothered by sneakers. Father Joaquin's steps were always deliberate, always steady and, most days, welcomed.

"*Mija*, are you sleeping?" He dragged the chair across the linoleum.

"If I was, I'm not now." She pushed herself upright, wincing as an ache sliced through her hips. That happened when Amanda daydreamed about *before*. She'd forget about the rock tumbler of a river that'd fractured her pelvis and left her with a splotchy scar kissing her temple.

The priest laughed as he folded himself into the chair. "I spoke with the doctor. He's happy with your progress. Mostly..."

"Well, tell him I'm sorry I'm not quite ready to do the splits."

She shifted in her hospital bed. The *'mostly'* was what the doctors couldn't see happening in her mind. "What's in there?" She gestured toward the plastic bag sitting between his feet.

"They say some senses bring you back to a memory. A whiff of salty air can remind you of a family vacation. Or, car exhaust can take you back to living in a big city."

"Do you have jars of smog in there?" Amanda swallowed an apology, hoping it would pick up the bitterness that coated her every word on the way down.

He chuckled. "I think when we find out who you are, we'll discover you're a famous comedian." Joaquin brought the bag up to his lap. "*Fresca o chocolate?*" Condensation clung to the side of the ice cream containers.

One side of her mouth quirked up. During one of his first visits, he'd asked if there was anything he could do for her. The words *'ice cream'* had tumbled from her mouth and he'd been sneaking it in ever since. Although, Amanda suspected it was with the doctor's blessing.

"Chocolate, although I doubt that'll bring up any useful memories."

He pulled the lid off the pint and passed it to her. "Oh no," he said, digging through the bag for a moment before producing two wooden spoons along with a book of baby names. "That's just a snack for us. This, *mija,* is what I'm hoping will help."

She shoved a large spoonful of ice cream into her mouth. The cold headache punished her at once, squeezing her brain in a vise that promised a migraine if she didn't slow down. At least she'd had that grimace to hide what was truly going through her mind.

How long could she keep up the charade of amnesia?

"What's a priest doing with a baby name book?" The ice cream rendered her tongue cold and heavy, the words came out in a lisp.

"Oh, the great lengths we go to for our flock." Joaquin sighed as he cracked the spine. "I ordered it online a few days ago."

"So, how's this supposed to work?" Amanda stabbed the frozen dessert with her spoon rather than look at the man. Growing up Catholic, she was at a serious disadvantage when it came to lying to priests. "You say my name, and I wait for the trumpets and angels singing?"

"Yes, definitely a comedian. Maybe it'll be that obvious, or maybe it will be more subtle, the desire to tilt your head toward me, or a pull in your heart." He licked his fingers and thumbed through the pages. "Or, maybe this is a huge waste of time and you'll feel nothing. In which case, you got a visitor and some free ice cream. Let's start at the beginning. Abigail." He glanced over the top of the book. "Abra, Ada, Adalyn, Adelaide, Adele…"

His accent, mixed with the melodic cadence of names, lulled her to the valley between consciousness and a dream. Amanda had spent most of her days here, visiting the time in the desert, back when David and Josh were still alive.

Back when *she* was still alive in some sense.

"Adrianna, Adrienne, Agatha, Aggie…"

Faking amnesia had been an impulse lie. Not one she'd crafted and molded. Not like the falsehoods that'd spewed from Josh's mouth.

Lies so well-nurtured they thrived on more than the truth. Hers was a baby fib, born of the child-like need to stick her fingers in her ears and *la-la-la* everything they said to her.

Ranchers had found her caked in mud and bleeding. She'd stirred, so they'd known she was alive, but when they'd tried to move her, she'd passed out from the pain. Amanda honestly didn't remember any of it; that was what Father Joaquin had told her on his first visit.

"Agnes, Ainsley, Aja, Alaina…"

When she'd finally woken up, the little Mexican hospital had hummed with jubilation. During her slumber, she'd managed to become the underdog, the long shot horse everyone had bet on. Somehow, she'd pulled ahead and crossed the finish line into consciousness. What was her prize?

"Alecia, Aletha, Alexa, Alexandra…"

Time lost all meaning.

It didn't matter if it'd been three weeks or three months. Day after day was the same. Doctors and nurses came in, speaking to her

3

in a language she barely understood. Staring at her with mournful eyes. Amanda could never tell if they were sad she was hurt or sad she was alive.

"Alexis, Alison, Alisha, Alissa…"

It was only when Father Joaquin had shown up she'd fully understood her situation. They knew she was American, but her injuries were so severe, they couldn't send her home. Not that she could tell them *where* home was. No ID, mixed with claiming no memory of who she was or where she came from, meant she'd stay with them until it was time for discharge or she got her memory back.

Why would she want her memory back? It was filled with nothing but loss, betrayal and heartbreak. Sure, Amanda had plenty of happy memories, but those were tucked so far away they were practically out of reach.

"Allegra, Ally, Alora, Amalie…"

The closer the priest got to her name, the more she wanted to take her broken body and run.

Her legs twitched, remembering her evening runs.

*Will I ever be able to run again?*

The ice cream churned in her stomach. A ringing in her ears grew louder, as if attempting to drown out the word that was coming.

"Amanda." He paused for a bite of ice cream.

Her name hung in the air. It floated over her, looking for a place it could sink in.

Did she hear the trumpets? Were the angels singing?

Instead, a cold numbness chilled her through the thin hospital gown and scratchy blankets. It felt different than the other names he'd said. As if she was standing in a bedroom full of pink lace, rainbows and kittens while she wore a nose ring, mohawk and thick black eye makeup. The name was hers, but it didn't belong to her.

"Azabeth, Azul, Azure." He closed the book and held it in his lap.

Her new friend studied her, but she fought to avoid his stare.

Was he looking for any changes in her posture? Checking her face for tears?

Amanda scraped the bottom of her ice cream container before bringing it to her mouth and slurping the last of the chocolate from inside. Good manners be damned, it gave her a reason to avoid eye contact.

"So, that's the *A's*," Joaquin said. "Anything, *mija?*"

She shrugged. "The angels and trumpeters were silent." Were they going to go through the entire alphabet of names? What would happen the day he started on the M's? Would her heart shatter when he said Mandy?

Would the name David called her be too much to cover up?

He bent toward her, resting his elbows on his knees and reached for her hand. His thumb gently caressed the tape holding down the needle poking into her skin. It was a much more intimate gesture than a priest should allow. "How are you? I mean really, no comebacks, no, what do you call it, snark."

On most days she existed, a living being that breathed. On other days, Amanda felt only physical agony, something she'd built her tolerance to and didn't need to hit the button for pain meds.

It was on those rare days when the emotional hurt was so all-encompassing and everything was clouded black she'd allowed herself to waft into a blissful, drug-filled haze.

"Do you believe in Purgatory, Father?"

"Some in the Church do."

Amanda glanced at him from the corner of her eye. "I'm there, and I should fight to pull myself up, toward Heaven, but really at this point, I just want to let go and fall."

Joaquin squeezed her hand, firm enough to show disdain at her answer, but not so much to hurt. "If God thought you were done on Earth, you would've died in that river. But you didn't. I might not know what you are called, *mija*, but I know *you*. You're a fighter, a survivor. You're here for a higher calling."

"Please don't give me the *'part of His plan'* speech." Her words fought against the growing lump in her throat. She wasn't ready to cry, not in front of Father Joaquin when an accidental confession would be picked up in the debris of tears.

He grinned, transforming his face from serious-handsome to relaxed, charismatic-attractive. How many *señoritas* had cried when he'd gone to the Seminary?

"His plan was never to cause you hurt. Maybe to truly find your calling you have to shed your former life."

*Like a snake shedding its skin.*

He stood and planted a kiss on top of her head. "Rest up, *mija*. I'll be back soon and we'll start on the B's. We've got a lot of names to cover."

She kept her eyes focused on the opposite wall. After the door snapped shut and his footsteps receded, Amanda allowed herself a deep gasping breath, as if surfacing from a long dive.

# 2

The baby-soft pink gave way to gray-blue as the sun rose. Throughout the day, the blue deepened until it ripened to bountiful orange, ready to burst as the sun set.

Amanda marveled at the sky's changing colors. What did the world outside her window look like without David? The Earth seemed to continue its rotation, despite the fact she wanted to get off the ride.

Father Joaquin's whistling bounced down the hallway before he opened the door. Perspiration dotted his forehead and he pulled at his collar.

"*Buenos dias, mija,*" he said. "I wished I'd picked a cooler day for this, but I didn't think you'd mind."

Several questions perched on her lips, all fighting to go first. Were they discharging her? Sending her home? Kicking her out? "What?"

"You need to start walking, to regain your strength."

"Oh no, I'm not walking around in a gown that's little more than medical-grade lingerie." It was more than modesty. Amanda hadn't left the hospital room since she'd woken up.

Joaquin held up a shopping bag he'd had hidden behind him. "I guessed your size." He put the bag on the bed and pulled out a pair of charcoal-colored sweatpants, a long, boxy T-shirt and a pair of sneakers that were, to her surprise, pretty close to her size.

*Not bad for a man sworn to celibacy.*

"Do you want me to ask a nurse to help you dress?"

Dressing herself.

Something kids fought for the freedom to do now frightened her. A middle of the night stumble on the way to the bathroom had caused agony so intense Amanda had passed out on the floor. Ever since then, the nurses hovered with hummingbird intensity.

"No, I can do it," she said. "But I might need a little help with the shoes. That bending over thing."

"Of course. I'll be right outside the door. Just call if you need anything."

Once alone, she swung her legs to the side. A dingy mirror stared back. She tried to avoid the reflection. While she was unconscious, they'd opted to cut off her long hair rather than spend time teasing out the muddy knots. She'd gotten lucky. The nurse given that assignment had done her best to save as much of her hair as possible.

Every time Amanda caught sight of her choppy, chin-length bob in the mirror, it made her feel more foreign. The girl staring back at her was no more Amanda Martin on the outside than she felt inside.

She eased the sweatpants up her legs, getting them just past her knees before gingerly putting her feet on the floor. Why was she so nervous?

She'd made several trips to the bathroom each day, but she had those three steps down.

This was different.

There were people out there. People she didn't know or trust. People who might try to hurt her or someone she loved.

Her heart beat with the ferocity of a captured bird.

*Breathe, Amanda, breathe.*

"Ten, nine, eight…"

"*Mija?*" Joaquin's voice was thick with concern.

"Get it together," she whispered. Amanda looked toward the closed door. "I'm fine, just taking it slow."

The shirt swallowed her; the arms loose enough to not pull at her IV. She called Father Joaquin back in.

"Not the most fashionable, I know." A deep line sliced through his brow when he frowned. "Okay, *zapatos*." He slid the sneakers on her feet with the care of someone handling a glass slipper. Or, in her case, a glass girl. "How does that feel?"

"There'd better be ice cream where we're going." Her cheeks wobbled as she drew her mouth up into a smile, like a weightlifter struggling with a heavy barbell.

"Yes, there is some tucked away in the cafeteria fridge just for you." The priest offered an arm. "Shall we?"

Amanda had only peeked outside her hallway before. The beige walls were broken up by cream colored doors. The strong scent of bleach and antiseptic cleaner nearly made her gag. Hospital staff beamed as she passed them, no doubt pleased that their long-shot of a patient was able to walk out of her room.

Albeit, at a pace where a snail could lap her.

"Where to?" she asked between pants.

"There's a nice patio garden. A short walk, then you can rest while we start on the *B's*." He waved the baby name book at her and tucked it under his free arm.

Maybe Amanda should feign familiarity with one of those names. Something to encourage Father Joaquin.

He pushed open the door leading to the garden. The sun and heat hit her. What month was it?

"Father, how long have I been here?" She'd counted at least two weeks, but in addition to the unconscious days, she'd spent many of those first few conscious ones in and out of a haze.

He hesitated, as if counting or deciding how she would receive the answer. "Four and a half weeks."

Four and a half weeks.

Had there been a funeral for David? Had his body been found as soon as the flood waters receded? And, Josh. Had Vargas killed

9

him quickly and left his body in the desert to be picked apart by vultures?

An ache grew in her chest and sunk to her hips. She gritted her teeth and took a slow breath, sending it to the sorest parts of her broken body, hoping the infusion of oxygen would quiet the screaming agony—physical and emotional.

She focused her attention outward. They wandered a winding, maze-like path. The air was hot and sweet. Bougainvilleas bloomed in vibrant pinks, their branches cascading over each other. The wind tickled the back of her bare neck.

Sounds of the hospital faded. Honking cars competed with a trickling fountain. Maybe it was being stuck inside a sterile hospital room for weeks, but Amanda had never seen a garden so beautiful in her life.

"Careful, these bricks are old and uneven," Joaquin said.

She looked down, forcing her attention on the red-brown bricks. Her IV pole skipped over them.

He helped her ease onto a wooden bench under a tree bursting with purple flowers. "Are you comfortable?" The priest pulled the pole closer to her.

Amanda nodded. The warm bench eased the soreness in her body.

"Wait here. I'll get the *helado* and be back in a moment."

She closed her eyes and allowed her body to feel anything other than hurt. After those days wandering the desert, the sun felt kinder, gentler. As if there were two stars orbiting; a cruel one that threatened to kill them and this gentle giant smiling down.

A bead of perspiration tickled her forehead before caressing her face as it slid toward her chin. So different than the sweat that had streamed from every pore.

As much as Amanda wished she'd died, life hummed all around her, nourishing her, making her feel weightless. Maybe she could do this. Maybe Father Joaquin was right, if her time on Earth was done, she would've died. But she hadn't, so what was left?

Should she tell him her name when he came back? The fresh air and sunshine was all she'd needed to remember her past?

Her parents would take her home, get the best physical therapy money could buy.

Then…send her off to prison.

What if she stayed in Mexico? Adopted another new name, new life. This one without the burden of searching for an ex-boyfriend who'd entangled her in his crimes, one without the fear of a drug lord lurking around every corner.

One without the heartbreak of losing the man she loved, right after learning he was close to betraying her.

Her eyes fluttered open at the sound of footsteps. Amanda expected to see Father Joaquin, but instead, the profile of a man caught her attention.

He was much taller than Joaquin. Unlike the clean-shaven priest, his cheeks were covered with a dusting of a beard. Rather than the cassock, this man was dressed in boots, jeans and a T-shirt.

*David?*

Her mouth went dry. Was it really him? Maybe he'd gotten out of the river and was looking for her. "David," she called, but the man continued walking.

Amanda stood quickly, ignoring the flash of discomfort. As much as she wanted to run to him, the best she could muster was a shuffle.

He disappeared around a corner, her view blocked by another flowering bush. With an eye down to avoid a stumble on the bricks, she tried to keep him in sight. With every turn, he moved farther from her, closer to the perimeter of the garden.

She tried to move faster, but her body betrayed her. The IV pole dragged behind her like a stubborn toddler.

At the next corner, she saw him again.

His back to her, he stood in front of a door at the outer gate.

"David, wait."

The man pushed open the door, falling into the stream of a busy sidewalk.

"No, no, no." She sped up her steps and took a corner too fast. The IV pole lodged in a deep crack, refusing to move. "Dammit."

Amanda grimaced, pulling the needle out of the back of her hand and abandoning the appendage.

She paused at the door. The city thrummed. Bustling with people and sounds and smells and Vargas' spies.

The bird in her ribcage stirred, warning her that danger lurked on the other side.

But...*David* was on the other side. She took a deep breath and pushed open the door.

Cars whirred by, just a few feet from where she stood. Sounds assaulted her. Honking and music and shouts and whistles. The smell of exhaust was interlaced with the sweet smell of frying dough from a street vendor.

Amanda leaned against the wall.

*Where did he go?*

She took a few wobbly steps in one direction, then doubled back, afraid to get too far from the door.

People passed by her; some staring at her with concern painted across their faces, others pushed past as if she were a ghost. Her throat burned from screaming his name.

Maybe she wasn't the ghost.

David was.

Panic seized her in a tight fist. Somewhere deep inside Amanda had held on to a thread of hope he was still alive. She looked down at her hands. They were empty except for the blood streaming down her left hand.

The thread was never really there.

A scream rose up on the busy street. Raw. Primal. Filled with an agony that permeated every cell, every atom and every soul. It echoed off buildings and the sidewalk.

The crowd gathering around her threatened suffocation. They moved in closer.

Amanda backed into the brick wall of the garden, a white-hot bolt shot through her core as her tailbone cracked against it.

It was only when the crowd parted, when Spanish words whizzed by her with the velocity of bullets, when arms cloaked in black cloth wrapped around her; that she realized the screaming was coming from her.

# 3

Torture was a word that sounded exactly as it felt.
Josh thought about that word.
A lot.

When they stripped him.

When they tied him up.

When the leather strap bit into his back.

Sometimes, it lulled him to sleep when the agony became so great all he could do was vomit and pass out.

Between beatings, Josh counted his inhales; relishing them while they lasted.

Why he was still alive? After he'd surrendered to Vargas, he expected to be promptly killed. Instead, he was thrown into the trunk of a car.

He'd come to in a dark room. It had felt subterranean, but he couldn't tell if that's how he felt, buried alive, or if his senses were accurate. They'd left him there for a week. Or a month. Or a day.

There was no daylight for time to get a foothold. A few pieces of stale bread were brought to him, and water with a sour tang he begged his mind not to analyze.

He wasn't back on the *hacienda*. Somewhere outside his cell were sounds of a city pulsating with life. Car horns and the hum of electricity called to him in the moments of dead silence.

Josh expected Vargas to show himself, but somehow the man stayed hidden. Licking his wounds. Or, preparing to inflict some on him.

Probably both.

He straightened at the sound of footsteps echoing in the hallway. Sometimes two sets visited him, others just one. This time, he counted three, maybe four sets of feet.

Light from the open door blinded him. He squeezed his eyes and tried to turn his stiff neck.

Two of the shadowed figures he recognized as members of Vargas' goon squad, the other was a smaller guy, wearing dress pants and a tie entered without acknowledging him. The fourth emerged last, like a diva awaiting her cue to come onstage to adoring fans.

"Josh," Vargas said, walking around his men. "My, how you've fallen."

Not much had changed since he'd seen the drug lord last. The man still wore beige linen suits, his hair was a little longer, likely grown out to disguise the fact he was missing his left ear.

"I don't know, I seem to be upright." Josh tugged at the chains anchored into the ceiling. He gestured toward the smaller man with his chin. "That my replacement?"

"You were good," the guy said. "But I'm better."

He tried to shrug, a less effective move with his arms over his head. "We'll see." He'd hid his theft deep within the books. Unless this dude had Wall Street experience, he wouldn't be able to uncover exactly how Josh had stolen from Vargas. "Why am I still alive, Rafael?"

The cartel boss put a cigarette in his mouth. "You don't mind if I smoke, do you?" He exhaled, a puff of smoke rising in a thin cloud. "It's refreshing to see even in your time of greatest need, you are still the same, the impatient child. Eagerly awaiting death, as you did Christmas morning."

It wasn't that Josh had given up the will to live. Quite the opposite. Locked in that cell, he found life to be even more beautiful. He'd find himself remembering the feel of a gentle, cool breeze on his face, the warming sensation of a kind sun, the pleasure of a woman's touch.

He even found himself recalling those days in the desert. How he'd grown to feel desire for Amanda that transcended the physical pull. Josh had to keep her alive, no matter what. It hadn't even been a decision to sacrifice himself to Vargas to give her a chance to escape. It had been an urge.

"I'd say the Vegas odds on me getting out of this alive are less than zero," Josh said. "Then again, I'm not really a betting man."

The man chuckled. "I love that your sense of humor is not… damaged." Vargas paced the small cell, exhaling clouds of cigarette smoke. "You should know, she didn't get away."

Nausea hit his empty stomach as if he'd been beaten again. Instead, it was his hope that was pummeled. Imagining Amanda alive, and semi-well had saved him during those beatings.

"That's a lie."

The drug lord shrugged. "Perhaps, but you don't have any way to verify it, so you're going to have to trust me."

"Where is she?"

Vargas paused his pacing, standing just inches from Josh. He inhaled a deep drag and blew cigarette smoke in his face.

The noxious nicotine churning his stomach even more.

"I don't have her. Not yet, anyway."

He examined the mental chessboard. There'd been no mention of David. Did this mean he was in the cell next to him, having the same torture inflicted? Or, had he died in the river? Josh had heard gunshots after they jumped. Maybe a bullet had found the man and he floated out to the ocean.

If that was the case, where was Amanda?

"I don't know how I can find her," he answered. "Seeing I'm a little tied up at the moment." He pulled at his restraints. "But perhaps my schedule will clear in the coming weeks, and I can make some calls for you."

It wasn't a good idea to taunt the bastard, but Josh was fresh out of shits to give.

Vargas' face lit up. "Oh but you're wrong. You *can* help me." He resumed his pacing. "I've got people looking for her."

"The U.S. is a big country," he mumbled. "I can't imagine a small-time crook like yourself can afford to cover that territory."

The cartel leader snapped his fingers and the largest goon stepped forward, his fist colliding with Josh's jaw so violently he felt it pop. Copper flooded his mouth. He flexed his jaw a couple of times, feeling it shift back into place.

"Lucky for me she didn't make it back to the U.S."

Blood dribbled from his mouth as he considered Vargas' words. How had she not made it back? They'd jumped. He'd seen them both go over the edge.

He opened his mouth to ask another question, but the henchman hit him again, this time an uppercut rattled his brain. When the ringing in his ears stopped, he pushed out the words. "What about Stephens?"

Vargas eyed the glowing end of his cigarette and pursed his lips. "What do you care about him? If you'd like company, I can have him brought here."

Josh teased apart the man's statements. Did that mean David was safe? Or, did it mean he was somewhere nearby? What'd happened after they hit the water?

A Spanish command flew from the drug lord's lips and one of the goons left the room.

Vargas wrapped an arm around Josh's shoulder, their foreheads touching in a gesture more befitting of friends than enemies.

The man smelled clean, a mix of tobacco and spring-fresh laundry detergent.

"You asked why you're still alive," he said.

A searing sting pierced Josh's side, the smell of burning flesh wafted between the men.

The drug lord pressed his cigarette deeper into his skin. "One of the most effective ways to capture prey is to smoke it out," he continued. "To make the animal run to you." He stepped away.

Josh's knees gave out, but he caught himself before the metal cut deeper into his wrists.

"We really should do something about your hair." Vargas snapped his fingers. "I'd hate for you to get lice."

The goon that had left the room stepped forward.

He fought to keep his eyes open, but darkness closed in. Josh jerked up at the sound of electric clippers and tried to pull away, but the man squeezed his jaw between rough fingers.

In a few quick moves, the man ran the razor over his head, capturing his blond waves and putting them in a box.

Even though he'd been nude for several days, he'd never felt so naked.

The drug lord backed to the door.

The small man, the replacement accountant, had already escaped the cell.

"*Muy bueno,*" Vargas said. "Now, let's send Amanda a message she will surely hear."

The biggest man stepped forward. The light from the hallway glinted off the blade of a knife large enough to disembowel an elephant.

"No, no, no." He retreated as far as the chains would allow him.

The man grabbed Josh's left ear.

A scream exploded from his chest as the blade sliced through the delicate cartilage. Agony pulsed with each heartbeat, spreading throughout his body, stealing his breath, robbing his body of what little nourishment he had left as bile rose up his throat. Blood dripped down his neck.

When the men left, all he could focus on was something new to count.

# 4

The darkness of the desert evening consumed everything around David. Thick clouds blanketed the night sky. His headlights were swallowed by the abyss stretching across the highway in front of him.

Even with his A/C on full blast, sweat from a day of scouring the riverbed clung to him, refusing to give up and evaporate as much as he refused to give up finding Mandy.

The lights of Pardon Falls on the horizon beckoned. On clear nights, it was hard to discern between the town and the stars. Tonight, with no illumination from above, it was easy to see the beacon pulling him home.

*Home.*

A word he hadn't used in a while. Not since he'd left Phoenix and settled along the Texas-Mexico border. His trailer was always just a place he laid his head each night. A place that held a uniform that never felt right when he put it on. A place that gave shelter to a man he didn't know, a man who drank too much, who held on to anger too long.

A man who betrayed a woman he loved.

He wasn't that man anymore, so he couldn't live in that trailer anymore.

El Capitan's parking lot was empty when he pulled in. He'd expected El Calchera would've called it a night if he wasn't waiting for him.

The bar owner was perched on a stool. A forgotten cigar pinched between his fingers, the ash gathered on the wood like dirty snow. El sat hunched over a newspaper, either intently reading a story or lost in thought. "Figured you'd be back a couple of hours ago," the man said, not taking his eyes off the paper.

"Went a little further east than I'd planned." David went around to the back of the bar, filled a glass to the rim with ice before adding water. The yeasty smell of beer tickled his nose. "Next time I might pack for a night or two. Stay down in Laredo maybe and see what I can find there."

El harrumphed and snubbed out his cigar.

They weren't necessarily friends. Comrades in grief was more like it. As both Mandy's boss and landlord, as well as Hank Snare's brother-in-law, David had felt an obligation to be the one to tell El about what happened on Vargas' compound. How Hank sacrificed himself to give them a chance to escape. It'd also been his responsibility to confess how he'd lost Mandy in the raging floodwaters of the Rio Grande.

After he quit the Border Patrol and made it his full-time job to find her, El offered him the *casita* Mandy had stayed, in exchange for tending bar on occasion. It stabbed at him every time he walked into the little house.

She was everywhere, and nowhere.

The bar owner pushed the paper aside and stared under bushy eyebrows. "You planning to stop when you run out of river, or you going to dig through the Gulf as well?"

"If I have to."

"Have you asked yourself what you're gonna do if you find her?" El asked. "David, it's been over a month. If there's anything left of Chicago, you probably don't want to see it."

His stomach spasmed at the guy's nickname for Mandy,

reminding him of what'd gotten them to this point. Josh Williams. A man he loathed, but somehow also respected. At the end, when Mandy was about to give herself to Vargas, Josh had stepped up.

It was hard to hate someone who tried to save their lives, but at this point, emotions sucker-punched him from all angles. He was getting tired of blocking them. "It's my duty—"

"Bullshit. Your duty is to snap out of it and live your life."

David refilled his glass, ignoring the whisper in his ear telling him he deserved a beer and instead listening to the shout of dehydration begging for water. "This *is* my life."

El shook his head and reached for the next section of the paper. "If she walked through the door tonight, what do you think she'd say to you?"

He'd often imagined a final conversation. One where he'd beg forgiveness at nearly betraying her to Fallon; but explaining his logic, he'd truly believed it was the only way to save her.

In this fantasy, Mandy would listen, she'd agree with his intentions and forgive him.

That was how he was able to tell real life from fiction. If she was alive, there'd be no agreeing, no listening patiently. No forgiveness. Instead, there'd be a Vesuvius-like eruption of anger.

"Right after she slapped me?" he sat on a stool next to El.

Before the man could answer, the bar door opened and a head full of thick dreadlocks peeked in.

"Oh good, you're back," Willa said to David, grabbing a seat on the other side of El. "Find anything?"

He shook his head.

The day after he'd moved in to her former home, Willa Sams had showed up, proclaiming to be Mandy's best friend in town. Tattooed, dreadlocked and pierced, it was hard to believe the two women had anything in common. But Willa had a stern take-no-prisoners attitude that could quickly transform into bake-a-cake compassion.

No wonder she and Mandy were good friends.

Willa rapped her knuckles on the wood. "That's good, right? In the no-news-is-good-news sort of way. No dead body means she might still be alive."

"Don't encourage him," the older man huffed before turning toward him. "David, quit chasing ghosts. Go home. And I don't mean back to the place where she lived, go back to your family."

He didn't answer. Instead, he grabbed a section of the discarded paper, and let the words float around his eyes while he pretended to care about what happened in the world.

David had thought about going back to Phoenix, but there was nothing left there. Sure, his parents would welcome him, but the rest of the town would treat him like the cancer he was. After he'd left, all he had holding him up with his anger toward Mandy. Really, that anger belonged more with him. He should've been there when she'd confronted Horace Foster about Katie Shelton's murder.

He snapped the newspaper, laying it flat on the bar top. Regret had a way of piling up like logs in a river.

"Giving up this fool's errand isn't giving up on Mandy," El said softly. "But keeping at it isn't going to bring her back. One day, you'll wake up as old and gray as me, wondering what the hell happened to your life. And, she will still be dead."

He opened his mouth to argue, but the man cut him off.

"You two get out of here, I'll lock up."

David followed Willa out to the parking lot, not ready to go home, but not eager to go anywhere that served alcohol. He didn't want to use the word 'addict' but some days, he felt the pull for a drink as deeply as the need for oxygen.

"Ignore him," she said, hopping on the trunk of her dirty sedan. "You still have hope. He's jealous."

He climbed up next to her, the heel of his boots hitching on the crooked back bumper. "Hope is a son of a bitch."

"Ugh, not you, too."

"No, I mean it," David paused. How could he explain that for every inhale, he could feel Mandy somewhere taking the exact same breath? "If she's dead, then she deserves to be found. Her family needs to tell her goodbye." The thoughts floating around his head refused to connect to words.

"But you don't believe that." Willa narrowed her eyes.

"Will you think I'm crazy if I tell you I think she's still alive?" he whispered. That was what hope did to him. It made him reject logic; Mandy had drowned in the Rio Grande. Her body had likely been carried out to the Gulf of Mexico.

Hope made him believe he could feel her. Like the sun. He couldn't see it at night, but it was still there.

"Half this town is crazy, and I've heard some wacky stuff," Willa said. "And that, my friend, isn't the nuttiest notion." She knocked his knee with hers. "I don't know her as well as you, but she is one bad-ass chick, so if she is out there somewhere, you know she's giving someone hell."

Hearing someone else talk about her made her feel even more alive. It justified her existence. Mandy didn't just live in his head, or heart, but she'd made friends. Friends who knew a different side of her, but a side that was her to the core.

Willa stretched and yawned. "I'm beat. When you find Mandy, will you tell her to get her skinny butt back here so I don't have to clean these houses by myself?" She jumped off the trunk and dusted the back of her jeans. "Don't give up on her. She would have never given up on you."

The woman's words echoed in his head as he drove home. Finding Mandy dead was still finding her. It still gave him a chance to apologize, to whisper he loved her.

He opened the door to the *casita*.

When would he finally take El's words to heart? When he could no longer smell her shampoo? Or, when he no longer found her hair draped across the pillow? Maybe when the faint lipstick stain on the coffee mug in the sink faded into oblivion.

David had a life before Mandy. A good one, but he just didn't know how to live it anymore.

# 5

David hadn't intended to sleep so late. His dreams were a loop of him and Mandy falling, hitting the water and surfacing empty-handed. It was like his brain was trying to tell him something. Show him a different angle, but he had access to only one camera.

The temperature was already crawling toward the triple digits and the sun had barely climbed the sky. If he was going to get a run in, he needed to get moving.

This was another way he felt her presence.

Running introduced her to him before they'd officially met, and it was a way for him to see her before he'd worn her down and convinced her to go out on a date.

The cadence of one foot in front of another fit the rhythm of his thoughts perfectly. He'd replay his search. Had he searched far enough up the banks? Had he missed a footprint? Was that a torn piece of her shirt, or a plastic bag that got away from a landfill?

David hit the highway, veering left toward the river. Even on the days when he didn't plan to walk along the edge of the Rio Grande, his body tugged him toward it. The music playing through his earbuds was a soundtrack to his psyche. It propelled him up the punishing hill, celebrated as he coasted down the other side.

The music stopped and Fallon Weatherby's name popped up on the screen. He sent the call to voicemail. His knee brace slipped on sweat and he tugged it back in place. Since the days spent walking the desert, his knee groaned at the smallest request. It flat-out screamed every time he ran.

Another pause, another flash of Fallon's name. Another decline.

He wasn't intentionally avoiding the FBI agent. It felt wrong to spend time talking with her while he was looking for Mandy. Like he was cheating on both of them.

Fallon had been nothing but kind. In those first days after coming home, she's followed him to the river, sweated alongside him, swatted at bugs, shook brush to scare off the snakes.

He could feel it pulsing between them. He knew that she knew David and Mandy had reconnected in the desert. Even though he'd asked Fallon out before Mandy had re-entered his life, his feelings for his ex were far from dead. They'd been revived, and, were thriving.

A car slowed behind him.

*Really? She's following me?*

David stopped, ready to give Fallon his usual *I'm-fine-please-quit-asking* speech, when a different voice called to him.

"If you're going to run on the frickin' highway, you should at least turn your music down." Shiloh Garcia leaned over her center console, smirking at him from the open passenger window.

Guilt flashed through him. He closed his eyes and let out a long exhale. He hadn't seen Shiloh since that night he'd gotten so drunk he'd slept with her, thinking she was Mandy. Sadly, that hadn't been his lowest point, but he could see the bottom of the barrel from there.

"Hop in, I'll buy you breakfast."

David braced himself on the open window, the air conditioning chilling his body through sweat-drenched clothes. "I, uh, got this thing," he stumbled over an acceptable excuse. "I'm training, need to get in a couple of miles. Raincheck?"

Shiloh pursed her lips, deep lines formed on her normally smooth forehead. "David Stephens, if you don't get in this car I'm going to call your mother."

He shook his head. The momma card worked every time, especially if Shiloh waved it. "I could meet you somewhere, let me finish my run and shower."

"Nope," she said. "No offense, but I think you'll come up with another excuse. Get your sweaty butt in my car now or I'll throw you in."

David pulled open the door and obeyed. Luckily his own smell covered any of Shiloh's scent that could kick him into a tailspin of remorse.

"You don't have to be so afraid of me," she mumbled after making a U-turn to head back to Pardon Falls.

He pretended her words were lost in the wind blowing through his open window. "How long have you been in town?"

"Got in yesterday afternoon," Shiloh said. The town breakfast spot came into view and she flicked on her blinker. "Was trying to find you then but everyone said you were out looking…"

David could hear the ellipses in her voice. Everyone in town knew what he did when he went to the river; they knew who he was looking for. Some even volunteered to join him. Despite Mandy's disappearance, he sensed Shiloh still harbored some ill-will toward her.

In the year since he'd seen her, she'd somehow managed to look younger. Could be that having lived with the secret surrounding her best friend's murder for more than a decade weighed her down?

Now that the case was solved, she was more like the girl he'd watched grow up. The pretty Latina's warm eyes sparkled and her long hair flowed over her shoulder in gentle waves instead of a tangle of curls.

Maybe he'd always felt it. The crush Shiloh carried for him. As her big brother's best friend, David thought of her as a kid sister. What would have happened if Mandy hadn't gotten off that bus in Phoenix? Would he have eventually found his way to Shiloh's bed? Would the anger she harbored over Katie's murder grown so strong that it overshadowed the person inside? Would Horace Foster, the hermit bookstore owner, have found another young girl to stalk and eventually kill?

Sure, Mandy broke a few dozen eggs when she left Phoenix, but some of the people she touched at least had an omelet to nourish them.

*And, all I had was egg on my face.*

With coffee and breakfast tacos in hand, they found a shaded table outside. They eyed each other over their cups.

Shiloh would open her mouth, as if to speak, only to instead shove a bite of chorizo in it.

Words would rise up David's throat, but he'd flush them back down with a large gulp of scalding liquid.

"So…" she finally said.

"You're not really the outdoors type. I doubt you came all this way for hiking or camping. What's up?"

She fidgeted with her cup, flipping the plastic lid off and snapping it back on.

He'd known her since she was a kid, and she'd never been at a loss for words. Not even when her best friend had disappeared and was later found dead when they were sixteen, not when a strange woman showed up in town and caught his eye. Not even when David lost his job for not realizing his new girlfriend was running from an indictment.

Shiloh took a deep breath and slammed her cup on the table, looking away before speaking. "I owe you an apology."

He tilted his head. "For what?"

"For what I did to you." Her voice broke.

David had only seen her cry once, after Katie's body was found. What could she have possibly done to him that rivaled that?

"You're going to have to help me out here."

She let out an exasperated sigh and picked at her napkin, rolling it into a tight spiral and twisting it around her finger. He then noticed what was missing. The cigarettes. He could read the nicotine-need written all over her face.

"That night." Shiloh unraveled the napkin, flattening it on the table. "I took advantage of you."

David straightened, his knee banging the table and causing their empty coffee cups to tumble. "Shi—"

"No, listen. You might think you did something wrong, but it was all me. I should've walked away, left you there, but I got jealous. Of her." Shiloh took a deep breath and looked behind her, but David could tell it was to hide wiping away a tear.

"I wanted what she had, and I took it, but I realized how awful that was, because what happened between us, wasn't what you and Mandy had. I took something from you and you ran away because of it. I lost your friendship, and so much more."

He put his hand over hers. "We were both pretty messed up for a while. Maybe even still a little, but Shi, you took nothing from me. Look, maybe we needed that night. In some way, we each needed to have that dark moment. Rather than suffer it alone, we suffered it together."

A sob escaped Shiloh's throat, which she attempted to mask in a laugh. More tears fell, and this time she didn't try to stop them. "That's the stupidest thing I've ever heard."

David relaxed at the glimpse of the old Shiloh peeking out. "Yeah, probably. Someone interrupted my run. That's when I do my best thinking. More coffee?"

"Yes, please."

When he returned, they sipped in silence, each studying the landscape around them. Bees buzzed in and out of a flowering bush, competing with the butterflies for the precious desert nectar. A mourning dove cooed, her melancholy song clashing with the brilliant sun and bright blue sky of the late morning.

"Did you come all this way to apologize?" David finally broke the silence.

"Well, that's part of it, but the other part is a job offer back home."

He winced. Were El and Shiloh *both* conspiring to get him back to Phoenix?

"I don't know, Shi."

28

"No, listen." She leaned forward. "Everyone misses you, especially after hearing you nearly died by a cartel leader. Dude, you got some serious sympathy points."

"I doubt they'll feel sorry enough for me to give me my job back."

"Not your old job, a new one. Eddie's going to call you in a few days. He's getting married; he'll ask you to be his best man. That's not all he'll ask. They're moving after the wedding, and he needs a bar manager."

"What about you?"

"I can be your assistant, but I'm going finally going to college and have a full course load in the fall. I won't have time to do both." She lowered her voice. "This isn't where you belong."

David draped his arm over the back of his chair and looked out over the dusty parking lot. Where he belonged was with Mandy. He had more memories of her in Phoenix, but somehow he felt the presence of Mandy Martin in Pardon Falls, not Mandy Jackson, the woman she'd pretended to be.

"You would have found her by now." Shiloh lanced his thoughts. "Getting on with your life doesn't mean you love her any less. Trust me on this. I know."

He heard her words, but he wasn't eager to really listen.

What if Mandy showed up in Pardon Falls? Was it asking too much to expect her to rise up out of the river and come back to him? Would she want him?

Williams had shared his ultimate betrayal right before he lost her. Before he had a chance to explain.

Was he searching for Mandy to save her, or to save *him*?

"Sometimes, losing the person you love makes you better. You want to be the person they thought you were," Shiloh stood. "I've got a long drive ahead and have to work tonight. Do you need a ride?"

He jumped, almost forgetting she was there. "No, it's not a far walk from here."

She smiled down at him. "Right, you're training for that thing," she teased. "Promise me you'll think about it when Eddie calls." She walked back to her car. "Dah-veed," she switched to the Spanish pronunciation of his name. "Living in the past isn't good for you. It's filled with ghosts, and if you hang out with them long enough, you become one yourself."

David sat there long after she'd left, after the sound of her car faded and the dust from her tires settled back into place. Shiloh was right, he couldn't stay in the past forever, but he wasn't ready to face the present.

Because, in the present Mandy was dead, and that was more than he was ready to handle.

# 6

Sunday supper at the Weatherbys' was a lesson in the branches of law enforcement. One of Fallon's older brothers sported a Texas Rangers badge, a point of pride for her retired Ranger father, and another worked for the DEA. She had a cousin serving as Sheriff and her oldest nephew was a rookie with the El Paso PD. Her black sheep brother, the lawyer, was across the state in Houston, the longest branch of the Weatherby family tree.

It was bad enough she couldn't escape being "one of the boys" during the week at the El Paso office of the FBI, Fallon usually found herself drifting between the men at her parents' ranch, cleaning guns and talking shop, and the ladies, bustling around the kitchen, swapping potty training secrets and asking her prying questions about her dating life. It felt horribly cliché. Sometimes, it took all she had to not hand a sister-in-law a gun to clean and a brother a kid with a diaper to change.

*This would be almost bearable if David would've answered his phone.*

Her calls had gone to voicemail too quickly for the message to not be received.

He didn't want to talk to her.

Seeing him at the hospital, fighting off the doctors, shouting orders at the police and Border Patrol agents swarming around him, she'd known he'd lost someone important. How important became clear when Amanda Martin was assumed dead, yet David kept going back to the river to look for her.

"Aunt Fallon!" The sing-song voices of a pair of five-year-olds cut through Sunday's silence.

Her niece Becca and nephew Will sprinted across the yard. She knelt down so they wouldn't take her feet out from under her when she was hit with their combined weight.

"Oh, my favorite people in whole wide world." Fallon inhaled their sweet scents with the slightest hint of little kid sweat. Working the human trafficking division was the toughest with the kids, especially those around their ages.

"Can we swing?" Will asked.

"No, let's race," Becca argued. "I've been practicing."

"We could climb the tree," Will suggested.

"I have an idea." Fallon pointed at the old porch swing hanging from a thick limb. "Let's race to the hill and hop in the big swing together."

Two little faces came to life. The three of them sprinted the hundred or so yards to the giant oak tree that stood sentry on her parents' property. It felt good to laugh and run.

When they got to the tree swing, they fell into it, giggling and gasping for air. Her long legs were no match for little kid energy.

With the kids cuddled on each side of her, she rocked the swing with her feet, enjoying the warm breeze and view of the city. This was her own little slice of Heaven. The smell of burgers grilling in the distance, a hot breeze lifting her hair and childhood innocence snuggled close.

"Where's your boyfriend?" Becca asked.

*Dammit.*

She should've known her sister-in-law was going to say something to her brother, and, of course, kids heard everything. In her feeble attempt at girl-talk, she'd shared with Denise that she'd reconnected with an old college friend, and this time it was different.

His gaze lingered on her a beat longer than it had in school.

Even she'd found herself smiling when his name showed up on her phone, her cheeks warming when he entered a room. Little things that weren't there when they'd been classmates at UT.

"He's not my boyfriend. He's a friend who happens to be a boy."

*And, he happens to be avoiding me like I'm a geeky love-struck thirteen-year-old with bottle-thick glasses and spinach in my braces.*

"Yuck, I don't ever want to have a girlfriend," her nephew chimed in.

"Kids, supper," Fallon's mom called from the back porch.

As the youngest of her siblings and the only one, aside from her twenty-something nephew, still single, she was often lumped into the 'kids' category. Lucky for her, everyone would be gathered around the patio or she might be seated at the kids table. *Again.*

The potato salad was ice cold, the cheese melted to a gooey blob. Sunshine burst on her tongue with the first sip of sun-brewed tea. Hidden in the depths of her momma's freezer, was a gallon of hand-cranked homemade ice cream. She didn't care if it looked like she was living a Hallmark card, she wholeheartedly embraced it.

"Hey, Fallon," her DEA agent brother Richard spoke through a mouthful of coleslaw. "What's the name of that guy caught up by Rafael Vargas?"

Her face warmed. The kids were just a warmup to the actual interrogation by her family. "David couldn't make it." It best to nip it before the prying began.

"No, that's your friend from college, right? I'm talking about the other guy. The one from up north."

Fallon stared at her brother, trying to read him, but all of the siblings had been taught at an early age the fine art of holding a poker face. The only reason she knew these details of the case was because David had refused to talk to anyone else until she'd gotten there.

It was a cross-agency issue, but in addition to working the wrong division, she wasn't high enough in the ranks to cross anyone other than some of the more chauvinist guys at the office.

"Josh Williams, I think." Of course she knew. Since David had come home and started his search for Amanda, Fallon had thrown herself into their world, eager to know every detail of the woman that drove him to search in the dangerous heat for her body. It was hard not to learn about Amanda without crossing paths with Josh's case file.

"Why do you ask?"

Richard put his plate down and braced his elbows on his knees. This was his tell. He was about to spill something juicy. "Got this CI, a real people pleaser, the best kind you can ask for." Her brother took a swig of beer. "Anyway, in our meeting this week, the kid didn't have anything good on drugs moving in, but he did tell me he'd heard Vargas was holding a *gringo*."

"How does he know it's Williams?"

"Said the guy used to work for Vargas, but then took off with a bunch of stolen money and two other kidnapped Americans. Word on the street is Vargas is pissed. He's trying to fight off rumors that he's weak so this Williams guy, let's just say I'm pretty damn happy I'm not him."

Fallon chewed on the inside of her cheek. "Where's he keeping him?"

Her brother shook his head. "Kid didn't know. Not at Vargas' usual place. Somewhere else. Somewhere hidden."

She took another bite of potato salad.

Mexico was a large country, and navigating its legal system was more complicated than figuring out the back roads. Maybe David would know something. Maybe he'd heard about where Vargas had other stash houses. Could this help him snap out of his fruitless search for Amanda?

"Can I see him? Your CI?"

Richard glanced at their dad and other brother. She'd crossed a line, asking to get involved in something that didn't involve her. While they'd never treated her unfairly, Fallon didn't quite belong among the men in her family.

"Sis, you know I can't—"

She waved off her question before her brother finished the rest of his answer. "Do me a favor though, see what else you can find out."

He nodded and the family went back to their supper, chatting about the heat, sports and politics.

After ice cream was served, Fallon volunteered for kitchen duty, shooing everyone else outside to enjoy the early evening breeze. As her hands scrubbed bowls and dishes, her mind scrubbed the options she had.

Could she follow her brother to his CI appointment and try to get the informant on his own? Or, could she reach out to some of her contacts in the *Fedareles* to see if they could help?

"Fallon."

She jumped at Richard's voice and dropped a bowl back into the sink, splashing sudsy water down the front of her T-shirt and jeans.

Her brother crossed the kitchen and leaned against the counter next to her. "There's one more thing." Richard's voice was low. "Vargas seems to think the American woman with them is alive, and he's looking for her. If that's true, we have to assume he's also after David."

All the wind left her lungs. Perspiration flashed on her forehead and her heart sped up as if she were sprinting a mile.

She looked at her brother, his mouth pressed into a tight line. His green eyes were heavy with worry. They were always closer than the other Weatherby kids, able to read each other's minds. Fallon wouldn't need to say it; Richard already knew David was more important than just an old college friend.

"I'll see what I can dig up, but sis, keep yourself safe for me. Okay?"

# 7

She felt his presence before she opened her eyes. One side of her bed dipped under the weight of his elbows and deep sighs filled the air.

"Hey." The word felt heavy on her tongue.

Had they drugged her?

"Who's David?" the priest asked.

Amanda took a deep breath and stared up at the ceiling.

*I'm a bit tired and loopy, my hand is throbbing, my head feels like it was run over, and I'm pretty sure I've damaged every bone in the southern half of my body. Thanks for asking.*

"I don't—"

"You were screaming his name over and over." His words came out harsher, less benevolent, more impatient. "If there's something you remember, anything that can help us—help you."

She swallowed, her throat still raw from the screaming. "Can I have some water?"

Father Joaquin poured a glass and handed it to her.

As she sipped, she tried to call up the memories. Chasing who she'd thought was David. Going outside the confines of the hospital.

The noises, the fumes. All the people closing in on her, stealing her breath.

Then he was there, Father Joaquin. Comforting her, trying to get the bystanders to give her room.

Amanda wouldn't go back inside, not without David. That was when the orderlies had come out. Her last memory was her friend apologizing to her.

"How long have I been out?"

"About twenty-four hours. They originally gave you a light sedative, but you woke up in the middle of night screaming, so you got something stronger."

"Sorry."

*Sorry for causing a scene. Sorry for being a nuisance. Sorry for being alive.*

"There must've been something, *mija*. Something you saw or heard that triggered a memory. Was it in the garden?"

How crazy would she sound if Amanda told him she'd chased the apparition of her dead boyfriend? In addition to thinking she was an amnesiac, would they lock her away in a mental institution?

"Maybe we could go back out there?" Joaquin continued. "This time, I'll stay with you and see what caused it. You might even remember more."

She shrugged.

What were the chances someone who looked just like David would pass through the garden again?

Joaquin could try to recreate it in hopes of helping his broken ward, but she shoved all memories of David deep into a place where they could be protected. A place where no matter how much prodding, no one was going to get to them. Because they were hers; all she had left of him.

"I'll ask the doctor if it would be okay. Don't move."

Amanda looked down at herself. She was back in the thin hospital gown. The IV had been moved from the back of her hand to the crook of her arm. She was tucked so tightly into sheets they doubled as restraints. "Don't think I'm going anywhere. And if I did, you could catch me."

When he left, the small room felt suddenly enormous. Joaquin wasn't a big man, but his presence took up an abundance of space.

Maybe this hospital room was an allegory for her life. A year and a half ago, her world was filled with family, friends and colleagues. It was filled with a gorgeous apartment in a tree-lined Chicago neighborhood overlooking the lake.

When she'd had to abandon that life and start a new one in Phoenix, Texas, she'd whittled it down to a small apartment, a few friends and David. After the fire, she'd left with even less, first stopping in El Paso before making a short life in Pardon Falls with Hank, El and Willa in her shrinking circle.

Then, it was just David and Josh, wandering around the desert. The clothes on her back, a gun and bleeding blisters.

Like a Russian nesting doll, each outer shell shed shrank her world. Herself. Was this the innermost doll? Lying there with nothing, not even her name?

"Amanda."

Her head whipped in the direction of Joaquin before she stopped herself. A word spoken just days ago that meant nothing was now filled with urgency.

She locked eyes with him. It was too late to deny her name. The recognition of it was written all over his face.

Joaquin closed the door behind him. "We have to go." He pulled open cabinets, rummaging through various medical supplies.

"Father Joaquin, what are you talking about?"

"We've only got a few minutes." The priest tossed the shirt and sweatpants over his shoulder at her. "Get dressed."

She stared at the back of his black shirt, sweat rings darkening his underarms.

He glanced over his shoulder. "*Mija*, I mean it. Now."

Amanda crossed her arms, the IV tugging at her sensitive skin. "Not until you tell me what's going on."

A curse fell from his lips and he gripped her shoulders. "There are two men here asking about an American woman."

She straightened in his pause. Maybe it *had been* David she'd seen.

"They work for Rafael Vargas."

The words hit her like a blast of arctic air. Her lungs froze. Her arms dropped to her sides, fingers numb.

"Help me with the IV." Her hands shook as she pulled at the medical tape.

Joaquin took over, handing her a cotton ball to put on the puncture while he pulled out the needle and strapped on more tape.

He turned, giving Amanda a moment of privacy to pull off the gown and tug the shirt over her head.

Her body throbbed when she swung her legs off the bed to put on her pants, but cold flash of fear at hearing Vargas' name numbed her.

"I still need help with shoes," she croaked.

Her friend was less careful this time, he shoved her feet in the sneakers, tying them quickly and haphazardly. When he stood, he pulled open a drawer next to her bed and opened the Bible. Instead of the Word of God, the book was hollowed out with a small gun nestled inside.

*Why is there a gun in my room?*

"Let's go." Joaquin tugged at her hand, but Amanda pulled back. "What?"

"How do I know I can trust you?" If it were true, if Vargas' men were just down the hallway, how could she be sure she wasn't being handed to them?

His face softened and he bent down to eye level. "I've been here since they brought you in, keeping you safe. If I were going to turn you over, I would've done it four and a half weeks ago. I'll explain everything later, but we have to go. Now. Quickly."

Amanda followed him to the door.

The priest pulled the door open, peeking out before grasping her hand and tugging her behind him.

An unsettled hush fell over the busy hospital. Nurses cut them sideways glances, tossing looks in their direction before gesturing with their eyes, as if silently signaling the safest route. They cut down a hallway and Joaquin dragged her into a medical supply closet.

"What're you doing?" she asked.

He pulled large, white bottles off the shelves with each hand, barely glancing at the labels before slamming it back. "You're still not healed. You'll thank me later." When he found what he was looking for, he slipped it in his pocket.

Joaquin speed-walked down the hall, forcing Amanda to do a Quasimodo-like shuffle to keep up.

"We're almost there," he whispered, hugging her close to him. "Out that door. A white car not far from the entrance."

Amanda couldn't tell if he was talking to himself, or her. Maybe both. She'd kept her focus on the floor in front of her, making sure her feet were on firm ground before putting any real weight on them. At the next adjoining hall, she spared a glance.

Two men stood at the nurses' station. The one with his back to her was tall, broad-shouldered and his long hair pulled back in a low ponytail. The man facing her was shorter, stockier, his stomach paunching over his belt buckle.

Her gaze found his and she stumbled into Joaquin. It was the same man who'd tied her up on a hot desert highway, who'd threatened to kill David if she didn't cooperate. The one who'd come to Josh's room with ill intentions, but was met with the business end of a champagne bottle.

He nudged the man next to him, gesturing in their direction with his chin.

"They see us."

She tried to pick up her feet, matching Joaquin's jog. Pain pulsed through her body with each step.

Spanish commands were shot at them from behind. The footsteps of the men came quicker.

The door was just a few feet away.

A few more steps until they were outside.

The swell of panic stirred in her chest. She took long, deep breaths, begging her body to not feel anything.

Not fear.

Not the gnashing of her fractured bones and wounded muscles.

Not even hope they would actually make it.

When they burst through the door, Joaquin dropped her hand and drew his gun.

She glanced behind her.

In a choreographed move, the men reached behind them and pulled out their own weapons.

The wail of a siren pierced her ears. As if by divine intervention, an ambulance flew into the parking lot, cutting off their pursuers, giving them precious seconds to get safely in the car.

Joaquin backed out of the space and flew over a curb, the car rocking as if it would tumble before righting itself and joining the flow of traffic.

"I don't think you really have amnesia," he said, looking in his rearview mirror instead of making eye contact.

"And, I don't think you're really a priest."

# 8

Fallon sat in the middle of the young women huddled together at a gas station parking lot. Most of the them were teenagers, but a few younger. Those were the ones that churned her stomach. If her team hadn't busted this trafficker these girls would be sold as sex slaves.

The sad thing was, for every bust they made, there were at least three that slipped past them, sending too many girls into hell on earth.

*Focus on the win. Focus on the win.*

She'd been telling herself to focus a lot lately, especially on anything *other* than David.

He'd finally texted her back. He was moving back home to Phoenix.

Fallon missed him as soon as she'd read his text, but at least he was further from the border. The physical space between them shouldn't bother her. He'd put up a barrier between them the minute he got back in the U.S.

Who was she fooling?

The minute he'd lost *her*.

The wall went up the minute he and Amanda had gotten back together. She just couldn't feel it from her side of the border.

The girls clustered around her started giggling.

Fallon's cheeks warmed. She'd been speaking to them in Spanish, asking if they were hungry, had anyone to call, had been hurt. But distracted with David, she'd mixed up all her words.

*Would you like to eat your family? Geesh, Weatherby, you know better.*

"*Lo siento.*" She smiled. It'd been a long night. A long few weeks. "*Estoy cansado.*"

These were the days when she wanted nothing else to do in the world but this job. To give a voice to the silent. While her team finding them sometimes resulted in being sent back to the heartbreaking conditions they'd tried to escape, she hoped it was a least marginally better than their future in the sex trade may have held.

"Weatherby, you telling jokes over there?" her partner, Jay Ford walked over to the group.

A recent transfer to Texas and the human trafficking division, his Spanish hit its limits after ordering a beer and asking for the bathroom.

Fallon told the ladies she'd be right back and pushed herself off the dirty ground, dusting the bottom of her black pants. It was hell on her clothes, but she found being on the same level as the victims instantly set them at ease. "Nah, just embarrassing myself." She joined him at the back of the empty truck trailer.

In the rising sun, she got a good look at what these ladies traveled in. A few backpacks were strewn about, amounting to the little possessions they'd been allowed to bring.

Heat poured out of the yawning doors, the meager holes cut in the sides of the truck did nothing for ventilation. She fought the gag reflex at the smell of human waste.

"Cattle travel in better conditions," Jay muttered. "How are they doin'?"

"Better than I'd be." She nodded to the driver, his arms wrenched behind him, his hands faintly paler thanks to too-tight handcuffs. "What's his ties?"

He ran his hair through his white-blond hair. His ears stayed in a perpetual state of sunburn. Jay was definitely having a hard time with his transition from rainy Seattle to the harsh southern sun. "Nothing good," he said. "Says this was his first go at it, thought he could use an empty truck for a different delivery service."

Fallon grimaced. She'd secretly hoped the man was connected to Rafael Vargas so she could learn more about what her brother had told her. Many drug dealers were beginning to diversify into human trafficking. More than a few times one of their busts would help the DEA and vice versa. "Can I have a few minutes alone with him?"

Jay quirked an eyebrow. He laughed and looked down at his feet. "You know you scare me, right?"

She couldn't help but notice how he looked at her, somewhere between fear and longing.

They wouldn't be the first partners in the force to hook up; she just wasn't interested in going there. Was it possible to need to have time to get over the notion of a relationship before moving on?

Fallon patted his arm. "And that's why we get along so well. Run interception for me, okay?"

She didn't wait for him to agree; and walked over to the portly man sitting on the curb.

His shoulders were rounded, his body trying to fold in on itself, and his legs were splayed out in front of him. His body odor accosted from three feet away, and something brown dribbled down the front of his shirt.

*Good God, how did he get any of these girls to agree to go with him?*

"So you're some sort of entrepreneur, huh? Guess you didn't spend much time working on your business plan."

"Suck it, sweetheart," he growled.

She ignored his taunt. "If you were working for someone else, it would mean they were the ones responsible for leaking that your truck would be coming across the border at about one-thirty a.m., because surely you wouldn't have ratted on yourself."

The man looked up through his long, greasy hair. His face was full of blackheads and pockmarks, his nose was so wide it looked like it was flattened against his face. Tobacco spit stained his beard. It never ceased to amaze Fallon how people's inside ugliness seemed to seep to their appearance.

"You're lying."

She shrugged. "How else do you think we had so many people waiting for you to cross? Our technology is good, but not *that* good."

The man spit a long stream of nasty brown saliva.

It was all she could do to not throw up on him.

"If there's people above you, talking would go a long way to making your future marginally more comfortable."

He harrumphed.

Dude was going to be a tough, ugly nut to crack.

"Okay, so let's say it's just you and a truck, and this brilliant plan to smuggle young girls into the country." Fallon hitched her hands on her hips and paced. "How did you recruit them? Did you just sit on a street corner with a sign that said 'Free Ride to the U.S.'?"

He shifted on the ground.

"Not sure how much experience you have in prison, but some of the guys in there miss their kids, and if they hear about what you were attempting to do, well...with budget cuts, guards are really overwhelmed and might miss something."

"What're you sayin'?" He peered over his shoulder, beady black eyes studying her.

Fallon opened her mouth to answer, but a low whistle cut through the air.

Jay's signal that Winslow was coming.

"You know, I'll let you fill in the gaps." She backed away. "But think about it, a little more information could save you some discomfort."

To her boss, life was a coloring book, with very specific, thick dark lines that were never to be crossed. They weren't even allowed to be touched. He preferred his agents to always leave a hair's breadth of space, enough for mistakes, for caution, and for him to step in and make the final stroke.

"Weatherby, I thought you were to get the victims' statements." He looked over her head as he spoke to her.

In the two and a half years that she'd worked for him, he'd

never once looked her in the eyes. She'd claim misogyny but he never looked the men in the office in the eye either.

"Yes, sir." Fallon flipped open her notebook, ready to give her boss the rundown, but he cut her off.

"Then why were you speaking with the suspect?"

She shifted. As she spoke with the man, she'd kept an eye on Winslow.

He'd chatted with El Paso PD, his back to the circle of women, the truck and the man seated on the ground. It wasn't the first time she'd concluded he had eyes in the back of his head.

*Maybe that's where he's looking when he's not seeing us.*

"Well, I, uh, had a few questions for him..."

"And, did you run those questions by me?" Winslow made micro-managing look like performance art.

"Sir, that was my fault, I told her I'd clear it, and I forgot to ask," Jay jumped in, trying to be her knight in a shiny, black synthetic weave jacket.

Winslow's gaze darted to her partner. He wasn't a fan of partners covering for each other. For him, loyalty ran only one way. Uphill.

Her boss' phone rang. Winslow spun and charged in the other direction.

"I didn't need saving," Fallon mumbled under her breath.

"No, but you didn't need an ass chewing later either," Jay said. "Get anything?"

She shook her head and glanced at the group of girls.

Other agents from victim services were with them now, giving them water and food, instructions on what would happen next.

Her job was done. Now it was time to go back to the office, file detailed reports that Winslow would rip apart for not including enough detail.

Fallon peeked at her phone. Quarter to seven. It was going to be a really long day.

With the phone to his ear, Winslow walked away and climbed into his car.

"Guess that's our cue," Jay said.

She took a step to follow him when the trafficker called out.

"Hey Blondie," the man shouted.

Fallon cringed at the man's voice. She took a few steps toward him, hitching her hands on her hips.

"They've got people on the inside, you know," he said.

She tilted her head and narrowed her eyes. "Who does?" Was this the lead up to a confession? A name at least?

"They all do. Keeping my mouth shut gets me more protection than snitching. So you can take all those empty promises and shove them up your sweet, self-righteous—"

A buzzing in her pocket drew her attention away from the man on the ground. Her brother Richard. He'd never call her this early. Unless…

"What's wrong?" she answered, ignoring the vitriol the man on the ground was spewing.

"Nothing, sis, calm down." The lightness in his voice did nothing to ease her nerves. "Just calling to invite you to breakfast."

Fallon pulled the phone back from her ear and stared at it.

Richard never called up out of the blue like this.

"Well, we just busted a trafficker and I have paperwork—"

"Does your partner still have a crush on you?"

*Seriously, does everything I tell Denise go straight to him?*

"Uh…" She glanced at Jay from her peripheral vision. Her partner watched her, his brow knitted. "Most likely."

"Call in a favor," Richard said. "I've got someone you're gonna want to meet."

# 9

The car weaved and jerked through the traffic. Ignored red lights and pedestrians.

Amanda clung to the dash to steady herself. She tried to take deep breaths, but her lungs were distracted by the rising panic.

It made sense Vargas would send people after her. She was surprised an angel of death hadn't visited her already, holding a pillow over her face or plunging a heart-stopping narcotic into her IV line.

She'd been so focused on her own loss to look outside her world. Maybe in some way, she'd subconsciously welcomed someone to end it all for her.

Or, so she thought.

It was in that moment, locking eyes with the men sent to kill her, she'd found what she thought she'd lost.

Her will to live.

Joaquin cut the small sedan to the right, bouncing it over the curb, barreling down a sidewalk before it hopped back down to the street.

"Joaquin," she said through gritted teeth, holding back the bile that rose with every hairpin turn. "Please don't add whiplash to my list of injuries."

His gaze darted to the rearview mirror before his shoulders relaxed a bit. "Sorry, that was just closer than I expected. You okay, *mija*?"

She nodded. Her mind hovered in a cloud of dizziness. The street flew by out the window. Strange faces blurred into buildings, which morphed into cars and trees. It moved too fast for her to get moored to any one image. "I'm going to be sick," she said through her fingers.

With one hand still on the wheel, her friend reached to the backseat and handed her an empty Styrofoam container. "Here."

Amanda flicked it open. The smell of leftover food was enough to give her stomach the extra push to the finish line. When she was done, she tilted her head back, trying to focus on anything other than where she was and what just happened.

*Horses. Baseball. Taking the SAT. Getting a root canal. Nails on a chalkboard.*

None of it worked.

She could still see the men. The one who'd tied her hands and put her in the van. The one who'd put a gun to David's head on a desert highway. The one who'd sat beside her on Josh's bed and traced his finger along her body.

"So, what's the plan?" she asked, holding the back of her hand against her mouth. "When are you taking me back?"

Joaquin spared a glance in her direction. He cut the car down a street no wider than an alley and doubled back into the flow of traffic. "I"m not."

The small car closed in on her. More bile stirred, but she pushed it down. Was she getting kidnapped all over again?

"What do you mean?"

"We've been compromised. Taking you back is not an option."

The car slowed in a crush of cars, motorcycles and bikes. Joaquin stuck his head out the window, shouting in Spanish and honking the horn.

Amanda twisted in her seat. So many faces, but none of them

were the men from the hospital. She unbuckled her seatbelt and opened the door in one move, but she wasn't quick enough.

"What are you doing?" He reached across her and pulled the door shut.

"What are *you* doing?" She narrowed her eyes.

The priest looked behind them. Like a guard dog, he was on high alert, his eyes constantly scanning the traffic around them. "Saving your ass, so sit still."

"Where are you taking me?"

"Somewhere safe, I promise. Amanda, *mija*, trust me. If I were one of the bad guys, you would have died a long time ago."

She reclined in the seat. What choice did she have?

She was in another country, a city she didn't know. A drug lord wanted her dead. The fastest she could move was a hobble and her head throbbed at any sudden movement. Or, sudden thought.

"We're getting out of the city," he added, as if sensing her frustration.

The traffic opened and Joaquin accelerated, but drove at a manageable speed along smooth, flat pavement.

Amanda tucked her panic away. She didn't need it right now, but she would again.

Vargas hadn't forgotten about her.

Josh may have stolen the opportunity for her to save him and David, but it was clear the cartel leader still intended for her to pay the price.

The jumble of the urban core thinned. Fewer cars, fewer people. The houses had more room to breathe.

Joaquin relaxed as they got further away from the city center. His head jerked side to side less often, and he didn't drive with his eyes glued to the rearview mirror. One hand even dropped from the steering wheel, resting on the gear shift between them, his fingers drumming along to some imaginary tune.

Somehow seeing him now, not as a priest but whatever he was, seemed much more fitting than the black shirt and white collar.

Like an actor shedding his role and stepping back into his real identity. Who was Joaquin Rios? Could she trust him as much as she'd trusted Father Joaquin?

"How long have you known my name?" Amanda asked.

His eyes drifted in her direction for a moment, long enough for her to see that he was equally shocked by the forwardness of her question and unsurprised. "Just a few days after you arrived. You were still unconscious, and had no ID. My niece is a nurse there. She called me to help."

She nodded. "Are you really a priest, or do you just play one to get amnesiac foreigners to trust you?"

His mouth pulled up to a smile. "You never had amnesia, and no, I'm not a priest."

"Why impersonate one? Why not just be Joaquin Rios?" She paused. "I mean, your name is Joaquin, right?"

"Yes, yes." The car slowed and he pulled off the road into a gated community. A man came out of the guard house, shook his hand and quickly ushered them through. "I'll wait until we're inside. We'll explain everything then."

*We?*

The neighborhood was neat, with modest homes from the desert section of the coloring box. Beiges, siennas, even a gorgeous turquoise that made her long for El's bar in Pardon Falls.

Most of the homes had bars on the windows and doors, as if the protection of an on-site security guard wasn't enough.

He pulled up to an ochre colored stucco house and followed a cobblestone driveway around to the back. A two-car wooden garage door lifted. One side was filled with a rugged SUV, the other empty.

Joaquin took the empty spot, killed the engine and popped open his door.

Amanda tugged on his arm, stopping him. "Promise me. Complete truths, no lies, no half-truths. I don't have it in me to figure out what's real and what's made up." Her head throbbed and flames of pain licked at her core.

A sad smile crossed his face and he nodded. "I promise. Just follow my lead when we get inside, okay?"

She wanted to ask him what *that* meant, but once he helped her out of the car, it took all of her concentration to walk through the door of the house.

The jarring car ride, the nausea, the flush of adrenalin; it was all too much.

The inside of the house matched the outside. Stucco with a large fountain in the middle of the foyer and skylights stretching across the roof three stories up.

The rooms surrounding the interior courtyard had windows with the same bars. Flowerpots clung to the iron railing on the second and third floors. It was as if they stood within a fish bowl made to look like the outside world, but still encased in glass.

"Is this your house?" Amanda could hear the awe in her voice.

Joaquin led her to a glass-top dining table that stretched along a sliding patio door and looked out over a small courtyard.

A twin fountain to the one inside sat outside, lush flowering plants tumbled down from pots and cacti and agave grew from the ground against a thick, tall stone wall.

"I stay here, but no, it belongs to my employer."

He eased her into a chair and pulled the bottle of pills from his pocket. With a quick glance at the label, he flicked off the lid and shook out a pill. "You'll need this."

Amanda didn't even wait for water, she swallowed it back, hoping it'd get to work as it slid down her throat.

"Wait here," he said before jogging up the stairs, calling out in Spanish, his words bouncing off the tile and stucco.

He was answered by another man, his voice deeper, the words more melodic. They spoke quickly. Quietly at first. Respectfully. Then the words got louder, each man talking over the other before they burst into the room.

The man stopped, his jaw dropped open when he saw her sitting at the table. He was older than Joaquin by about thirty years. Weight gathered around his neck, face and gut, but his legs and arms were thin.

She lowered her gaze and tugged at her short hair, as if trying to hide behind it. Did she look that pathetic?

"Amanda Martin, Alfredo Alvarez," Joaquin said, as if their names were all they needed to know.

"Hi." She gave a half wave.

The older man's face reddened, but she saw his struggle to calm himself. "*Mucho gusto*," he said. "Forgive me; this is a bit of a surprise." Alfredo cut his eyes to Joaquin. "I wasn't given much notice."

"Makes two of us," she said. "Normally I wouldn't drop in like this without a bottle of wine or a fruitcake."

He paced. "What do you know?"

"That Joaquin only pretends to be a priest and stashes guns in Bibles." She paused, taking a deep breath, staring at her hands. The puncture wound from the needle in the crook of her arm had bled through the bandage, warm red blood streamed down her arm. "And, Rafael Vargas isn't happy I'm alive."

# 10

David hadn't been back to this part of the river since the dogs and dive teams had left. He told himself there was no reason to return here.

She was somewhere else. He had to move forward. Look further east where he had a chance of finding her.

That was the lie he'd told himself. The truth he couldn't imagine facing, especially now that he'd quit drinking, was *this* was where he'd failed her. In their fall he let go, lost her in the raging Rio Grande.

This pebbly riverbed was more than where he'd lost Mandy. It was where he'd lost his desire to live.

Not just exist, but to *live* in the fullest extent of the word.

Shiloh and El were right. He had to move on. Move away. But the feeling he was abandoning Mandy weighed so heavily on him, he'd sink straight to the bottom.

He walked closer to the river. It flowed lazily, as if unburdened by love.

By loss.

David knelt. His hand hovered just above the water. He could almost feel her, as if the river had consumed part of her essence.

"Hey," he whispered. "It's me. I'm sorry."

There were so many things he was sorry for. Where should he start? Not standing by her in Phoenix? Sleeping with Shiloh? Or, nearly turning her in to Fallon?

Letting tequila mean more to him than her? Losing her in the river?

They were all acts he'd spend a lifetime berating himself over, but they weren't what made his breath hitch.

David cleared his throat and started again. "I'm sorry, Mandy, but I have to leave. I tried, baby, I did. I wanted to bring you home, let your parents bury you, but you're gone."

A bird swooped down, riding on a current of air just inches above the water before taking flight up the canyon wall across from him.

He followed it with his gaze, watching it land at the place where they jumped. The bird sat on the edge, cocked its head to the side and dove down again.

Is that where she was now? Was Mandy's spirit soaring and diving, being lifted by the wind?

Was she telling him it was all right? Nothing hurt anymore; not the sunburn or the blisters, not even the pain he caused.

The bird landed on the shore next to him. One beady eye studied him before it cocked its head to let the other eye get a look.

Suddenly, Mandy felt closer than she'd felt in months.

Maybe he was wrong. He just needed a little more time. She spent over a year looking for Josh, and while she hadn't achieved what she'd set out for, she'd found him.

How could he quit her when he'd only been looking for a month?

"I can stay," David said to the bird. "If you want me to, I can keep looking."

The bird pivoted and hopped away, leaving little triangular footprints in the loamy sand.

Going home didn't mean he was giving up on her.

She wasn't here, that was obvious.

The one place he could still find her was in his heart. David had to nourish that place, feed it love and hope. It wasn't in Pardon Falls; it was back home in Phoenix.

There he could keep her alive.

It only took minutes to pack his meager belongings. The *casita* had never felt like his home, and every day it felt less and less like Mandy's home.

He tossed his stuff in the back of his truck, but the few things Mandy had left behind, he tucked them into the seat next to him.

It was only late morning, but David found El at the bar. With his bifocals sliding down his nose, the bar owner studied an inventory list rather than look up.

"You finally going home?" the older man asked.

He had a question perched on his lips, but the man answered it before it could take flight.

"I've been seeing people coming and going since before you were born." El sat the paper on the bar top and laid his glasses down. "I know what a goodbye looks like."

He pulled out a barstool and sat across from the man. "Thanks for letting me stay here." As soon as he sat the keys down, he felt homesick for the little house that just moments before felt so foreign.

El shrugged him off. "Where you headed?"

"Back home, to Phoenix. A friend of mine is getting married, wants me to take over his job managing a bar."

The older man furrowed his brow, two white, bushy eyebrows joined together. "You sure about this?"

It was David's turn to shrug. "I thought you wanted me to get on with my life."

"I do. But I want it to be *your* decision. Not something you're doing because I told you so and someone offered you a job. Coffee?"

"Sure." He nodded.

El poured them each a cup and heaved himself onto the barstool next to him. "Are you ready to go back?"

David studied the steam rising off the black liquid. Would he ever be ready to go home? Was Phoenix even ready for him?

He sat up the night before letting the various scenarios run through his head like running football plays. A defense man has his tight end covered, go for the running back. Running back not paying attention, see if he could sneak it to an offensive lineman. At some point, if every man was covered, he had no choice but to run it in himself.

It was time to run it in. To run home.

"If I waited until I was ready I'd be older than you."

El chuckled.

They sipped their coffee in silence.

David's phone buzzed in his pocket. Fallon. He was going to wait and call her when he was far enough on the road he wouldn't be tempted to turn back.

She'd be disappointed with his decision to leave, but she'd also understand. He was just too broken for her to try to put back together.

He sent to the call to voicemail and wrapped his hand around the warm cup.

"Answer me this," El said. "Are you running from something? Or, toward something?"

He wasn't so much afraid of Fallon. David was afraid at what almost happened with her.

Every time he saw her in those days after he'd gotten back, disappointment looked back at him. He'd stood her up and reconnected with Mandy, and not in a friendly ran-into-her-at-the-store connection. He'd fallen much deeper for her than he could have ever imagined.

How much more could he do to Fallon?

"Both," David said.

El chugged back the last of his coffee. "Fair enough." The man pushed himself off the stool and went back to inventorying his liquor behind the bar.

He stared down at his nearly empty coffee cup. Starting over and going back home. It was weird to think the two could go together. That he could move forward and backward at the same time. He was thwarting some law of physics. Then again, he'd somehow survived Rafael Vargas and three days lost in the Mexican desert.

He'd thwarted a lot of laws.

"You have my number, right?" David asked.

The old man nodded.

"Promise me if you hear anything you'll call me. Even if it seems crazy or you think it's a rumor. I can be here in about six, seven hours." He studied El. The man had aged decades in the month that he'd known him.

How did *he* look in El's eyes? The last time he'd studied his reflection, his face was thinner, but the sunburn had faded. Circles seemed to permanently darken under his eyes and a few more gray hairs peeked out.

"Go home, David. Let your momma take care of you. Find a lady who loves you, have babies and forget about this."

"I can't forget about Mandy."

"I'm not saying forget about her. Forget about this fantasy of finding her. Living in the past guarantees you'll never be in the present."

"Promise me you'll call," David repeated.

El's light blue eyes locked with his. Was the man checking his sanity? Looking for wildly twitching eyes? Anything he could use to write David off as a victim of sunstroke and madness?

The bar owner pressed his lips tight and nodded. "Don't expect to hear from me, but yeah, if it means you'll get the hell out of my bar, I'll call ya."

Leaving Pardon Falls wouldn't take more than a few minutes, but David paid attention to every step. The burst of light as he left the darkness of El Capitan into the bright South Texas sun. The crunch of the gravelly parking lot as he backed out. Plumes of dust rose up behind his truck, preventing him from looking back.

The town retreated from him until finally he was alone on the highway.

No buildings, no cars.

No Mandy.

# 11

Neither man joined her at the table. Alfredo leaned against the doorway, his ankles and arms crossed. He seemed friendly enough, but his posture told her he wasn't happy she was there.

*Makes two of us.*

Joaquin hung back near the kitchen.

Now that she knew he wasn't a priest, he looked odd in the black shirt and collar. Like a little kid playing dress up in his dad's suit.

Amanda's heart finally stopped pounding. Her shoulders relaxed. The throbbing in her head and dull ache in her gut were becoming bad memories. The pain pill must be taking effect. "So, are we going to sit around in awkward silence. Or, do one of you want to tell me who the hell you are, and what I'm doing here?"

A slight grin tugged at Joaquin's lips, no doubt amused by her let's-get-this-party-started forthcomingness.

Alfredo, on the other hand, scowled. He turned to Joaquin, spoke in quiet Spanish.

"Your English is much better than my Spanish." She interrupted whatever he was saying. "If you're going to talk about me, do it in English so I don't get a headache trying to translate."

Joaquin covered his mouth to hold back a laugh.

"Okay, I asked him how you are supposed to help us if you have amnesia," Alfredo said.

Amanda gnawed on her lip. Help? How could she help anyone? She could barely put on pants and tying her own shoelaces was somewhere between winning the lottery and walking on the moon on the likely-to-happen scale. "I don't have amnesia," she said. "Never did."

Alfredo narrowed his eyes. "So, you're a liar."

Joaquin hissed in quiet Spanish.

She didn't understand the words, but it felt like something in her defense.

"I'm not perfect, and sure, a lie is sometimes much easier than the truth." She shifted her gaze to Joaquin. "Thank you for saving me, probably more times than I know. I'm sure I owe you any help I can provide, but who you are and why I should trust you?"

The men looked at each other again.

Alfredo sat in the chair next to her.

Joaquin stayed back.

His sudden distance made her feel exposed, naked. She'd gotten used to having him by her side, whether it was chatting about how she felt or translating for doctors, Joaquin was always there. Why was he now abandoning her? "Joaquin? What's wrong?"

He took the chair next to her. "Nothing, just giving you space."

Was he being respectful of the panic attack she had outside the hospital?

Alfredo took a deep breath. "As you know, Joaquin is not a priest. He assumed that role because his true career could get him killed."

Amanda looked at Joaquin. Her mouth pursed to form a question, but the man ducked his head, dropping his gaze to his feet.

"He's my best investigative reporter, and he's been undercover for some time," Alfredo said.

"Investigating what?" she asked.

"Not what, *mija*. Who." Her friend spoke softly, as if the house might be bugged. "Rafael Vargas."

The drug lord's name rattled her spine. It was the second time she'd heard it that day and a tiny flush of adrenalin flew through her body.

"Journalists here are murdered for speaking the truth," Alfredo said. "So we hid him in the priesthood."

"We?" Amanda asked.

"Alfredo owns the paper," Joaquin said.

She nodded as the words soaked in. This wasn't the first time she'd heard cartels murdered reporters for speaking out against them.

"I dropped in your lap and you want to get my story?" Amanda tried to connect all the dots, but they were fuzzy and moving around. Some of them were falling off the map completely.

The men exchanged glances.

They held their promise to speak only English in front of her, but instead a conversation of sighs, blinks and nods passed between them. It was obvious they've known each other for quite some time.

"Yes..." Alfredo drew the word out.

Joaquin reached for her hand. Rubbing his thumb across the back of it. This time, that gesture didn't feel intimate.

Now, it was reassuring. Warm. Calming.

"There were three of you, no?" he asked.

His question somehow made her daydreams more lucid. She really had been lost in the desert. Josh really had sacrificed himself to save her. David really had drowned in the river.

A rogue tear streamed down her cheek. "Yes," she whispered. "I'm the only one who survived."

Now that she said it, the dream felt concrete. Like a television signal finally coming in tune. No longer floating in the ether, she was forced to say the words out loud.

She'd survived.

They died.

Joaquin popped out of his chair and knelt beside her, still holding tight to her hand. "This is hard, Amanda, I know," he paused and dropped his gaze. "I wasn't deceiving you when I said you still have a purpose in life."

She swallowed and wiped her face with her free hand. A purpose would give her a reason to not be angry every day when she woke. It would give her a way to honor David and Josh's memory. A purpose would help her heal; give her broken body a goal as it repaired itself.

However, a purpose could also expose her. Make her rely on legs that radiated fire with each step. A purpose could cause her head to ache with the ferocity of a thousand stinging bees.

Amanda studied Joaquin. The gel that had slicked his hair was starting to give in the humidity, letting loose a churning sea of waves. He couldn't have been much older than her, but lines were already working their way across his forehead.

He stayed by her side, when she'd pretended to be asleep, when she'd refused to talk, when she'd lied about not knowing who she was.

Joaquin had never let her down. He never got angry, never questioned her amnesia. Never called her a liar.

She pressed into the table, pushing herself up.

"*Mija?*" he whispered, standing to give her a hand.

"I'm okay. Sitting too much." She shuffled across the spacious kitchen, careful to place her foot firmly on the rug covering the tile floor. The only sound was the tinkling of the fountain.

Natural light illuminated the house, despite no naked windows looking out. The high wall enclosing the back patio protected them from watchful eyes through the glass doors. Frosted glass let light into the kitchen, but kept movement a secret.

The men were silent.

Alfredo kept his eyes on the table, but Joaquin hovered nearby, like a parent letting a child take her first steps.

He watched intently, close enough to catch her if she stumbled, but he wasn't going to help unless she asked.

When Amanda visited her memories, reliving them, she often spent time with David and Josh in the desert, when they were alive. Sometimes, she'd revisit Vargas' office, when she'd snuck in with a gun.

It was during these trips that she'd correct her aim, calm her fears and quiet her screaming conscious before pulling the trigger, this time striking Vargas squarely in the forehead instead of his ear.

There was no doubt she had the desire to help them take down Vargas.

She leaned against the counter, the edge of it biting into her lower back. "It takes everything I have to stand up," she said. "Bills pass through Congress faster than I can go to the bathroom." She pulled back the hair at her temple, giving the scar a clear view of the room. "There's always a throb that radiates from here. Sometimes it's low and manageable, sometimes it's so bad I want to cut off my own head." Amanda glanced around the empty house, waiting to see if any ghosts sprang up from the corners. "And, I have panic attacks when I go outside. How can I be any use to you?"

Her doubt was in her ability to be anything more than a liability.

"I know you're scared, but—" Joaquin said.

"I'm not scared. I'm broken." She tried to swallow the lump in her throat, but it was stubborn.

Joaquin stood against the opposite counter and crossed his arms. His dark eyes bore into her.

As much as she wanted to break eye contact, she couldn't let him win; with words or stares.

"You're not broken," he said.

She laughed. "Oh? Have you guys been lying to me about the head injury and fractured pelvis? Because, I am starting to really sympathize with Humpty Dumpty." She tried to laugh again, but the emotion took a hairpin curve. It picked up speed down a steep hill of self-pity and crashed into a wave of regret, splintering the wall she'd built around her heart into a million shards. The tears came quickly. Like flood waters washing over the desert floor.

Joaquin wrapped her in his arms.

"I'm sorry, Joaquin," Amanda sobbed. "I wish I could help you, but I just want to go home."

He loosened his embrace and held her at arm's length, ducking slightly to look her in the eye. Sadness was smeared across his face.

He had really hoped she would help. The time he'd spent next to her in the hospital could've been used nurturing someone else, a stronger source who wouldn't stand in a stranger's kitchen crying for her mom.

"It's okay, *mija*, I understand. You're safe here. Rest tonight. Tomorrow I'll start working on getting you home."

*Home.*

The word buoyed her heart. Like her name, it was a word she'd used all too casually, but now it felt dense with meaning.

With hope.

# 12

The knock on her door was so quiet Amanda thought she'd dreamt it.

"Are you sleeping?" Joaquin's whispered voice came through the wood.

She sat up in the bed. The darkness outside her window was fading into a baby blue. If she'd slept, it was so brief and dreamless she didn't notice it. "No, I'm awake."

He came into the room and sat at the foot of her bed. Dressed in a T-shirt and basketball shorts, he looked almost unrecognizable. His hair stood up on one side and dark circles cushioned his eyes. Joaquin yawned and rubbed the stubble on his face.

"Slept that good, huh?" she asked.

"It's been years since I've had a good night's sleep. What about you?"

"Do you ever wonder if this is how it's always going to be? The days of peace and quiet are a thing of the past?"

Joaquin's shoulders lifted with a deep breath and he looked up at the ceiling. "I'm not sure they were ever really there."

Amanda winced and studied her fingernails. She'd only spent a couple of months living in fear of the drug cartels. What was it like living in constant fear of them? Was it like the hum of white noise? Something loud and all-consuming at first, but softens to a dull roar, only to feel its absence like a chilling silence when it was gone. "I'm sorry," she said. "I'm letting you down."

He looked at her, a half smile tugged at his lips, but it didn't make its way to his eyes. "I'm the one who should apologize. That's why I'm here. I didn't want you to leave thinking I lied to you just to use you. I couldn't tell you who I was in the beginning because we didn't think you even remembered who you were. We were afraid it would only make things worse."

"I lied to you." Her voice was sharper than intended. "Don't apologize because I knew who I was the moment I woke up." She craned her neck to look out the window.

The sun was now rising, coloring the window in deep orange and yellow. This time yesterday she was still in her hospital bed.

This time last year, she'd been in Pardon Falls, biding time to find Josh.

This time two years ago, she'd been suffering through a Chicago heat wave with her life fully intact, her philandering boyfriend using her to cover his crimes.

Her life had changed so much she didn't recognize it.

Didn't recognize herself.

"You really want to go home?" Joaquin's voice was flat.

Amanda guessed he'd hoped she'd had a change of heart overnight. She'd hoped so too, but her heart was so numb if a change was coming, it couldn't feel it. "I do," she whispered.

He nodded and patted her knee. "I'll take you to the Consulate today. That's the safest way..." Joaquin didn't finish his thought, but he meant the safest way for her to get back without Vargas' people intercepting.

They sat in silence for several minutes. It didn't feel like an ending.

She'd had plenty of those. Goodbyes were best if they weren't spoken. The words only diluted what was in her heart.

*Thank you for staying by me. Thank you for nursing me back to health. I'm sorry I let you down.*

Her heart wasn't ready to give flight to those words. They were baby birds, not ready to leave the nest. If she pushed one out, it would fall to an early death.

"You know so much about me," Amanda said. "But what I thought I knew about you was wrong. So, tell me about the real Joaquin Rios."

He shrugged and looked at his hands. "How do you sum up a person in words when their true nature lies in their actions and deeds?"

There was so much truth there. It was what Amanda had spent the last year and a half of her life doing. To let her actions override her words, especially the ones she'd said at Josh's urging to help him commit securities fraud.

Joaquin stood and stretched. "We've got a little time before the Consulate office opens. Want some breakfast?"

"Actions are driven by desires," Amanda said. "All of mine since Chicago have been about bringing Josh to face a jury. What's driving you? What's your desire?"

He pivoted from the door. "The cartels run this country as if it's theirs. It's not, it's mine and Alfredo's. It belongs to the children on the streets. It belongs to the men and women who work long hours to give their children a better life. It even belongs to the wealthy, those who earned their money the honest way. They don't get to steal people's families because it suits them." He pulled the bedroom door open. "I'll start breakfast. Join me in the kitchen when you're ready."

The meal was a solemn affair. Alfredo sat hunched over his plate, shoveling his *huevos rancheros* into his mouth.

Joaquin stared at his phone, his face either relaxed and pleased with what he read, or puckered into a deep scowl. He took a bite, thumbed through his phone; took a sip of coffee, swiped at the screen.

Amanda picked at her food. Not that it didn't smell delicious, or her stomach didn't beg for a bite of non-hospital food. Physical pain from her injuries was melding with the emotional ache of telling Joaquin no.

After the men were done, she scooped up their empty plates despite their protests. She had to keep busy, because otherwise, she might change her mind.

With the dishes soaking, Amanda looked out the patio doors. The back courtyard was flush with life. Birds bathed in the outdoor fountain. Butterflies flitted from flower to flower. The sky over the tall stone wall was a brilliant, deep blue.

"*Mija*, ready?"

She jumped at his voice beside her. She wasn't ready to go home. She wasn't ready to stay and help.

The car ride to the Consulate was less rushed than their getaway from Vargas' men. Like watching a movie in reverse, the city grew as they moved closer to the center. Buildings inched closer together, people multiplied, more cars sprung up around them on the road.

The sleeping panic stirred within her chest, curious as to what was going to jump out of the side streets. Amanda silently hushed it, told it she was going home. Once she walked into the Consulate she'd be back on American soil, where Vargas couldn't reach her, and just steps away from her family. It would also be time for her to finally pay for her part of Josh's crimes.

The panic called her a liar, and rolled over and went back to sleep.

Traffic slowed to a standstill. Exhaust from the cars rose up in dirty waves, permeating the inside of the car with hot, stifling air. The American flag beckoned ahead of her. Waving coyly at her in the loose breeze.

Sweat trickled down her chest. Perspiration flushed her thighs, the sticky sweatpants were a sauna for her legs.

Joaquin cursed and pushed up in his seat, as if trying to see over the cars.

The traffic lunged forward, but then abruptly stopped. The squeal of brakes and crash of metal filled the air and his car lurched.

Amanda gasped as the seatbelt cut into her pelvis. Tears rushed forward, but she squeezed her eyes shut, refusing to let them fall.

A tangled mix of Spanish and English curses fell from her friend's lips. "Are you okay, *mija?*" he asked, before looking up in his rearview mirror. "Stay here while I see the damage."

She nodded and took deep breaths, sending oxygen to the center of her body. If it worked for women in the throes of childbirth, then it would have to work for a cracked pelvis as well. At least she hoped.

While Joaquin argued with the man who'd rear-ended them, she watched the traffic start and stop around them.

Old and young men pushed carts through the traffic, selling juices and frozen treats. Children knocked on car windows, their palms out asking for any bit of money.

These were the people Joaquin had talked about. Mexico belonged to them, and in some cases, it was all they had.

Amanda didn't have much more, at least not sitting there in a traffic jam wearing the only clothes she had, but once she got home, her parents would help her rebuild her life. She'd have so much more than these people.

What did her actions and deeds say about her now?

She jumped at a knock at her window.

A little boy stared, probably no older than six or seven. He smiled shyly at her, his little teeth glowing against his tanned skin.

She rolled the window down, trying to think of the words she could say to him.

*I'm so sorry, I can't help you. I have no money and no bravery.*

"*Hola, como estas?*" was all she could think of.

The boy handed her a blue velvet box. It was large, a jeweler's box that could hold a necklace or bracelet.

"*Para mi?*" she asked. Amanda wanted to call out to Joaquin to see if he had any money he could give the boy, but a quick glance behind her told her he was still arguing with the other driver. She looked back to the window, but the boy was gone. She looked out the driver's side window. Nothing.

Ahead of her was more cars, the same men pushing their carts of treats. More gangs of kids rushed from car to car.

The box sat in her lap. Why would he deliver something and want nothing in return?

Her heart banged against her ribs. It didn't want her to open the box. Her blood rushed through her ears, the thrumming drowning the sounds outside the car.

She lifted the lid.

A white notecard stared up at her from a bed of yellow string; the words "Silence is Golden" penned in beautiful calligraphy.

She picked up a piece of the string.

Not string. Hair. And not yellow.

Blonde.

Amanda brushed it out of the way. Her fingers scraped against something waxy. Not waxy. Detached.

Her breath pushed out of her lungs. She drew her fingers back, afraid to see more of the ear, the part where it was hacked away from its owner.

Joaquin pulled open his door and flopped into his seat, still muttering under his breath.

She could hear him speaking, but he sounded far away. Everything felt distant. As if the car didn't exist, the traffic wasn't there. The only thing in the world right now was Amanda and the box shaking in her hands.

"Amanda, what's wrong?"

Her head jerked in his direction.

The scowl was back. "Where did you get that?" He gestured to the box.

"A kid." Her voice came out in a soft whisper. "Turn around."

"What's in it? Why?"

She passed the open box to Joaquin.

He glanced down at it and blanched, snapping it closed and covering his mouth with his hand.

The flag at the Consulate office hung straight down, lost in the still air. If she hadn't seen it earlier, she would haven't been able to discern the red and white stripes, the blue box with its cluster of stars. It had turned its back to her. The same way she'd considered turning her back to Joaquin. Turning her back to Josh.

"I'm not going home," Amanda said, looking straight out at the traffic. The cars around them started to move, but theirs sat still, despite the disapproving honks. "Josh is still alive."

# 13

Fallon had to hand it to her brother. He was a freaking
genius.

The senior center was thrumming with activity. Of
course it was, since it was only a quarter past seven. If the meeting
was twelve hours from now, the place would be a ghost town.

Richard was seated against the window looking out over a lap
pool. He spoke with a man across from him, their heads close.

Fallon waited at the entrance to the dining room, giving her
brother a few extra minutes with his CI. She looked across the sea
of elderly ladies, wearing matching track suits and similar white,
short curly haircuts. The men all wore the same short-sleeved
button-up shirts, their glasses cases peeking out of the top of their
breast pockets.

This was the perfect place for a DEA agent to meet with an
informant.

Her brother looked up and waved her over.

His informant stood when she approached, and waited until she
was seated before easing back into his chair.

*This guy has better manners than my last five dates.*

"Berto, this is Agent Weatherby of the FBI," her brother said.

She nodded at the young man across from them. He was every sense of the word *young*. Couldn't have been more than twenty.

His face was soft, little patches of beard strained to grow on his cheeks. His hair was smoothed down flat against his forehead, framing insanely long eyelashes.

"Is this y'alls regular meeting place?" she asked. The sound of splashing caught her attention. A group of ladies in skirted swimsuits climbed into the pool. Fifties music blasted from a boombox on a chair. Water aerobics time.

"Yeah, Berto volunteers here." Richard shoved a forkful of scrambled eggs in his mouth.

"Volunteers?" Fallon couldn't help herself. The word launched from her mouth before she could catch it.

"Yeah, you see, it was part of my community service, right," the boy said. "But, these old people are awesome, man. They don't treat me like I'm some hood rat or nothing." It was written all over his face. The boy truly loved it here.

"So yeah, I help them out wherever they need me. I do some laundry, gardening, help out in the kitchen, and sometimes I play dominos with the guys."

"Tell her about the crocheting," Richard said. His eyes crinkled, a sure sign this was more play than work.

Berto blushed, possibly the deepest crimson she's ever seen on a human.

*Well, outside of David's post-desert sunburn.*

Fallon swallowed that thought. Heart attacks were horseplay compared to her brother. If he could have fun with a CI, she could too.

"Aww, man, why'd you have to go and tell her. Now I've got no chance with her," Berto said with a wink. "If you'll go out with me, I'll crochet you a tissue box cover."

Her brother and the kid burst out laughing.

It took a moment for a giggle to bubble up her throat. The past twelve hours didn't give her much to laugh about. It felt good to get the cobwebs out.

"Okay, okay, all serious now," Richard said, wiping tears from his eyes. "Tell her what you told me."

Berto glanced behind him and leaned over the table. Even though there was zero chance someone in here would accuse him of being a snitch, it was obvious he lived looking over his shoulder. "I don't work for Vargas, but I know people who do, people close to me. I hear them talking."

"I don't need to know the drugs part, save it for Richard, but about the people. The Americans?"

The boy drummed his fingers on the Formica table. "Yeah, Vargas' former accountant, man, glad I ain't him."

"What do you mean?" she asked.

A voice grew suddenly loud outside.

Fallon darted her gaze out the window. The water aerobics instructor stood on the side of the pool and demonstrated exercises for the ladies.

"Like they have him chained up somewhere, whipping him and cutting body parts off and shit." The boy slapped his hand over his mouth. "Sorry, and stuff."

She pressed her lips together and glanced at her watch. Jay could only cover for her for so long. The conversation needed to move along a little faster. "Okay, so they're torturing Williams. What have you heard about anyone else? Does the name David Stephens ring a bell?"

Berto twisted in his seat, his back to the table.

Fallon cut a glance to her brother, but he kept his eyes on his informant.

The boy swiveled back around and pushed off the table, looking over their heads. Satisfied it was safe, he settled back in. "Yeah, I've heard his name."

He spoke so softly that both Fallon and her brother moved closer to hear him.

"There's eyes on him. They said he left the border though, headed to Phoenix, but I don't know why he was going to Arizona, I thought they were staying in—"

"Phoenix, Texas, not Arizona," Fallon said. Numbness crept up her body. Her feet froze in her shoes, goosebumps broke out beneath her jacket. "Why are they watching him? Williams is the one who caused all the trouble, right?"

Berto shrugged. "Yes, and no."

"There's a lot of machismo around the drug trade," Richard said. "Vargas lost valuable ground among his peers and he's trying to reclaim it."

"Yeah, the chick with them, she shot his ear off." Berto's voice rose with excitement.

Fallon looked at her brother and lifted an eyebrow.

*Amanda?*

Everything she'd seen about the woman made her think she was a typical city girl. More concerned about shopping than helping people out. Or, shooting someone's ear off.

"Vargas likes being good-looking," Richard said. "Disfigured and discredited. Doubly dissed, doubly pissed."

"Okay, but what does that have to do with David?" Fallon felt the need to plead his case. Information could flow both ways. If she convinced this kid David was innocent, maybe he'll blab.

"He's got a lot of ground to make up," her brother mumbled.

She took a deep breath. "They're not just watching him, are they?"

A look passed between the two men.

Berto's face whitened and he gnawed on his lower lip.

"Go ahead. Tell her," Richard said.

"The guy going after him is good. Orders are a clean shot, in and out."

All the sound in the room got sucked into a tiny hole in her gut.

Berto's words were the only sound in Fallon's ears. She glanced out the window.

The women bounced in the water while making circles with their outstretched arms. Their instructor silently counted down and then demonstrated the next move.

A waiter moved among the tables, wordlessly checking on the guests.

She had to get to David. Get him to stop ignoring her.

"Fal, you okay?" Richard closed his hand over hers.

"Yo, I'm sorry, I didn't mean—"

Fallon shook her head. "No, no. Thank you, this is — I've got to, Richard, thank you, Berto." She pushed up from her seat.

The boy stood again. "You never asked why they are cutting up the other man."

Didn't really matter. Nothing mattered other than getting to David. "Because he betrayed him?"

"Yes, but man, this is the messed up part. *El Jefe* is sending bits of him to that *chica*."

*The chica?* "Amanda died in the flood."

"Boss-man doesn't think so. Rumor is she's alive."

Fallon should thank him. Tell him she appreciated the boy putting himself at risk for her. For David.

If she opened her mouth, she might vomit. *This* was why she didn't do relationships. Especially with people in law enforcement.

"Sis, you okay?"

She swallowed her panic. "I will be once I talk to David. Thank you both."

She was two tables away when Berto called out to her.

The boy was still standing, but glanced down at his feet. "What are you going to do about the woman?" He looked up at her. His brow was furrowed, eyes narrowed with worry. "She's all alone over there."

She grimaced and cut her gaze out to the pool. Water aerobics was coming to an end. "You said yourself it's a rumor. I can't chase after rumors; I have to follow leads that are tangible. Right now my friend needs me." She was nearly out of the dining room when the kid spoke again.

"What if it's not a rumor?"

She paused and spoke over her shoulder. "Amanda Martin got herself into that mess. She can get herself out."

# 14

The closed box sat on the table between them like a curse.

Joaquin was still ashen, as if seeing a dead body, or a detached body part, for the first time.

Alfredo held tight to his coffee cup, the steam stopped rising long ago.

Amanda stared at the lid, but saw what it held inside. She parsed through the messages Vargas had sent in that brief exchange with the boy.

*Silence is golden.*

Did he want her to quietly go home?

No, he wasn't one to send her on her way with a wave and shouts of *bon voyage*. Most likely the silence he spoke about was *her*.

Josh was alive.

At least he had been long enough for the drug lord to cut off his ear and send it to her.

Vargas knew *she* was alive. No surprise there, since two of his men had found her in the hospital.

The man was toying with her. Like a cat playing with its prey before devouring it. What good did that do to the outcome?

The cat still got its meal. The prey still succumbed.

Instead of sending the boy, he could've sent an assassin.

No, Vargas wanted her to *feel* the fear, to *see* the end coming. He wanted to swat at her and terrorize her before ultimately gobbling her down with a satisfied purr.

The message that worried her the most was the one she'd been struggling to say aloud since they arrived back.

The safe house was no longer safe.

"He knew where we were headed." Those words had been hovering around them since they'd returned. She might as well bring them in for a landing. Amanda kept her eyes glued to the box, afraid to look at either man. Could one of them be working for Vargas? It hurt her head just thinking about it.

"We made the most logical play," Joaquin said, shaking his head. "Vargas is a master strategist. We got you out of the hospital, so the next place you'd go is home. And the way for you to go home—"

"Is through the U.S. Consulate." Amanda exhaled. They'd done *exactly* what the drug lord had expected, rather than her being betrayed. Again. "So the traffic jam…"

"Was most likely caused by him," Alfredo said. "And the man who rear-ended you, that was probably no accident."

The man had been arguing with Joaquin right up until the boy had given her the box, then he handed over a wad of *pesos* for the minor damage and left. It was all part of the game.

She nodded. "Okay, I'm in."

"You wouldn't help us before, but *now* you will?" Alfredo's voice dripped with sarcasm. "How generous of you."

Amanda tried to find the words to explain her sudden change of heart. It wasn't that she didn't want to help earlier, she'd been afraid she couldn't. If she'd tried, she'd fail them. Not just fail *them*, but get them killed like she had David and Josh.

Or…

Just David.

Now that she knew Josh was alive, she couldn't leave. Not without trying to bring him with her. It didn't matter if he never saw the inside of a jail cell. It didn't matter that he'd stolen money, twice, and drugged David in an attempt to get her to leave with him. What mattered was he'd sacrificed his own freedom for hers.

Amanda could've pretended she didn't see the box for what it was. She could've gone to the Consulate and would've been back in Chicago by evening, nestled in her childhood bed with her parents peeking in on her like a newborn baby. She would've had freedom, but she'd never be free from her conscience.

She took a deep breath and pushed the box out of her line of vision. "Do you know anything about the time we were kidnapped, and our escape?"

The men shook their heads.

"There was this bond that formed among us. In the desert. We wanted to strangle each other, but we would also walk through fire for each other." Those days felt so long ago, yet as fresh in her memory as the morning's breakfast. "I was prepared to die."

Joaquin's sudden intake of breath made Amanda pause.

"I was going to give myself to Vargas so Josh and David could get home. Josh stopped me and surrendered himself in my place." Tears stung her eyes. She hadn't cried for Josh. Not in the way she'd mourned David.

Had she really started to see Josh as a goal, and not a person?

She sniffed and straightened her back. "So, yes, I couldn't help you before because I was afraid I'd fail you. Now I can, because if I don't, I'll fail Josh."

Joaquin grasped her hand and squeezed.

Alfredo sipped his coffee, his gaze glued to the box with Josh's ear. The man nodded and glanced up. "You're doing exactly what Vargas wants."

"I know." Amanda held his gaze. "I've beaten him before, but I can't guarantee I can do it again. You want to take down the cartels. How? Vargas has many people loyal to him, both in the U.S. and Mexico. How do you know who to trust?"

The men glanced at each other, a silent conversation passing as smoothly as the spoken word.

"You're right, *mija*," Joaquin said. "It's difficult to know who to trust. The police aren't the same here. Politicians with good intentions don't last long."

"The only untouchable is the clergy," she said.

Joaquin flashed a quick smile. "Mostly. We have those within our network we trust. They're all like us, people who are tired of being afraid."

"Where do I fit in?"

"We need you being you," Alfredo said. "We need you visible, out where Vargas can see you."

"I sit on a park bench and wait for him to kill me?" Amanda shook her head. "That's not going to help me find Josh."

"What do you suggest?" Joaquin asked.

She reached for the box, cupping it in her hands. Vargas could've killed her, but he hadn't. This was for sport.

Amanda had to play Vargas' game, but better than him. Smarter.

"How many properties does Vargas own? Can you get me a list? He must have Josh somewhere nearby."

"You're suddenly in charge?" Alfredo's face flushed red.

Joaquin held a hand in front of his boss, quieting him. "Yes, we can get you a list."

"I doubt he's at the *hacienda*, we took it out of commission when we left," she said. Amanda glanced down at the clothes she's worn for the past twenty-four hours. Having a wardrobe, no matter how small, was a luxury she missed.

"We'll get you some more clothes, too," Joaquin added, as if reading her mind.

"I'll go with you. I might as well start being visible."

Alfredo left in a grumble. Was he upset that not only had she come back, but she'd come back with her own list of demands? Or, was he bitter that she chose to get involved for Josh rather than for them?

Joaquin watched his boss leave. "I'll be right back," he said before following the man into the other room.

Alone in the kitchen, she opened the box again. She needed to see it. If Josh was still alive, David could be as well?

What happened if she found him? Walk in and negotiate with Vargas? Rely on Joaquin and Alfredo's network to arrest him?

How much of Josh would be left? He was missing an ear, but what other injuries had been inflicted?

"Ready?"

Amanda snapped the lid closed, but by the look on Joaquin's face, he'd still spotted her looking at it.

"You don't have to do this. I can still drive you to the Consulate. It'll be safer now."

She stood, wincing. When had she taken meds last? Was it too early for another?

She shook two pills from the bottle. "I'm good, let's go."

The drive to the shop was short and uneventful. She felt strangely serene, safe and invincible. Maybe it was the message from Vargas, knowing he was out there watching her. Amanda feared being found, but now that she had been, what else was there to worry about?

Death?

She'd already lived through that, a few times over. Torture? Agony flooded her body every time she stood or sat.

The only fear that floated around her heart was for Joaquin. His involvement with her would end in the same way it had for Josh. Or, David.

The little clothing store was bustling.

Joaquin clung close to her as she perused the women's section, grabbing a handful of basics, just enough to get her through a few days. How long would it take for her to find Josh? How long would Vargas keep him alive?

Her eyes caught her reflection in the mirror outside the fitting room. The scar on her temple was starting to fade to white, but there was still the angry red bullseye in the middle of it. Whatever was responsible for this scar was her last memory in the water.

Amanda's hair hung in jagged edges around her chin. On someone else it would be an edgy, stylish cut. On her, it seemed like a disguise. Despite the ruse, she felt exposed. Naked.

Maybe this was good. They wanted her to be visible. Vargas

would have no trouble spotting her. She looked at the clothes in hands. A pair of dark jeans and a couple of tank tops. Perhaps she should grab some neon-colored shirts as well. Maybe with a flashing arrow pointing down at her.

Joaquin was never more than a few feet away. He stared at the screen on his phone, but Amanda could feel his eyes on her.

"We've got the list," he mumbled to her when they approached the checkout.

"Good," she said, picking up the bag containing her new wardrobe. "Let's get to work."

# 15

At the end of his first week at Riley's on the River, David had only a slightly better handle on the operations of the bar. Just when he thought he'd figured out the management of the employees, Eddie would add in maintaining the inventory.

Once he got that, it was time to greet the customers. He pulled double shifts every day trying to soak it all in. To ensure he'd be so exhausted when he got home, he wouldn't feel guilty for abandoning the search for Mandy.

Guilt had a way of sucker punching him when he least expected it. He was working on the employee schedule when he'd heard Mandy's name whispered in his ear. Or, he'd be counting bottles of liquor in the storeroom when he'd see her walk by out of the corner of his eye.

Riley's was packed full his first weekend night. David had to twist and turn to walk through the bar.

Shiloh worked two sections, moving so quickly among the tables that the most he saw of her was a blur of dark hair.

How much of the busy night was the result of a late summer

cool front rather than the fact that Phoenix's most notorious screw-up had come home with his tail between his legs?

Probably a little bit of both.

The bar was full, but the spot where he and Mandy had stood the evening of their first date sat empty, as if it were a shrine to the woman he loved, betrayed and, ultimately, abandoned.

"Hey, how you doing?" Shiloh fanned herself with her tray. "You know you could've taken tonight off."

David shrugged. "Keeps me busy."

She grabbed her waiting drinks and loaded them on her tray. "All right, but promise me you'll take care of yourself. I worry about you." She pivoted and was absorbed by the mass of thirsty patrons.

He worried about himself, too. New routines were tough. Especially new-old routines. Twice that week he'd caught himself pulling up to the police station on his drive to work. He kept his eyes peeled on his run for Mandy's jogging form, half a block ahead of him, teasing him. Driving by the newspaper office where she'd worked, he'd crane his neck to see if her robin's egg blue Bronco was parked out front.

David was surprised the people of Phoenix were eager to greet him. Shiloh was right. Something about getting kidnapped by a cartel leader and being the lone survivor erased his past discretions.

Former teachers and coaches came by his house. Old classmates stopped by after work for a beer. Even the police chief had come by for lunch one day. The man had walked right up to him, stuck out his hand and looked him straight in the eye. "Welcome home, son," he'd said.

The buzzing in his pocket pulled him away from the busy bar. El Calchera's name flashed on the screen. David had managed to only call El twice since coming back to Phoenix.

"Hey El, hang on, let me go outside." David pushed his way through the crowd.

The side patio was just as loud. He finally found a quiet place to talk across the parking lot near the dumpsters.

"Can you hear me?" he said.

"David…nothing…see…okay." Static filled the gaps between the older man's broken words.

He looked at his phone. The signal wasn't the strongest in the parking lot, and El was likely at the bar or his house, neither being the primo spot for cell service in Pardon Falls.

"You're breaking up."

The man paused, and this time spoke louder. "This is…*casita* broken…kids probably."

David tried to put the two sentences together while he paced the dirt parking lot. Had the casita been broken into? "El, are you okay?"

"Yes, yes." Suddenly the man came in loud and clear. One of them must have hit a spot of service. "I'm fine. I went down to the *casita* this afternoon and it was broken into, stuff thrown everywhere. It's probably nothing but some drunk kids, but in the thirty-five years I've lived here, never seen that."

The words took a moment to sink in. For being a desert outpost a stone's throw from Mexico, Pardon Falls was a pretty safe town. Everyone knew everyone else and looked out for each other. Could it be a coincidence this happened now? To the place where he'd lived? Where Mandy had lived?

A shiver crawled up his back vertebra by vertebra.

An outburst of laughter brought him back to Riley's. To the warm summer evening, to the locusts calling out to each other from the treetops.

"But you thought it was enough to call me," David said.

El exhaled over the phone. "I don't know what to think anymore. But I never ignore my gut, and my gut told me to give you a heads up."

"Thanks, man. I'll keep you posted."

David didn't go back inside when he ended the call. He walked to the edge of the parking lot, where the sounds of the Tejas River rushing by drowned out the bar noises.

Had it been a mistake to come back to Phoenix so soon? Instead of kids looking for valuables, could Mandy have survived the Rio Grande and made her way to the last place she called home?

A branch snapped behind him. He whirled, his eyes trying to adjust to the blackness of the riverbanks and the lights of Riley's. His breathing slowed. The hair standing up on his arms told him he wasn't alone.

David went back to the parking lot, eager to get back into the pool of light. He was three steps away when a man stepped out from behind the Dumpster.

*Probably just a drunk making a nature call.*

"Hey, how's it going?" David called, less concerned about the man's well-being and more interested in if his assessment was true.

The guy was backlit by the lights of the bar. He could only make out his silhouette, but a glint of gray metal bounced off the gun in his hand.

Was he getting robbed his first week on the job? The little Glock nestled in his ankle holster suddenly felt warm, as if the metal of his weapon felt the presence of one of its kin. He didn't want to use it. Didn't want the gun to go off and spark a round of gossip about how he was to unfit to run a bar.

David held his hands up in the air. "I'm unarmed. I can reach around to my back pocket and get you my wallet."

"I'm not here to rob you." His words were thick with a Spanish accent. "Well, not rob you of money. *Señor* Vargas sent me to collect on your debt to him."

The name slammed into him with the force of a freight train.

"Debt?"

He scanned the parking lot.

A couple walked out of the bar and to the opposite end of the lot. Not that their presence would scare this guy off. In all likelihood, they would just get hurt.

"Your life." The man said it bluntly, as if he were asking for repayment of a few dollars.

*Keep him talking.*

David needed a little more time to deescalate. "So y'all must be done with Williams, then. How long did you torture him?" He shuffled to his right, enough to put him in the line of sight of the patio, but not so much to make the gunman nervous.

"We're not done with any of you." He took a step toward him.

David tilted his head. Any of them? Who else was in danger? Did this extend to El? Willa? Shiloh even?

"But for you." He came closer. "We will end it quickly. You will not suffer like the others."

*There he goes again, talking like there are multiple people in play.*

He gritted his teeth. Not at the possibility of facing his own death, he'd made peace a thousand times over. It was the hint of what he *didn't* know.

A figure made its way down the steps from the back patio. In the flash of a cigarette lighter, Shiloh's face lit up in the night.

"How did the others suffer?" he asked, raising his voice, hoping it was enough to get her attention so she could call 9-1-1. His pulse beat against the strap of his holster, reminding him it's there, begging to be used, but he'd be dead before he could grab it.

David kept his eyes focused on the guy, but watched Shiloh study him across the lot. He kept his hands stayed up in the air, hoping she'd get the universal gesture for *I've-got-a-gun-pointed-at-me.*

She tossed aside her cigarette and moved toward them, holding a hand up like a gun.

David cleared his throat, hoping that would be affirmation enough. *Just go inside, Shi.*

She took another two steps, this time moving to the man's right.

*Dammit, Shiloh.*

Using a combination of hand signals and mouthing silent words, she threw incomprehensible instructions his way.

*She's been watching way too many cop shows.*

"*Señor* Williams still suffers," he said.

David cut his eyes to Shiloh.

She continued her slow progression, pulling her drink tray out from under her arm.

"But *señorita, el jefe* has something special planned for her."

Shiloh paused at the same beat as David's heart.

"You should know by now she's dead."

Laughter from the bar sliced through the silence. The gunman shifted his gaze.

David tackled him, grabbing the hand with the gun and banging it hard into the packed dirt. After a couple of hits, the weapon loosened from the man's grip.

"Shi, kick it away," he shouted. With his free hand, David tugged up the leg of his jeans to draw his weapon.

A fist collided hard with David's cheekbone, knocking him back before he could grasp his gun. The man laid another punch in his gut, sending all of his air rushing out of his lungs.

The goon pushed David off him and hopped upright. A distinctive ting rung out in the air.

David scrambled to a crouch.

*Of course the guy has a knife.*

A howl of gunfire went off over his head. Shiloh pointed the gun over the treetops. "Hey asshole, you know what they say about bringing a knife to a gunfight?"

Voices behind him competed with the ringing in his ears. Even over the music, a single shot would be a beacon.

The man looked past them. "She's alive. For now." He ran behind the Dumpster, the night swallowing him whole.

# 16

D espite his years being a cop, David hated seeing the dancing red and blue lights.

The hum of radios competed with the chattering frogs.

Bar patrons clustered in the parking lot, talking about who saw what; the fish tales already spinning up.

He glanced over at Shiloh, who was talking to an officer. He'd expected her to be shaky, but she calmly answered questions, nodding her head and pointing to the thick woods outside Riley's.

David had given his statement first. Not that he had much to offer. Hispanic, at least judging by the accent. Shorter than him, but stockier. Aside from a quick profile view, the man's face had been enveloped by the dark night.

"Capt—" The Chief caught himself before letting David's previous rank slip from his mouth. His former boss had rushed up to the bar right before getting into bed, so he donned an odd combination of a pajama top, jeans and slippers. "David, you doing okay?"

"Yeah, Chief." He answered, keeping his eyes focused on the woods. Spotlights bounced around the darkness. "Y'all finding anything?"

The man shook his head. "He must've had a vehicle stashed somewhere nearby. Be a few days before we can get dogs out here. By then…"

"Yeah, I know," David said.

It took everything he had to not go running after the gunman. To find out what he knew about Mandy, to offer himself as a hostage if the guy would promise to take him to her.

Only two things could come from giving chase; ruining any chance for the dogs to find a trail, or ending up with a knife in the gut.

Was the man only toying with him? Telling him a vicious lie in his final moments, robbing David the opportunity to die in peace.

He didn't die, and whether the goon meant to or not, he'd given him the slightest bit of hope that Mandy was still out there.

Hope served with a side of cynicism.

No matter how it was sliced, it'd leave a bitter taste.

The officer talking to Shiloh flipped his notepad shut and handed her a card, not like she really needed it. A town as small as Phoenix everyone already had everyone's cell numbers.

"Why do they always want to give victims blankets?" she asked, sauntering over. "It's fricking summer. Idiots."

David laughed. "It's for the shock."

"Yeah, well the shocked one will be that *pendejo* if he ever shows back up here," she mumbled, pulling a cigarette from her pocket. Her hand trembled slightly when she lit it, telling him as unfazed as she tried to seem, it still shook her.

"Thought you'd quit smoking," he said, the words sharp enough to make a point, but with a rounded edge.

"My lack of willpower probably saved your life," Shiloh paused and dropped her half-smoked cigarette, snubbing it with the toe of her sneaker. "I guess I was a little nervous about how this was going to work out, with you here and all."

David was a little nervous about it as well. While she'd checked in on him and worked a few hours one afternoon, this was their first full shift together. Would it resurrect old feelings?

Old regret?

The chief walked over with the other officer.

Shiloh shuffled, moving away from David.

"Well, son, I think we're about done here," he said. "Make sure you lock your doors and keep your gun nearby tonight, you hear?"

"Yes, sir," David said. Not that he was going to get much sleep.

Once the police left, the majority of the crowd dispersed, leaving the bar nearly empty for the last hour. Which suited him fine. Closing duties with a subdued crowd gave him a chance to mentally chew on what Vargas' guy had told him.

He'd searched all along the Texas side of the river, but what if Fallon's original assessment was right? What if Mandy had made it out the Mexico side of the river?

She would've woken up alone and afraid. There was far less along the Northern Mexico border than the South Texas border. She couldn't have survived that harsh landscape for long, not without some help.

But, from who?

"You keep wiping that same spot and you'll wear a hole in it." Shiloh's voice made him jump.

"Sorry, just thinking."

She hopped onto the barstool. "I heard what he said. About... her. Do you think he was telling the truth?"

David took a deep breath. He still felt strange talking to Shiloh about Mandy. "I dunno, he could've just been messing with me. But..."

"There's also the chance he's not."

Shiloh pulled out another cigarette and tapped it on the counter. "What are you going to do about it?"

That was what he'd been asking himself since the man had run off. He'd have a better chance of finding a needle in a haystack on the moon than one woman in all of Mexico.

Then again, she'd managed to find Williams. With her days numbered, did he have what she did to find her?

The one advantage he had was not being under indictment and wanted by the SEC. David could go through more official channels, get the backing of the law enforcement agencies that searched the Rio Grande for her.

"Would it be too early to ask for some time off?" he asked.

She stuck the fresh cigarette in her mouth and lit it, her hands steady again. "We were going to fire you anyway. Too much drama."

# 17

The music reverberated around Josh's cell, falling lightly on his ear. It was hard for him to think of his ears as a singular term.

*Ear.*

It didn't feel right not being plural.

His hearing on one side was muffled. Sometime during one of his anguish-filled unconscious moments, someone had come in and bandaged it.

It was most likely less out of concern for Josh's comfort and more they didn't want him dying of a staph infection before they were done with him.

He pulled at his restraints. If they were worried about keeping him alive, they should do something about the gaping sores encircling his wrists.

When had he last had a tetanus shot?

The tunes grew louder, pouring in from above. It was jubilant. Full of celebration and happiness. Was there a wedding party walking by?

What would the blushing bride think if she knew a naked, bald, maimed American lurked just below her feet?

*She'd probably puke.*

Two sets of footsteps shuffled above his head, only reaffirming what he'd suspected about being underground. A large door groaned open, and snapped shut with a dreadful *thud*.

If sounds could kill, he'd be dead.

The door to his cell was pushed open and the new accountant strode in with Vargas' biggest goon following, dwarfing the already short man.

*Did they give this guy growth hormones?*

The strongman tugged on the lightbulb chain, flooding the cell with a yellow glow.

"Hi New Me," Josh winced at the offending brightness. "I see you brought someone to help you reach up high."

The accountant said something to the other man, who left the room and returned with a pail of water.

"You reek," his replacement said. He tossed the water at him.

He opened his mouth, hoping at least a splash would slide down his parched throat. Instead it hit his chest with an icy explosion, forcing air from his lungs. The cold was both refreshing and excruciating. As it drained down his body, his skin crawled with the sensation of a million stinging ants. Josh looked down to confirm an army of ants was actually attacking, but instead found his skin red and puckering with goose pimples. "Sorry, the shower facilities in this shit hole are nonexistent," he sputtered.

New Josh grabbed a chair and flipped it around, straddling it and resting his arms across the top.

He'd been fondling the chair with his eyes from across the room. Imagining its smooth wooden seat cupping his ass. How it'd feel to let his arms hang down, blood flowing to his fingertips, turning his skin from white to pink. He fantasized often about how it would feel to lift his feet off the dirty floor. To give them a break from holding his body upright.

Josh had whispered sweet words to it, hoping it would move across the room seductively to give him what he wanted more than anything else in the world. To sit down. All that time courting this chair, and this asshole comes in and defiles it right in front of him.

"Williams, you listening?" New Josh asked, snapping his attention away from thinking impure thoughts about a *chair*. "Amanda got our message."

A shiver rocketed through his body. He hoped it was an aftershock from the ice bath, but it was most likely from her name.

In Chicago, when they'd worked together, they could always read each other from across a room. That ability to pick up the subtlest glance, the lightest nod. He'd assumed their connection was a surrogate for intimacy, rather than love Amanda. They just *got* each other.

The time in the desert had made him realize maybe it *was* love, feeling like she was the other part of his soul *did* mean more than physical attraction.

Josh had tried to telepathically warn Amanda to get to safety. Hoping that wherever she was, Vargas' men wouldn't be able to get close enough to give her his detached ear.

Maybe their connection was only in person. Maybe when they weren't in the room together, they were just two people sharing this ride called life together.

Nothing more. Nothing less.

"She's not really the kind of girl to swoon over body parts." He hoped the smart-assed comment would cover any concern that might've crept across his face.

The man dragged his finger across the top of the chair.

Josh almost moaned with desire.

"You shouldn't think that about her," the account said, pushing off the chair, discarding it like a rebuffed lover. "After all, she literally had freedom staring her in the face, but she decided to save you." New Josh paced in front of him. "I don't get it, personally. Why would she do it? You steal a lot of money, then leave, letting her take the blame."

He stopped in front of Josh and grabbed his balls, squeezing and pulling to the point the room filled with a blinding light before letting go.

Fuzzy stars raced around the edges of his vision.

"No, you can't be that good in bed." His footsteps echoed

around the cell. "I plan to ask her. As soon as she gets here, I want to find out why she would risk her life for a piece of shit like you."

Josh bit back at the nausea rising up his throat. Was she still mad about Chicago? Or, was she pissed that he'd drugged David and tried to get her to leave with him?

Knowing Amanda, she'd gotten her panties in a wad because Josh wouldn't let her sacrifice herself to Vargas?

"I have a few words of advice, New Me," Josh said. "You're not Amanda's type, she likes guys over five feet tall, for one thing. So if you think you can waltz in and take my place in her bed; not happening."

The accountant laughed. "I don't think she'd share a bed with you anymore. Not since she learned who you really are. But, enough talk about women, let's talk about something more important. Money."

His stomach dropped. There were only two things keeping him alive; Vargas' vengeance quest for Amanda and his desire to get his stolen money back.

"I'm close to figuring out how you cooked the books," the man paced as he spoke. "Such a funny phrase. But in a sense there's truth to it. Before you, it was just raw numbers. Money in, money out. Then, you applied heat, threw in some spice and, *voilà*, you stole thousands of dollars from your employer."

"Will you say that again, but with a Julia Childs' voice?"

His replacement snapped his fingers and the goon laid a heavy fist into Josh's lower back.

Agony radiated from his kidney and air fled from his lungs.

"You don't care for your own life, obviously," the accountant said. "I don't have a lot of seniority with *Señor*, but I can make you a promise. If you'll tell me where the money is, I'll advocate for a swift and merciful end for Amanda."

Josh's lungs finally opened, letting precious oxygen rush in. He studied the man.

The guy had just enough white hair peppered in to put him north of forty, but his face was full and unlined, making it look as if two ages battled for dominance. The accountant's eyes were hidden behind round, wire-rimmed glasses, magnifying the brief flash of sincerity.

"I can't," he said. Even if he could remember where the money was stashed, there was no guarantee this man wasn't lying.

Or, telling the truth.

Or, lying about telling the truth.

The accountant narrowed his eyes and nodded once before letting out a low whistle.

The door above him opened again, and shut gently. Slow, hesitant footsteps echoed overhead.

"Do you believe in karma, Josh?" his replacement asked.

The goon walked out of the room, leaving them alone.

There was something about his words, the sound overhead and absence of the strongman that made Josh shiver despite the stuffy, dank cell. He tugged at his chains, but unless he suddenly developed superhero strength, it wasn't budging.

"I do. I believe everything comes back to us." New Josh laced his fingers behind his back and faced the door. "I believe every good deed is met with good, and every evil deed…"

A man peeked around the door. Fear and anger danced in his eyes.

The last time Josh had seen Manuel, he'd two hands. Now, he covered the stump of his arm with the cuff of his shirt.

The goon followed him in. He grabbed Josh's wrist, his grip so tight the metal dug into the sores.

Josh kicked, trying to keep him away with the little energy he could muster, but the henchmen laid another punch into his gut.

This time bile exploded from his mouth as if someone stepped on a tube of toothpaste.

The strongman unlocked the cuffs and threw him to the floor.

He pushed himself upright on his knees. His feet tingled with relieved pressure. He walked forward on his knees, stopping directly in front of his replacement.

The man who controlled whether he'd end the day with his remaining body parts intact.

"Wait, wait," Josh said between gags. "I'll tell you whatever you want to know. Just please, not my hand."

The account bent at the waist, getting eye level with him. "That was never up for negotiation. Your fate is sealed. You are only in control of what will happen to Amanda."

He snapped his fingers again.

The goon held Josh's left hand high over his head and handed Manuel a machete.

"Manuel, no, *por favor*! *Lo siento*! No! No! No!"

Manuel lifted the blade high.

Josh closed his eyes and started screaming long before the blade came down.

# 18

Amanda cleared the steam off the bathroom mirror, but it instantly clouded over again. She stared at the ghostly reflection of herself. A cold shower would've been more refreshing, but the heat had loosened her sore muscles.

She ran her hand over the mirror again, bringing her face back into view. Could she do it? Was she fooling Joaquin and Alfredo? Herself? Could she survive a desert now? Or, a flood?

*Or, failure?*

She sniffed, tamping down the treacherous thoughts. David was lost, but she could still find Josh.

The tile cooled her bare feet as she padded around her modest room. Amanda pulled on her new jeans and tank top, glancing out the second-floor window while she finger-combed her wet hair.

The house backed up to a desert foothill. They were in a small neighborhood, but the homes had breathing room between them. As if they were united, but still stood alone.

Was that how she'd join Joaquin and Alfredo's team? To stand with them, and apart?

A pang of homesickness squeezed her heart with nostalgia for the desert. Then she, David and Josh had been a team, but also stood apart.

Amanda took a deep breath and closed the curtain on the waning day.

For the first time in weeks, she felt normal. Like someone who could take care of herself. And, others. Maybe it was finally being honest with Joaquin, or it could've been getting out of the hospital and putting on real clothes. Or, maybe having a purpose, something to focus on other than the hurt.

She popped the lid off the bottle and pinched two more pills, swallowing them back with a gulp of water from the sink.

*No, I feel normal because I can't feel anything.*

What was the recommended dose? Probably more than she was taking. Did it matter how doped up she was? Josh needed her.

Amanda found Joaquin and Alfredo in a room lit only by the blue-white glow of a computer.

They murmured between themselves as Joaquin appeared to type coordinates into an online map, zooming in before shaking his head and moving the map with his cursor.

"Anything good?" She leaned on the back of his chair to get a better look at the screen.

He exhaled a long, frustrated sigh and shook his head. "He has everything from gas stations to palatial estates registered under him or his aliases." Her friend picked up legal pad full of scribbles. "And, that's just in Northern Mexico. We're excluding the properties in Texas, Arizona, and the coastal states." Joaquin tossed the pad back on the desk and kicked the chair back, causing his face to nearly collide with her's.

Amanda jumped back. Although he'd held her hand, helped her to the bathroom and comforted her during her panic attack, that had all been when she'd thought he was a priest.

She reached over him and grabbed the pad. His spiky handwriting filled each line. Some with addresses, others had names of businesses or what looked like GPS coordinates. "How in the world does he own this much?" she muttered.

"Stolen, or given to him, when people couldn't pay their debts.

The ones in the U.S. are places where he can hide his true business," Joaquin answered her while typing another address. His eyes landed on hers. "I believe Josh Williams set several of those up."

*Of course.*

As much as Amanda felt the tug to save Josh, she'd spent too long being angry with him. Feelings of *getting-what-he-deserves* crept up like a bad habit refusing to be broken.

Nothing on the page made sense to her. A headache tugged at her right temple, fighting through the God-knows-how-many pills she'd taken. This one would've been completely debilitating if she wasn't already heavily medicated.

She sat in an armchair tucked into the corner of the office and closed her eyes.

The men continued their hushed conversation as if she weren't there.

"What about places between here and the Consulate office?" Amanda pinched the bridge of her nose. Not that she thought it would help ease the throbbing, she was just hoping to give her body something else to focus on for a bit. "They wouldn't have gotten to us so quickly if they weren't watching."

A gasp answered her.

She opened her eyes.

The men stared back.

Alfredo's jaw dropped, exposing a piece of gum he'd been gnashing.

Joaquin lifted one side of his mouth into a proud-papa grin. "He owns an abandoned restaurant three blocks from the Consulate." He whipped the chair around and rolled it over to her, grabbing her upper arms. "*Mija*, the traffic, the accident, all happened right outside its front door."

She tried to find the words, something between jubilation and disgust. Did Josh know he was mere blocks from American soil?

"Okay, let's go." Amanda tried to push herself up from the thick chair, but Joaquin held tight to her arms, holding her in place. "What? What are we waiting for?"

He looked over his shoulder at his boss, then turned back to her. "We don't go there. You don't go there."

She narrowed her eyes. "Who does?"

Alfredo stood. "There are people trained for this."

"I thought you wanted me to be visible." She pulled out of Joaquin's grip and pushed out of the chair. Her sore body started to complain, but she mentally told it to shut up.

"This is different." He hopped up, blocking the door out of the study as if she'd make a run for it. "That was to draw him out. This is a raid."

Alfredo pulled his phone from his pocket and spoke in quick, clipped Spanish sentences.

Amanda crossed her arms and swallowed her rising anger. "Joaquin, he needs me. If he sees other people he doesn't know, he's going to just think it's another one of Vargas' games."

"And, I promise, as soon as we have him, we'll bring you there."

Alfredo finished his call and pulled Joaquin aside.

They spoke in hushed Spanish, with their backs to her.

The only way to make her feel even more like an outsider would be walking into a soundproof booth.

She dropped her arms with a frustrated sigh and went into the kitchen, looking for something to clean. Unfortunately for her, Alfredo kept a tidy house. Amanda pulled open the oven. The blackened, sooty bottom was a gift from heaven. It would be just the distraction she needed.

Under the sink she found a treasure trove of cleaning supplies. With her body set to scrub, she let the soothing, repetitive motions calm the panic stirring in her stomach.

What if they failed? What if they got there and it was too late?

*Or, what if it's a trap and I sent good people with families, into a horrifying situation?*

"Food doesn't taste any better based on how spotless the bottom of the oven is."

Amanda jumped at Joaquin's voice. Her head banged the top of the oven. How much time had passed since she started working on it?

"Calms the nerves," she said, standing and pulling off the gloves.

He walked past her and opened the fridge, pulling out two beers. "Yours is more productive than mine." He twisted the cap off one and handed it to her. "Please know it's for your safety."

She took a sip.

*What's the rule about eleventy-billion pain pills and beer?*

"I know. I just feel so useless." She took another longer sip. "I laid in bed all those weeks doing nothing and now that I can do something…"

"You're ready to save the world." Joaquin flashed a smile with the bottle touching his lips. It made him look so much younger, as if a heavy weight of life was lifted.

"Just my little corner of it. I'm surprised *you* didn't go running out the door."

He laughed. "No, I have the bigger challenge keeping you safe. Not many men were up to the task."

She pulled back on the plastic glove, aiming to snap him with it, but he jumped out of her reach. The teasing felt like flimsy veneer covering warped, ugly wood.

It was all a game, a distraction to keep her from worrying about Josh.

Maybe it was also to keep him from worrying about the people he'd sent after Josh.

"What if this isn't it?" she asked. The mood in the kitchen took a nosedive. "What if Vargas isn't there?"

*Or Josh?*

Joaquin's face tightened. The amusement that had lifted his cheeks and lit his warm brown eyes dissipated.

Amanda hated to snuff the moment of lightness, but the question had to be asked.

He opened his mouth, but shouts of their names interrupted him.

They jogged back into the study.

Alfredo leaned on the desk and the computer screen showed a

grainy hallway. The publisher had earbuds on, mostly listening but every now and then giving a short command.

"What is this?" she whispered.

"The team," Joaquin breathed.

They watched the silent film on the computer. Whoever wore the helmet cam walked through a doorway, and down a flight of stone steps.

A shiver flared throughout her body.

Joaquin reached for her hand, squeezing it twice.

When the team reached the bottom step, a long hallway stared back. Their lights only illuminated a few feet in front of them.

The combination of the jolting camera and fear churned the beer in her stomach. Blackness nudged the edges of her vision, threatening to pull her into unconsciousness, but Amanda pushed back.

Once the camera fell on Josh, she'd be out the door.

No matter what Joaquin tried to do to stop her.

The man with the camera paused at a door. He looked at the men behind him, backing up before kicking it in.

Gray spotlighted around the room. He walked forward, toward a stone wall. Even in the black and white picture, she noticed the slimy wetness of water. In her head she could hear it tinkling; drip, drip, drip.

Gloved hands reached out and pulled heavy chains toward the camera. Then the camera pointed down. A large blackish puddle darkened the stone floor. The same hand reached out, touched it, then rubbed it between his fingers.

Alfredo sucked in a breath and crossed himself.

"What?" she didn't feel the word leave her mouth.

Joaquin squeezed her hand again. "That's blood, *mija*. Lots of it, and it's still a fresh."

The computer screens suddenly pulled away. The room tilted, as if she were on a carnival ride. The floor rushed up, racing an eruption of panic.

# 19

Amanda and the frozen image of Josh's blood were in a staring contest. She didn't want to be the first to blink. Couldn't be.

The inky puddle on the screen taunted her. Daring her to look away.

They hadn't yet confirmed it to be his, but she didn't need any official reports. The ear was confirmation enough. But…an ear couldn't have bled that much.

What else had he lost?

A glass of water appeared beside her, connected to Joaquin's hand.

She glanced up. Worry knitted his eyebrows so close together they became one and his mouth was pressed so firmly his lips were white.

"It's not good for you to do that." His voice was tight, as if holding back a scream.

Amanda understood; she felt like screaming too. She might have if she hadn't passed out, or if she didn't worry she'd get sick.

"How are you feeling?" He'd been hovering since she came to.

"Considering I still have most of my blood and both ears, peachy."

Joaquin fell into the chair beside her and switched off the monitor.

The room went from gray-lit to nearly black. Only the artificial light from outside peeked in from around the edges of a heavy curtain.

She'd been trying to talk herself into shutting it off for the past hour, but her hand wouldn't obey. All she could do was sit and stare at Josh's blood. How late were they? Had they missed him by hours, minutes?

Seconds?

If she'd taken a faster shower, or no shower at all, would she have come to the conclusion about where he was being held sooner?

"It looks like he was moved by an underground tunnel. Our team followed the, um," Joaquin paused, not saying the word. "We lost it and the tunnel forked. They would have split up to go after them—"

"But it's not worth the risk." The words sounded as sour as they felt.

"*Mija…*" His term of endearment was full of apology.

Amanda faced him.

His normally tanned complexion had a tinge of green. Was it seeing all the blood? Was he worried about her fainting spell?

Lucky for her, the beer plus pain pills kept her from feeling too bad.

For now.

She wasn't looking forward to how she'd feel when they wore off.

*Who says I have to let that happen?*

She shook her head, both at her self-destructive thoughts and Joaquin's guilt. "No, it's the right call. It could have been a trap." Amanda paused; it was going to take all her strength to push the next words out. "Josh might already be dead."

What was the next step? Sit and wait for some sign of Vargas? Of Josh?

If her ex was still alive, the cartel leader wasn't going to give him up, not without a fight.

Not without Amanda.

She'd made a fool of him twice.

He owed her payback.

"I think you should go home." Joaquin's words shattered her thoughts.

"What? Why?"

"This was a bad idea, using you to find Vargas." Her friend stared at his hands as he spoke. "I've been covering this man for years. We shouldn't have asked this of you."

She pushed herself to her feet, hesitating for a minute to give the room time to stop moving.

The *help-us, don't-help-us* back and forth was giving her whiplash.

"Instead of finding Josh or Vargas we find an empty cell and some blood and that's it?" Her voice rose with her temper as she paced the dark room. "Come on, Joaquin. You didn't sit beside me for weeks to give up after one try."

He sat hunched over, his arms rest on his thighs and hands folded together.

She flashed back to how he'd looked sitting beside her, as if in contemplative prayer. Maybe posing as a priest wasn't so much as a disguise; as an alter ego.

"You don't know what it's like." His voice as soft as the darkness. "For someone to die because of you. Because of mistakes you've made."

The flare of her fight snuffed out in the breath of his words. She'd had a feeling there was more to his story than he'd initially shared. As a former public relations executive, she knew lots of reporters. Their weapon of choice was the written word, but Joaquin felt different. Like a war correspondent. Or, a vigilante.

"Actually, I do." Amanda sat back in her chair and reached for his hand. "I never told you who David is. Was."

"You don't—"

"Yes, I do. After Chicago, I ended up in a town in Texas, called Phoenix. It was meant to be a temporary stop before I went looking for Josh, but I met a man there. David." She grinned at the thought about their meeting and the early days of their relationship. "Against my better judgement, we fell in love." Her smile tumbled with her heart. "Long story short, I hurt him, ruined his life, and when he found me again along the border, he got pulled into my mess." She swallowed the knot in her throat, preparing the way for the words she had to say. "He died, in the flood, because of me. Because of my mistakes." She couldn't breathe life into the heartache of her colleagues in Chicago, but the haunting of that shooting would live with her forever.

"I'm sorry for your loss," Joaquin said.

"Thank you, and I'm sorry for yours."

His gaze shot up from his hands. His Adam's apple bobbed as he swallowed. "It's that obvious?"

"Written all over you."

Her friend crossed the room to the window and pulled back the curtain. "I always thought I had something in common with the villagers in the Middle East. Those who lived in constant fear of extremist groups. I wanted to tell their stories, but to do that, I needed someone who could speak their language. What I didn't realize is religious zealotry can make people…unreadable. My interpreter and I went into a village. The cafe owner was secretly a bomb-maker and when Wassim went in to see if he would talk to me, the man spooked and blew them both up." A tear made a crooked path down his cheek.

"It wasn't your fault," Amanda pushed the words out.

"No, but he was studying medicine to become a doctor before I showed up. He had the bad fortune of being fluent in English, and like me, he wanted to make his country a better place." This time his words wavered, as if unable to fight off the escalating emotion. He looked back out the window. "I robbed the world of a good man, who might've become an amazing doctor, someone who would've saved other people's lives."

She walked up behind him, but he didn't move.

Outside the window was the back courtyard of the safe house.

What did Joaquin see? A war-torn country? A young man with his whole life stretched before him, a life that ended much too soon?

Amanda touched his arm. "What if he did save other people? What if the bomb was meant for a crowded market, or a school? That might not make it better, but…"

He glanced over his shoulder. "Thanks, *mija*."

Maybe this was why he stayed behind with her. Like a soldier returning from battle, he suffered post-traumatic stress.

Did she? If she were honest with herself, Amanda had probably had it since the shooting and bombing in her office in Chicago. She'd only told herself she ran after Josh, but deep down, she'd run because she was afraid.

Fear was a bird of prey. It circled overhead, looking for a weaker creature to swoop down and sink its talons into. Fear passed over anything that resisted.

She'd been preyed on by fear long enough.

No more.

She was ready to stand up, be stronger, even if it was only by perception, and fight back.

"Tomorrow I want to go into town. I want to hold my head up high, walk around, be seen," she said. "Dammit, if I need to I'll ring a bell and shout Vargas' name."

Joaquin dropped the curtain. His face was just inches from hers, his eyelids half closed. "Amanda."

She shook her head. "Don't even try to talk me out of it."

"It's dangerous. You could be killed."

"I'm already dead," she said, retreating from the room. "And, the dead can't die."

# 20

Fallon parked in the garage of the downtown office building housing the El Paso branch of the FBI. She killed her car engine and rested her forehead against the steering wheel. It took every bit of restraint to drive into work when her body tugged her to Phoenix.

Overnight, David had finally answered her frantic texts and calls. She pulled her phone out of the cupholder and checked it again.

*I'm fine. Just busy. Talk later?*

Was she expecting the tone to soften on her drive in? That maybe he'd added more to it, something a little less self-absorbed.

"Hi, Fallon, good to hear from you," she mumbled, shoving her phone into her laptop bag. Several steps away from her car, she clicked the fob. "How are you? How was the trafficking bust you've spent weeks preparing for?" She caught her reflection in the garage elevator and took a deep breath. Red crept up her neck from her blouse.

Fallon smoothed her hair. The humidity made her curly hair frizz out of control. A low chignon was the best she could manage on a day when her temper flared like sunspots.

The elevator dinged to the building lobby. She got out of it and crossed to another one.

What was really making her angry? Was it David's evasiveness?

Searching for a woman who may or may not be dead? A woman who definitely deserved to be in prison. The fact that she was trying to warn him about a hit, and he wouldn't even return her damn calls?

The gold reflective doors revealed the red was now covering her cheeks. Fine.

*Screw a positive, reassuring talk, you'll just learn you're going to die by voicemail. That'll get his attention.*

Her office was already abuzz with activity and it wasn't even eight o'clock. Phones rang, agents scurried about and the hum of electronics enveloped her into the chaotic fold.

Fallon thumbed through her phone for David's number, hitting the call button a few doors down from her office, hoping to be safely ensconced behind a heavy wooden door when the call went to voicemail.

"Fallon." David picked up on the first ring. His voice sounded lighter, almost lyrical.

Was he laughing?

Well, he wouldn't be when she was done with him.

"Where are you?" The question came to her in stereo.

She crossed the threshold into her office and skidded to a stop.

David sat at the guest chair, the ankle of one leg resting above the knee of the other, the shaft of well-worn cowboy boots peeking out from under dark jeans. He held his phone to his ear with a sexy smirk slapped across his face.

"What're you doing?" Fallon ended the call and dropped into her chair. Framed pictures of her niece and nephew lined across her desk formed a wall between them.

"Came to catch up."

"Bullshit." She didn't even feel the word primed to leap from her lips.

David rested his forearms on his thighs. He wore a light denim button-up shirt, the sleeves rolled up showing his tanned arms. His hair was longer, almost shaggy. A look she hadn't seen on him since they were in college.

The covering of salt and pepper hair on his face indicated it'd been a couple of days since he'd shaved. The dark circles cushioning his eyes betrayed that was also how long it'd been since he'd slept.

"Okay, you're pissed." David spoke to the floor before shifting his eyes to meet hers. "I deserve it."

She jumped up from behind her desk and closed her office door. Then stared at him with her hands on her hips.

He kept his head down, eyes on the floor, but his gazed flickered up to her. If he had a tail, it'd be between his legs.

Fallon took two steps in his direction and whacked the back of his head before taking the other guest chair. "You jerk. Do you know how worried I've been? I'm starting to feel like a stalker when all I want to do is make sure you're alive."

"I know. I'm—"

"I know you're working through some stuff, and I'm more than happy to give you space, but when I call, you *damn well* better answer." She kept her voice down, but the finger she pointed at him indicated the volume she wanted to use.

"I promise—"

"No, you'll do more than promise. You will. Because you pissed off some serious people and I'm not leaving you a voicemail to tell you there's a price on your head." Fallon sucked in a breath as David met her eyes. When they'd been classmates in college, that used to happen a lot. Not telling him off, but her breath catching every time she looked at him.

The handsome star quarterback as a criminal justice major who actually went to class, and did more than merely went, but participated in discussions and class study groups. He'd been different than the other jocks, who all tended to just hang out with one another. David was as comfortable in the classroom as he was on the field. Maybe more so.

"Wow, sorry, I didn't mean...You came here and I rip you a new one. When did I become my mom?" Fallon tried to laugh off her tongue-lashing, but in truth, she would've done it all again. "And, then I just blurt out someone's trying to kill you."

"I wish I could tell you that's news to me."

The heat that'd been plaguing her all morning dropped to a dead cold. "What do you mean?"

David lifted his head, but kept his shoulders hunched. "I went back home; took a job at a bar. Went outside the other night to take a call and got jumped. Lucky for me, a friend came out for a smoke break."

"Are you okay?"

"Got the wind knocked out of me. He got away though." He straightened and draped an arm over the chair. "Your turn. What's your intel?"

"A CI for my brother told him Rafael Vargas wants to tie up loose ends."

He nodded, as if absorbing the information. "The guy that came after me was a bit chatty. Said Vargas has Williams."

"Seems to be consistent with what I heard." Fallon spoke slowly, picking at a cat hair on her pants.

"Did the CI say anything else?"

Guilt flashed through her body. Just how chatty was this assassin?

She felt like a kid caught in a lie. Then again, an omission wasn't technically a lie, especially if it was done for the good of her friend. Right?

All he needed to know was his life was in danger. David didn't need to worry about Josh or Amanda.

They were trapped in Mexico, or maybe even dead already.

"Ah, well, he said Vargas is trying to regain some ground in Mexico. He's madder than a wet hornet. You got away. He wants to show the other bosses he's not weak."

David opened his mouth, but a swift knock on her door interrupted them.

"Fallon, busy?" Jay stuck his head in. "Oh, sorry, didn't know you had company."

"Oh no, come on in." Her voice might've been a little too loud and jubilant. "Jay, you remember David, right? The Vargas kidnapping…"

*The one that lived.*

"Oh yeah, hey man, how you doing?" Her partner strode in and offered David a hand. Jay's mouth pulled up in mostly a sneer.

Not a shocker. A thin mask covered his jealousy.

Fallon wore it, too. Whenever Amanda Martin's name came up.

"Not bad, I was in town and thought I'd catch up with Weatherby." David stood between them, the awkward silence hovering, ready to drop. "Fallon, do you have a few more minutes? Then, I'll get out of your hair."

Her partner cocked his head, silently asking if she were okay.

She pulled one side of her mouth up into a smile for Jay. "Sure. I'll catch up with you in five?"

He backed out of her office with a nod.

David perched against the edge of her desk. "There's one more thing."

Her heart fluttered.

"The man sent after me—" He cleared his throat. "He said Mandy's still alive. Luckily, I don't think Vargas has her. Yet."

Fallon's heart slowed, doing what her training had taught it to do in stressful situations. She backed up against the windowsill. Didn't want to be too close to him. He might smell the lie on her. "Oh?"

"She's got to be across the border. I'm going over there tomorrow." David dropped his head. When he looked up, his eyes glistened. "I've got to find her before they do."

Her lungs froze. She could protect him here, but the minute he crossed the river, there was nothing she could do. At least, not from El Paso.

She weighed her options. Could tell him what she'd heard from the CI, but that would send him sprinting across the border. Or, maybe tell him Berto had said Amanda was already dead and crush him.

There was the third option, to neither confirm nor deny. Fallon had learned this trick from plenty of suspects. "How will you even know where to look?"

He grimaced. "Where was the first place I went when I was found?"

She remembered the call. David had been found and they'd rushed him to the hospital. He was so agitated they'd had to restrain him for fear he'd jump out the back of the ambulance.

"So you're going to check all the hospitals?"

"She won't be hard to miss."

Fallon nodded and pushed past him, rounding her desk. The certificates of being a good and dutiful agent stared at her from the wall across her office. She refused to look at them, to feel them judging her. They might as well tell her to pull them off the wall and discard them with her career.

She shook her mouse awake and opened her email. Her fingers typed up a quick note before her mind could talk them out of it.

What good was vacation time if she never took it?

"Let me go with you."

He ran his hands through his hair and looked out her window. "Fal, that's not a good idea."

She leaned on her elbows. "Oh? You wandering around Mexico is? You're emotional, you won't think clearly. You need someone logical with you. And, your Spanish sucks. I'm going."

"Don't you have a case you're busy with?"

"Not anything that can't wait."

David braced his arms on the back of the guest chair and let his head hang down. "It's not fair to make you do this." He spoke to the seat. "Especially not after...us." When he looked up at her, remorse was painted across his face.

Fallon swallowed. What was worse, being discarded by David for his ex or seeing that he knew what he'd done to her, and it hurt him?

She waved off his hurt. Waved off *hers*. "There was never an '*us.*' Like I said, you're not thinking clearly. I'm going with you."

# 21

Amanda sat in the shade of the giant fountain at the center of town. Droplets of water sprayed her.

It was only a quarter after eleven, but the cafés lining the square were starting to fill up.

Children laughed and played, using their precious lunch break from the classroom to run off some energy.

A man hocked large, helium-filled mylar balloons displaying cartoon characters she recognized from her youth.

"How are you doing?" Joaquin spoke into her ear.

She looked down at her borrowed phone.

He'd insisted they stay in constant communication, so sitting there donning earbuds made her look like a normal person enjoying her music on a warm, late summer day.

"Why is it I'm sitting out here roasting and you're sipping coffee in the shade?" She peered across the plaza and saw him laugh from a table tucked away in the corner of a café.

"You wanted to be seen, *mija*."

The oversized glasses slid down her face on a stream of sweat.

Joaquin had wanted her to throw on a baseball cap, but Amanda had pushed back, afraid of being *too* incognito. Now she was spending her time scooting around the hot concrete in search of the smallest slice of shade.

"Have you heard anything else from the tunnels?" she asked.

A new team had gone back to search under the restaurant owned by Vargas for any sign of Josh.

She watched her friend shake his head. They tried to keep words to a minimal, which suited her just fine. She felt sluggish, like the sleepy-drunk from having too much wine.

Or, too many pain pills.

It was preventative. That was what she told herself. What if she had to make a run for it? She didn't want her physical limitations preventing her from chasing after someone. Or, running from them.

The sun crept around the fountain, casting its rays down on her. "I'm scooting around to the other side," she whispered to Joaquin.

This side of the square was the business side. Various shops morphed into each other. A little food mart became a shoe store, which turned into a book shop. The outer wall of the hospital sat in the adjoining block. It wasn't the same side she'd run out of, but the back end.

In her slightly-clearer state, Amanda saw the top of the beige adobe wall was encrusted with what looked like multi-colored jewels, sparkling in the sun. She lifted her glasses to get a better view. Broken glass was built into the wall; a whimsical, economical, if not sinister, security system.

*Is it to keep someone out, or in?*

The tops of the trees in the hospital's courtyard swayed in the breeze. It felt like ages ago when Joaquin had walked her out there and she'd seen the ghost of David.

*Has it just been a few days?*

Was she overdoing it? Moving around as much as she was? Fainting? Sitting in the hot sun with her head injury? Did this amount to a suicide mission?

A man and woman walking down the street toward the hospital caught her attention. The woman stood out, with her curly blonde hair hanging loose down her back. She was tall, thin but athletic, as if her body was made for not just competing, but winning.

The man was also tall and lean. They both wore aviator sunglasses and dark jeans, he in a white T-shirt, she in a sleeveless one.

There was something cohesive about this couple.

He looked so much like the man from the courtyard that day, the one she'd thought was David.

A flash of sadness coursed through her body. With her focus on Josh the past few days, Amanda had put aside mourning for David. She couldn't let herself succumb to that, not yet. Not when she could still save Josh.

They turned away from her, walking toward the main entrance of the hospital. It was most likely the same man. He was probably visiting a family member there, and had left through the garden courtyard the day. Should seeing him again make her feel more sane or less sane?

Suddenly, her view of the plaza was obscured by thick, silver balloons. Latex, and a faint chemical smell filled her nose. The phone was tugged out of her hands, yanking the earbuds with it.

A man scooted close to Amanda. Dark, round glasses perched on his nose, making his eyes appear largely out of proportion with the rest of his face. His hair was thick, wavy and dark, but there was a harshness about him. "You've cut your hair," he said.

She studied him more intensely in the latex cocoon. "Have we met?"

"No, forgive me, Amanda, for the over-familiarity. We have common acquaintances." His voice had a formal, nasally tone.

Amanda stole another glance.

He had a slight build, and his head came to her shoulders.

"And you are…" Amanda said.

"Here with a message." He studied his fingernails. "*Señor* Vargas requests your acquiescence."

She withheld the shudder at the drug lord's name. Were the two goons from the hospital nearby? She craned her neck to the side and behind her. Nothing but the fountain and more balloons.

"I'm alone," he added.

Was her heart pounding as audibly as it felt?

"And why should I do that?" A cartoon mouse floated between them.

"*Señor* harbors no ill will toward your new friends," he said through the mylar character.

Amanda would never look at that mouse the same way again.

The heat of the balloon enclosure was suffocating.

Shouts of her name rang around the plaza, distant.

Her lungs tried to draw in air, but she choked on the overwhelming latex and helium gas.

The man spoke again, but his words bled together, twisting themselves around the balloons. "Prospera Pass." Spanish merged into English, but neither really made sense. "Find a way. Alone."

"What?" More balloons filled the distance between them. "I didn't understand. Where do I pass?"

"It is time for you to repent, Amanda. Confess your sins."

As quickly as the balloons had descended, they were gone.

In his place was the cellphone he'd tugged from her hand.

The sun filled the blue sky. The fountain roared behind her with gushing water.

Older men played chess at picnic tables, couples snuggled together, young moms hurried by with babies strapped to their chest.

"Amanda!" Joaquin's shouts gave her an anchor. "What happened? The call just went dead. I came running this direction and two police stopped me, thinking I'd stolen something from a shop."

She took a deep breath, calming her fluttering heart. "I was seen." The words came out hoarse and shaky.

"And?"

"Where's the cathedral?" Her body flushed with a cold sweat.

"What?"

"He said I have to confess. Something's there." She started walking, unsure if she was even heading in the right direction.

Joaquin's face was slack, obviously still processing everything that'd just happened.

Was this too much for him?

"Come on, Joaquin, we have to go."

He pointed down a street to her left.

She took off running. The first few steps, her body resisted, pulling her back, wondering what the hell she was doing. By the time she'd gotten down the end of the plaza, the runner in her took over, telling the hospital patient to get out of the way. Adrenalin spread through her veins like fire, incinerating the hurt.

Joaquin's footsteps thundered behind her, his breathing coming in uneven gasps.

The spires of the church came into view, calling her forward.

What was she going to find inside? Not Josh; that would be too easy. Maybe something that could help save him.

A clue.

A lure.

Amanda didn't slow her pace up the front steps.

The heavy wooden doors groaned open.

Inside, the church was dark, quiet. Empty. Prayer candles sat lit, proof that earlier someone had come in and left money to pray for a loved one.

To pray for her?

Joaquin paused behind her, muttering a quick prayer in Spanish before crossing himself.

She lifted up on her toes, her eyes quickly scanning the inside of the church for the confession. Finally, she found it, tucked away on the right hand side of the nave.

The side for the priest sat open, but the parishioner side was closed.

She pushed open the thin wooden door. A box rested on the stool. Dark brown with a gold floral inlay on the top.

Joaquin grabbed her arm. "We should call someone."

Amanda could see it, the bomb, his interpreter. "No," she said, shaking her head. "This isn't it; Vargas wants to kill me himself." Her heart slowed. The feeling of it beating was heavy, a thick thudding as it anticipated what she'd find inside.

With a silent prayer, she lifted the lid. Red rose petals stared up at her, soft against the harsh corners of the box.

She reached in, but hesitated before brushing aside the petals, as if she already knew what lay beneath and didn't want to see it.

Something cold froze her touch.

A hand, severed at the wrist, held the skeletal remains of a rose devoid of petals. A thorn pierced the thumb.

Her breath fled her lungs.

The confession booth grew smaller.

Amanda backed out, pushing past Joaquin. She slipped on the step down from the booth, her legs unable to hold her anymore she landed square on her butt.

The box fell beside her, spilling its contents on the stone floor.

Tears flowed freely down her face, not from the pain shooting up her spine, it was nothing compared to what Josh was enduring.

If—when—she found him, would there be anything left?

# 22

Good thing neither David nor Fallon were bleeding. The way the staff at the small hospital avoided them, they'd be dead in no time.

His Spanish wasn't perfect, but it was passable, and he knew all the greetings and terms of respect.

Fallon, on the other hand, had minored in Spanish in college, but even her textbook use of the language wasn't getting much response.

The young receptionist eagerly greeted people who came in, whether they were seeking assistance or visiting a loved one. Anything to keep her from having to talk to the two *gringos* asking questions.

It was a small hospital, but it was in a large enough city to have a heavy, secure door sealing off access to the medical ward. The panels would swing open, offering David a peek inside.

Doctors and nurses hustled, orderlies moved patients and equipment, janitors worked to keep it sterile. Every time the door opened, he'd stare, trying to soak in as much as he could before it clicked shut.

Would he catch a glimpse of Mandy? Lock gazes with her hazel eyes. See her long brown hair, sun-bleached blond from their time in the desert.

Did he really think he'd see her smile again?

Driving overnight to El Paso, sitting down with Fallon and telling her Mandy was still alive had been an act fueled by hope.

Hope that she'd offer to help him. Hope that his gut instinct was right.

Hope that the woman he loved was still alive.

Fallon walked back into the lobby. Patience wasn't her strong suit, so she'd gone outside to call some of her friends with Mexico's national police to pull some strings.

"Any luck?" he asked.

"I'm starting to get dizzy from this run around," she mumbled, her eyes focused on her phone as she typed out an email. "I'm trying one more person."

As she worked on her message, he watched a woman and her son enter. From the way the boy held his midsection and the grimace on his face, he suffered from a very upset stomach.

The mom checked in with the receptionist, offering up how long her son had felt ill, his symptoms. When she mentioned the vomiting, the boy got sick on the floor, as if by the power of suggestion alone. That sent the receptionist into action, buzzing on the phone asking for a janitor to clean up the mess. The mother tried to rush her son to the bathroom, but she only succeeded in spreading the mess throughout the lobby.

David tugged Fallon's elbow, pulling her out of their path and closer to the door leading to the interior of the hospital.

"Ugh," she said, cupping her hand over her mouth and nose. "There is nothing worse than the smell of puke."

A beleaguered, elderly janitor pushed through the door, muttering under his breath.

The receptionist choked as she shouted orders, her own face taking on a greenish tint.

The door into the medical ward closed at a lumbering pace, as if it were an elephant in no hurry.

"Come on," he whispered.

"What?" she said.

He nodded toward the door.

"We can't go back there," she whispered back. "We'll get caught."

Fallon had said she wanted to help him. Was she helping him find Mandy, or helping to make sure he didn't create an international incident? Once upon a time, he'd followed every rule to a tee. Rarely breaking from an agreed upon play. Never cheating on a test. Always filling out the paperwork perfectly.

But where had that gotten him?

A career-ending football injury. Dashed law school plans. Fired from the Phoenix Police Department.

*Following rules be damned.*

"Fine, stay out here and text me if anything happens." David slipped through the door and away from Fallon's protests.

The interior was busy, but not harried. He walked down the hallway, back straight, eyes forward, as if he knew exactly where he was going. Body language was always a clear clue to him someone was doing something wrong.

When he passed the nurses' station, they didn't register his presence. Until he cleared his throat.

An older nurse looked up, her brows knitted together. Through broken, elementary Spanish, he asked if an American woman had come in within the last month.

The woman scowled and shook her head. Either he'd butchered his question beyond comprehension, or Mandy had never been there.

While the woman looked up at him, she didn't make eye contact.

An alarm beeped in a room down the hall, and she scurried away.

He stood there a minute, contemplating whether he should search patient rooms in case she was in a coma.

The door leading to the lobby opened, the janitor pushed his cart through.

Fallon peered in, turning her hands up.

David shook his head and held up a finger, mouthing "One more minute."

A nurse and doctor walked up to the station, speaking softly and quickly.

He could barely make out their rapid-fire words. "*Habla Ingles?*" he asked, wishing Fallon would have joined him.

The doctor nodded. "A little."

"I'm looking for a woman, late twenties, American, long brown hair. She may have been injured in a flood last month. Did she come here?"

The doctor glanced at the nurse, pausing.

This didn't seem to be a question that needed thought, it was a simple yes or no, but the man seemed to weigh his options.

"No, not alive, dead. Excuse me." The man pushed past him, his eyes on a medical chart.

The nurse gave David a sad, sympathetic smile before following.

That wasn't the look of someone telling a family member their loved one was dying. It was someone who wanted to say more, but couldn't.

Had she been here? Was she still here?

It was more than obvious the doctor had lied.

The janitor walked toward David, humming a tune deep in his throat.

"*Señor, perdón,*" he said, reaching out a hand to stop the man. He used the same words on the janitor as he did the first nurse.

"*Sí, sí,*" the janitor said. "*Un sacerdote tiene su.*"

He shook his head. All he could understand was someone had her. "*Un sacerdote? Como?*"

The man dropped his head, as if in prayer, and crossed himself.

David needed all the prayers he could get, but now was not the time.

"*El padre,*" he said. "*En la catedral.*" The janitor steepled his fingers.

It all clicked. She was at a church. Of course, they would take care of someone lost.

He thanked the man, shaking his hand so hard that the janitor's whole body shook. Then jogged back down the hall, hitting the exit button for the door. "Got it," he said to a worried-looking Fallon. "She's at the church."

She pressed her lips into a tight line and crossed her arms over her chest. "Are you sure it's her?"

"Only one way to find out." David strode out of the hospital, heading toward the city plaza.

She jogged just a few steps behind him.

The plaza was full. People milled about, sitting around the grand fountain, enjoying their lunches in one of the many cafes lining the square.

Vendors pushed carts selling food, drinks and trinkets.

He craned his neck trying to look over the buildings for the tale-tell spires. A bell sounded behind him. Deep, a bass sound that reverberated in his chest. A higher-pitched clang followed. He glanced at his watch. Noon.

David sprinted down a street toward the sound, his boots slipping on the worn-smooth cobblestones. Like running in a touchdown, he pivoted and rolled around the people as if they were a defensive line keeping him away from the end zone.

From Mandy.

The bells rang even louder inside the church.

He paused just inside the door, giving his eyes a chance to adjust to the darkness and waiting for Fallon to catch up.

Candles flickered. Pulling him in, pushing him back. Light streamed in through the stained glass windows. The disciples, the Virgin Mary, a cross. He took two steps forward down the aisle, Christ on the cross pulled him to the pulpit.

"What's the plan?" Fallon asked.

He sucked in a breath. The plan was to shout her name until somebody showed him where they were keeping her. But, that would send her into hiding. This needed finesse. Patience. "Your Spanish is better, see if you can find the priest," David said. "I'm going to look around."

Her footsteps echoed in the now quiet church as she headed

down the aisle toward the pulpit. He walked over to the baptismal fountain. Touched the small circle of water in the bottom.

"David."

He wiped his hands on his jeans and joined Fallon at the entrance to a transept. A confessional with both doors open faced them. A spattering of red colored the beige stone floor.

She squatted down and picked up a handful of discarded rose petals. "I'm no expert in Catholicism, but I can't think of a single reason for these to be here."

David crouched next to her, rubbing a petal between his thumb and forefinger. "I can." He tossed the petal back to the floor and stood, swallowing the curse that wanted to leap from his lips. "We're too late."

# 23

The change in the air alerted Josh he'd been moved.

*Moved or dead.*

For the first time in his life, he wanted death more than life.

He refused to look at his left arm, didn't want to see the bandage that covered where his hand used to be.

This new cell was brighter. Hay covered the floor. The stone wall was gone; now he was held in a room with thick wooden walls. Light streamed in through a dirty window overhead.

The warm scent of manure mingled with crisp, fresh air. An olfactory yin and yang.

*A barn is a penthouse suite compared to a dungeon.*

Josh pulled himself to standing, clutching his arm tight against his chest. He expected pain to radiate from every synapse, but so far it felt...numb.

There were no sounds of the city. No cars. No pulse of life. Wherever he'd been moved was far from civilization.

He walked the perimeter of his new cell. His legs shook, muscles giving out every few steps. Like a newborn colt tottering on nascent limbs.

Heavy wood grunted as the door behind him was pulled open.

Vargas entered, alone, with his hands behind his back. No enforcers following behind.

Josh was not restrained.

Either he wasn't considered a flight risk, or there was nowhere for him to flee.

"Ah, I thought you'd be awake by now." The drug lord stood in the middle of the room.

Josh pushed his back against the wall. Rough wood and splinters dug into his back. "Where—" He stopped. His voice came out in an excruciating rasp. Had he screamed his voice raw?

"Do you want to know where you are?" his former boss asked, his tone soft, as if speaking to a child.

He nodded. Tried to swallow, but bile shot up like a flare of magma.

Vargas closed the distance between them and stood next to him, gazing out the window. "Prospera Pass," he said. "High up in the Sierra del Carmen Mountains. The air is clean, cool. Views are stunning." He turned, his light green eyes narrowing. "And when I'm done with you I'll simply throw you off a cliff."

His words were said with such normalcy, such flatness, as if stating the obvious.

Josh took a step to the other wall, but his ankle gave out. He tumbled, his left arm shot out as if to catch him, but there was nothing there to catch and he fell hard on his stump. "Shit." He groaned and cradled his arm. Nausea punched at his stomach.

"Careful, Josh." Vargas crouched next to him. "We've got you stitched up and the bleeding stopped. You don't want to tear your stitches, do you?"

He took deep breaths, gritting his teeth to keep from getting sick. The fall ignited the fire that burned at his stump. It hadn't been extinguished. Only smoldering. Now it flared. Threatened to consume him.

"Here, sit." The cartel leader pulled him into a seated position. "It hurts, doesn't it?"

Josh didn't want to acknowledge the physical agony, instead he wanted to address a searing worry plaguing him. "Where's Amanda?" He had to take a breath between each word to give them power.

"Not here, not yet. Truth be told, I don't know if you'll still be among us when she arrives." Vargas stood. "Or, I guess I could say, I don't know how *much* of you will be left. But no reunion for you two, not this time. Not on Earth at least." His former employer reached inside the pocket of his beige linen pantsuit and pulled out a small bottle and a case. "Today, I come with a gift for you," Vargas opened the case. A syringe came into view. "You've given me two incredible gifts, with which to send Amanda a message, and I thank you for that." He stabbed the needle into the bottle, the shaft of it filling with liquid as he pulled the plunger. "You know better than anyone I am generous, but my generosity does have a limit." He smiled.

If Josh's life was a horror movie, blood would've dripped from Vargas' teeth as he loomed over him.

He scooted to the side, splinters sticking in his bare buttocks from the wooden floor. "Wha-what is it?" Fear rattled his teeth.

Vargas thumped at the syringe. "This is enough morphine to kill you." He squeezed the plunger and a quarter of the liquid squirted from the needle. "This will put you under for about twenty-four blissful hours." The man knelt in front of Josh.

Tobacco tickled his nose. More liquid narcotic dripped from the end, less than a quarter remained.

"This will take the edge off." He held the needle upright and stabbed at the plunger.

The last of the medicine shot Josh on the cheek and dribbled down his face. He wanted to sweep up a few precious drops and lick them off his fingertips.

The drug lord flipped the syringe upside down and stabbed it into Josh's thigh, then flicked it sharply on its side, breaking off the needle with a sickening snap.

A scream rose up and tore through Josh's mouth.

"But this is what you're going to get, unless you tell me where my money is." Vargas stood and took two steps back. "I want your thoughts to be clear and not under duress. Think about it, I'll be back after *siesta* and we can talk."

His former employer retreated, taking the morphine with him.

And, Josh's will to live.

# 24

The faces staring back at her reminded Amanda of a nightmare. The kind where she'd find herself standing onstage, about to give a presentation but realizing she wasn't prepared. It was the typical nightmare of Type A personalities.

Only now it was her reality.

After they'd gotten away from the cathedral, Joaquin had driven them back to the safe house, making calls and sending text messages along the way. He'd taken a circuitous route, passing by some landmarks twice to make sure they weren't followed. By the time they arrived, the living room was full, quiet.

Solemn.

Alfredo and Joaquin took turns speaking.

Amanda could only pick up a few of their words, but she heard a few she knew. Vargas. Cathedral. *La mano*.

She'd lost sight of Josh's hand after they got back to the house.

Joaquin had passed it off to someone who'd passed it to someone else. Then the simple brown box was gone. What were their plans with it? Give it a proper burial? Throw it away?

"Just tell them everything that happened," Joaquin said. "I'll translate."

With a deep breath, Amanda recounted sitting in the plaza, hoping to be seen. The guy who'd ensconced her in helium balloons and grabbed the phone out of her hand, cutting off her ties to Joaquin.

A man in the corner asked Joaquin a question in Spanish.

"Have you ever seen this man before?" he translated.

"No, he wasn't anyone I'd seen at the *hacienda*. He didn't introduce himself, but he looked like your typical businessman." She tried to recall the conversation, but a headache squeezed at her temple. The adrenalin that'd flooded her body earlier dried up. Exhaustion lapped at her like lazy waves.

She was about to recount what'd sent her running to the cathedral when she stopped. A sliver of the man's words had fallen out of her memory and she fumbled around in the dark recesses of her mind to try to find it.

*"Mija?"*

"There's something I'm forgetting." Amanda closed her eyes and rubbed her temples. An aching ember warmed the center of her body. The pills were wearing off. If she didn't take more soon she'd be incapable of moving. Or, thinking.

A few of the people shuffled, tilting to their neighbors and whispering. It didn't matter that she couldn't understand the words. Suspicion and skepticism were universal languages.

This was the dream. Forgetting an important part of her speech in front of an audience. Standing in front of strangers relying on her to bring down a cartel leader was akin to standing there naked.

Maybe worse.

The dream spun into a gruesome nightmare, as the image of Josh's hand flashed across her memory. He needed her. They needed her. Her once-good memory had betrayed her.

*I'm supposed to pass something along? A message?*

"I'm sorry," she said, her voice hoarse and broken. "I need some air."

Amanda pushed out of the room and hurried out the back door.

The patio was quiet. The sounds of the city didn't float up the hill. Much like the garden of the hospital, this was a miniature version with a smaller fountain. Flowering vines covered the beige stucco wall, growing big and bushy with spent buds retreating behind wild, colorful blooms.

She leaned against the wall, the heat of the day seeping into her muscles and bones. Closed her eyes and inhaled. Warm sweet nectar, the smell balanced by the hot, flint smell of the stone.

Joaquin appeared in the doorway. "You okay?"

It was a simple question, one meant to convey concern for her well-being, but instead it was the spark to her simmering temper.

"You tell me. I'm picking up body parts of my ex-boyfriend like dirty socks. I want to move and act normal, but if I stand too quickly, I feel like my bones are liquifying, and now *this*." She rubbed her temple where something had struck her in the river.

It'd been the epicenter of her headaches, but was it a black hole for information as well? Was she truly at risk of losing her memory? Her mind?

"I've never had trouble remembering, and now I can't recall something he told me. Something important."

Her friend crossed the small courtyard and wrapped his arms around her. Warm and safe, enough pressure to calm her nerves, but not too much to suffocate her. His breath tickled her ear and Amanda froze, trying to fight the urge to pull out of the embrace.

Joaquin released her and held her at arms' length. "We've asked a lot of you, and you've done very well. Just help us find where Vargas is hiding and I'll get you home."

She backed away and faced the sun, closing her eyes but still seeing the glow behind her lids.

*Home.*

Just a few days ago, all she'd wanted was to be back in Chicago, seeing her parents for the first time in over a year. How has her disappearance changed them? Would they even recognize her now? Would they love the person she'd become, or was it better to let her live in their memories?

Joaquin reclined against the fountain, his legs crossed at the ankles. His brow only loosened slightly, but the tension traveled down to his lips. His words might have indicated that she'd be going home, but his face told the truth.

If she made it through this, even if she was able to go home, it was no longer the place Amanda belonged.

Where *did* she belong? Home no longer felt like a physical space. Phoenix felt like home, but much of that was because of David. Pardon Falls had inklings of home, but it was because of her friends; El, Hank and Willa. Even the desert felt like home, those few days lost and wandering with David and Josh.

*David.*

Their time together had been brief, but he was her tether, keeping her grounded. Losing David was like losing *home*. She could build a new life, but it would never be the same. Amanda was homeless.

Her forehead flushed with sweat. The edges of her vision pulsed with fuzziness. She leaned against the wall and closed her eyes. It'd been too much.

The plaza, the man, running to the church, Josh, the people, and now this, the unexpected assault of grief.

It hit her with the impact of a train. If she'd prepared herself for it, she could've hidden from Joaquin, found a quiet place to rock and hold her head.

"Amanda, you all right?" He gripped her arms, holding her upright. "Do you need water? Your pills?"

She nodded. "I overdid it, that's all."

His worried look jumped to a new level.

The corner of her mouth lifted into a half-hearted grin.

In Chicago, she'd seen her fair share of homeless people. People who once had families and friends who loved them. People who, for one reason or another had found themselves parting ways with the life they knew.

She was one of them now. Fully letting go of her old life gave her freedom. Freedom to put concern for her own well-being on the back burner. Freedom to do something truly selfless.

"Tomorrow, can we go back to the plaza?" she asked as Joaquin led her back inside. "I want to see if I can remember."

Being homeless gave her the freedom to do whatever it takes to help Joaquin, and maybe, if she were lucky, be able to join David in the afterlife.

# 25

There weren't many guests at the hotel David had chosen. No holiday loomed, the summer still beat down with the brutality of a dictator and the economy of this town was as dry as the desert surrounding it.

What the hotel did have going for it was a perfect view to the town's cathedral.

He sat on the long, second-floor porch. Taking up residency there after searching every corner of the cathedral for Mandy.

When they'd finally found the priest, he swore an oath to every saint he could think of that he wasn't aware of who left rose petals on the floor. He'd stepped out to check on a sick parishioner. No, he didn't lock the church when he was gone; a place of worship was always open.

The man seemed as concerned as David that something nefarious might've taken place in his church with someone posing as a man of God.

"That was the best shower in the history of showers." Fallon fell into the chair next to him. Her hair hung in long, damp ringlets, and her face was scrubbed free of the little makeup she wore.

He hated having her with him and he needed her at the same

time. It was wrong to ask her to help him find another woman, especially since a couple of months ago, he'd finally decided to move on, and it'd made sense to move on *with* Fallon.

In some way, it still made sense to move on with her. David was past the point of making sense. Even to himself.

"See anything?" she asked.

The sun had called it an evening. The blue-gray blanket of twilight clung to the day, refusing to give up to the night.

"Nah, a few ladies went in for their evening prayers. Kids playing and some teenage boys were sneaking beer." He perched his feet on the railing, rocking the chair back.

Fallon rested her forearms on her thighs as she scanned the plaza. "Do you think we're being watched?"

"Sure as hell hope so." David paused to swat at the pest buzzing in his ear. "Why else would I be out here feeding the mosquitos?"

Fallon pulled her hair back and wrapped it into a loose bun, tucking the ends in. "I can't figure out who has her. This whole town is acting like we're the first *gringos* they've seen in decades."

"Which makes me think she's still here."

They sat in silence for several minutes. Darkness won out over the twilight, the mosquitos gave up assaulting their prey, and the priest locked up the cathedral.

This was the moment he'd waited for. The church to be alone, without the watchful eyes of the clergy. To see who might use the sacred ground for sinful purposes.

Fallon took a deep breath. She started to speak a couple of times.

Sitting there in the soft yellow glow of the streetlights, David could pick up on her thoughts just by how she fidgeted in the chair or picked at her fingernails, only to *tsk* at herself and drop her hands in her lap.

She pushed her chair back, the screech silencing the crickets and blocking his view to the church. "Come on, let's get some dinner. I'll buy."

"Thanks, but I'm not hungry, you go ahead." He tilted his head to try to look around her.

She crossed her arms and shifted her stance, blocking him again. "You haven't eaten all day."

"You keeping tabs on me?" His voice jabbed with a sharp edge.

"As a matter of fact, yeah." Fallon fell back into the chair. Her mouth was pressed so tight her lips had gone white. "You're not thinking about drinking, are you?"

David stared for a heartbeat, then shifted his gaze back to the church doors. "No," he lied. In fact, that was all he'd been thinking about since watching the teenagers sneaking beer.

He wasn't at risk of breaking sobriety. At least he didn't think he was. Not as long as he sat there on the balcony. If he went downstairs, he might not be in control.

His feet might take him to the closest liquor store. He might find the Spanish words to ask for a bottle of tequila and a six-pack of beer. Then he might perch himself on the stone steps of the cathedral waiting for Mandy to show up.

Nope. He wasn't thinking about drinking.

Somewhere deep inside his mind, he was already doing it.

"Really, Fal, I promise, I'm fine."

"Want me to bring you something?"

"That would be great."

Fallon pushed past him, but he reached out and grabbed her wrist.

"Thank you. For everything. For believing me."

The tautness she'd held in her face disappeared, washed away in a tide of sadness leaving just the unblemished smoothness of sand. She nodded and the door slammed behind her.

Clanging from the bell tower rattled out the time. Nine o'clock.

They'd pulled a couple of eighteen hour days since setting out to look for Mandy. Up before the sun stirred and collapsing into bed late into the night. Picking their way through small border towns, some not much bigger than a few homes, others bustling cities. This town sat somewhere in between, big enough to hide her, but not so large he couldn't stake out a prime target.

As the city quieted, David's eyelids grew heavy.

It seemed like Fallon was gone just for a few minutes before she reappeared with a Styrofoam container full of food.

He rallied long enough to convince her to go to bed, but once his belly was full and the night air cooled, he found his chin resting against his chest.

When he woke, the courtyard was softly lit in a yellowish-beige. Low, thin clouds raced across the sky. Pigeons cooed as they pranced around the fountain.

David stretched, his back popping. His neck was so stiff it took him several turns to get it loosened up enough so he could peer around the corner to the church.

He pulled his phone out of his pocket to check the time, but only an angry red battery sign stared back.

At the first chime of the bell, the flock of pigeons fluttered.

At the second and third, he stood, stretching his arms high overhead, touching the ceiling of the balcony.

The fourth chime brought hushed voices echoing around the empty plaza.

The fifth, the voices grew louder, maybe even below him.

He could almost make out English words.

With the sixth, David leaned over the railing, trying to get a better look beneath him.

When the clock struck seven, two figures emerged. A man and a woman. He was slightly taller than her, with a head full of dark hair. She was thin, almost skinny, wearing a simple tank top and fitted jeans. The woman walked slowly. Her light brown hair was cut short, blunt, as if done by someone who'd never spent a day in beauty school. She didn't seem self-conscious by it. Quite the opposite. She walked with her head held high, shoulders back.

It was the posture of someone in charge. The posture of someone on a mission.

The posture of someone he followed out of the desert.

## 26

The plaza was nearly empty, only a few shopkeepers readying their stores for the day bustled about. Pigeons cooed and fluttered, fighting over the tiniest morsel on the ground. Orange lit the sky behind the buildings on the eastern edge, the sun not quite stretching to reach over their rooftops.

Joaquin walked next to Amanda, but he didn't speak or reach out. The sound of his breath was her only companion.

The conversation with Vargas' man played in a constant loop. A loop with a giant, gaping sinkhole in the middle.

He'd wanted her to surrender. Alone. That much she remembered. And, to find a way, *somewhere*. If she was to do this, go wherever Vargas wanted, and turn herself over, her new friends, Joaquin and Alfredo, would be safe.

"Anything?" he asked.

Amanda shook her head.

Joaquin had advocated for coming back early in the morning.

She'd wanted to replicate the entire exchange. Same time of day, sitting in the same spot, hoping the same man would show up and encase her in balloons to give his ominous proposal again.

Neither was going to work.

She'd sat up all night trying to conjure the words he'd said, the place he wanted her to go. It was as successful as flying a kite on a calm day.

The clanging church bell snagged her attention. The thought of returning to the place where they found Josh's hand made her stomach invert. Sometimes, evil invaded good. Just as sometimes good shone through darkness. "The cathedral," she whispered, afraid her words would assault the quiet of the morning. "I'd like to go to the cathedral."

Amanda set off down the side street, not waiting on Joaquin's acknowledgement. Truthfully, she needed to be alone. A few precious moments to herself. To try to call up stubborn memories. To find the courage to abandon the man who'd stayed by her bedside. Betrayal wouldn't come easily.

Like the previous day, the church was empty. Cool. Dark.

She paused in front of the candles. "Do you have any change?" she asked Joaquin.

He dug some *pesos* from his pocket and handed them to her. "What can I do?"

She lit a candle and closed her eyes. Tried to call up a prayer, but nothing was coming yet. "I just need a few minutes."

He nodded. "I'll be back here. If you need anything, shout. I'll be there in two seconds."

Amanda made her way down the aisle, stopping just a few rows back from the dais. Sun filtered in from the windows high overhead, a celestial play of light battling darkness through columns of illumination.

She studied the stained glass; the story of the crucifixion, the disciples, the heartbreak of the Virgin Mary. Caught herself studying the figure of Judas, the one who'd betrayed Jesus.

Was that who she was now? Was she really contemplating becoming Joaquin's Judas to find her own Judas?

Rather than take a seat, she lowered herself to the kneelers, wincing at the biting pain in her pelvis. It'd been at least twelve hours since her last pill. She needed to be as clear-minded as possible, even if it meant she felt like she was being ripped in two.

With her hands steepled and her eyes closed, Amanda took a deep breath, inhaling all the church scents; incense, leather and pulp from the hymnals, a bit of dust.

When she'd started sneaking into Mexico to look for Josh, she'd visited the church of each town she searched. It wasn't that she was overly religious, but it'd somehow made her feel safe, as if checking in with the "Big Guy" so he knew where she was. But also to beg forgiveness, and ask for guidance.

Now, she felt like screaming angry accusations instead of humble prayers. Why hadn't Josh just jumped?

If he had, he and David would've gotten to safety. Instead, they'd lost time and David lost his life.

It'd been her decision, *her* choice to face Vargas. Even if the sentence was torture and death, she would've been in control, albeit in some very small way.

*Where was God then?*

Why didn't he intervene? Stop Josh from doing what she'd decided to do. Now she was being forced to hurt others, to sneak off to…

"Dammit," Amanda murmured. The place still wasn't coming forward. She took a deep breath and cleared her mind, pushing away the anger at Josh, the blossoming remorse for Joaquin.

Her tangled feelings for David, grief and hurt, formed such a tight knot she couldn't pick them apart. They'd just have to sit in the corner in the back of her mind.

No prayers were coming to her. No asking for strength or forgiveness. No requests for guidance or riches.

All she needed was a word.

*Please, tell me what I'm forgetting.*

Kneeling in the cathedral with her eyes closed, Amanda found herself back in the plaza, back to the fountain, the sun's heat beating down on her. People swarmed, kids ran and played, the balloon vendors filled the sky with their helium-filled goods.

Then he was there. Vargas' emissary.

Except this time, she slowed down the exchange. Picked apart his comment about her hair. He'd seen her before, or at least a picture of her. Vargas wanted her and her alone. And then…

She mentally slowed his words. Pros… It was two *p's*, the hard sound of the consonant stuttering in her mind. *Prospera.* The word came into her mind with the suddenness of a clown jumping out of a box.

Amanda mentally fist-pumped. There were two words he said, but the second one was hiding like a scared kitten, refusing to come out. It was okay, she'd coax it out later with milk and soft words, but for now she had something.

Was it something she'd offer to Joaquin and Alfredo? Or, something she'd keep for herself, to follow instructions and find a way to Vargas, to Josh, alone?

The echo of footsteps pulled her from her meditation.

Joaquin must've grown worried. How long had she been there?

A second set of footsteps chased after the first. These more urgent, accompanied by Joaquin shouting in both English and Spanish.

Her mind commanded her legs to stand, but they weren't following orders. Amanda pushed up with her arms, stiff-legged and wobbly, holding on to the back of the pew to see what was going on.

A man walked in the darkness between sunbeams. He was tall, with sturdy, sure steps. Not the gait of someone looking for quiet contemplation, but someone with brash determination.

When he entered the cone of light closest to her, he stopped.

She swayed and her fingernails dug into the wood. Her heart didn't know whether to stop or sprint. Was she seeing a ghost? Had she just died?

His name tingled her lips. She never thought she'd say it again.

Not aloud. Not *to* him.

"David?"

# 27

Having coffee at a sidewalk cafe was too pedestrian for the conversation Amanda needed to have with David. Too casual to sit there with someone she'd thought had died. Too...normal.

Joaquin wandered around the plaza, sneaking glances in their direction while chatting up shop owners and passersby.

Once she'd said David's name, her friend had understood and offered them space to talk. By the close proximity of his hovering, he obviously wasn't willing to relinquish her to him.

A blonde woman sat on the bench around the fountain, her head bent over her phone. It was the same woman she'd seen the day before, the one walking into the hospital with the man she now realized was David.

He'd introduced her quickly before asking Fallon to give them some time.

The woman looked her up and down and pursed her lips. A deep line bisected between her eyebrows.

Who was the ex-girlfriend; her or Fallon?

The waiter dropped off their *cafes con leche*.

David squeezed her hand before dropping it to lift his cup for a sip.

She couldn't stop staring. It'd only been a few weeks, but it felt like she was seeing him anew. The way his eyebrows perfectly framed his dark brown eyes. How a smattering of gray dusted his dark hair, hair that now curled around his collar. How his dimples appeared before he broke into a wide grin. Committing it all to memory.

They hadn't spoken yet.

Not anything significant, beyond ordering coffee and the *is-it-really-you's*.

Was he as nervous as she? He studied her as intently.

A memory hit Amanda and she gasped, then dropped her gaze to his torso. "You were shot…" She could see it. Them running to the cliff. Him pitching forward, grunting.

"A graze." He shifted in his chair. "Nothing a few stitches couldn't fix." David paused, his stoic mask slipped. "But, you…" He brushed her hair from her temple, exposing the scar. "My God, Mandy, I'm so sorry I couldn't find you. If I would have dove under one more time…"

She shook her head, knocking his hand away in the process. "It's okay. It was chaos. Everything happened so fast."

David glanced down at the table. The warmth that'd been growing between them cooled. Like a ghost passing between them.

"There's—" He stopped and furrowed his brow. "Williams was right. I was going to turn you in, but I was angry. In a bad place. I hate myself for what I almost did to you."

The apparition solidified. The guilt he carried should have dragged him to the bottom of the river. Maybe it had. Maybe it anchored him to that spot on the Rio Grande, dragging him back every time he tried to leave.

Amanda placed her hand over his. "You were only doing what I was planning to do myself." She cupped his cheek with her free hand. "I break the law, you uphold it. It's what we do."

Seeing him alive, her anger vanished. But the space it took up filled with dread. Worry that Vargas would take him from her and send David back to her piece by piece stole the jubilation from their reunion.

A quick smile touched only his mouth, too shallow to make it to his dimples or eyes. "I have a million questions running through my head."

Amanda glanced down at their joined hands. "Me too. Just talk. Tell me everything. I just—" her voice broke. "Never thought I'd hear your voice again." She took a sip of her now lukewarm coffee to wash down the lump. "I don't care if you just read the menu to me. Talk."

*So I don't have to.*

David told her about climbing out of the river. How a park ranger checking flood levels of the Rio Grande had seen him and stopped him from repeatedly diving in to look for her. Divers came out. Her parents flew down. Ultimately, they'd declared her dead, accepting that her body was washed far downstream.

She winced. It was better for her family to mourn her and try to heal, but it still hurt to think they'd given up. "Well, I was unconscious for a couple of weeks, so that's practically dead."

"I couldn't accept it," he said. "*Didn't.* For weeks I walked the riverbanks. Searching for any sign you'd gotten out. But too much time had passed. I stopped searching to save you, started searching to bury you. Then Shiloh convinced me to go home."

Amanda expected her body to bristle at her old foe's name, but instead she felt warmth toward the woman. Appreciation that Shiloh was there to look after David when she wasn't. "How did you end up here?"

He took a deep breath. His gaze drifted down to their joined hands. "I was working at Riley's, and had gone out to take a call from El and got jumped by a guy Vargas sent to kill me." The words came out of his mouth in one quick breath. As if they were scared kids on a high dive, if he didn't push they wouldn't jump.

Amanda stiffened. Her worry solidified. The familiar flutter of panic beat against her heart. *This* was why she needed to do it.

Why she needed to send him home. Without her.

She dropped his grasp, instead busying her fingers with twisting the paper napkin. That didn't settle the rush of adrenalin picking up speed through her blood like a barreling avalanche. Amanda needed to go.

Now.

Her chair screeched as she pushed away from the table. *From him.* "I'm sorry, I thought I could—I can't do this." Tears coated her words.

She speed-walked across the plaza, ignoring David's shouts.

"Mandy, please, baby." He caught up easily and lightly gripped her arm. "Talk to me. What is it?"

Before she could answer, Joaquin jogged over, proving that he'd kept a more watchful eye than he'd let on. "*Mija,* everything okay?"

David tried to get in her line of sight, but Amanda kept spinning away from him, afraid that looking into his eyes would rob her will.

"What did you do to her?" Joaquin asked, he reached for her, but she shook out of his grasp as well.

"Nothing, we were just talking."

She spun and took two steps away.

Fallon glanced up, but went back to her phone, at least pretending to.

It was already starting, the tug of war she'd been so afraid of the moment David had stepped into the light. The overwhelming desire to be with him battled her sense of responsibility to save Josh. To protect David.

There'd be no clear winners, but it was certain she would lose.

"She's been through a lot," Joaquin said. "More than you could possibly know."

David pushed out an exasperated sigh behind her.

In her mind's eye, she could see him rake his hand through his hair. That was what made her ache more than her broken body and battered head. He'd thought he'd won. He got the girl and despite all they'd been through, they could finally start building a life together.

"Look man, I appreciate what you've done for her. And I promise, once I get her home, I'll make sure she gets the best care possible."

The steamy air of the early morning froze, as if he'd said something taboo.

Joaquin's face was pinched tight, but David's was slack. Each man waited for her answer. Each man hoped to walk out of the plaza with her.

Each man was going to be disappointed.

Fallon stood and started a slow approach.

"Mandy?" David's voice was quiet, pleading. "Say something."

Joaquin shook his head and looked down at his feet. "You haven't told him."

The blonde woman now stood behind David, her mouth turned in a deep scowl and her eyes pinched together, a deep crease forming between them.

"Tell me what." His voice was low and strained.

Amanda took a deep breath. Eyes were all on *her*, waiting like she was a soprano taking the stage.

Where should she start?

Whose heart does she break first?

"Josh is still alive."

David's eyes widened, but then he moved his face back to neutral before dropping his gaze to the flagstones in front of him. "I know."

It was her turn to lose control of her jaw. "You know?"

He nodded. "That was the other thing the guy Vargas sent for me said." He reached for her, but she jerked her arm back. "Come on Mandy, he's likely dead by now."

Amanda took a step backwards, stumbling on the uneven stones.

Joaquin lurched forward, reaching out to steady her, but not letting go once she regained her balance.

*A strong tug of the rope in his direction.*

"Maybe, but he sacrificed himself for me, for us." She stepped away from her friend, further away from David. As if she was getting a head start on a race. Amanda looked David square in the face, trying to not fall into those dark eyes, to not weaken and lose the strength she needed. "I'm not going home. I'm staying here. To

149

find Josh." She shifted her gaze to Joaquin, her heart breaking at the look of genuine concern etched in his expression.

She was a baby bird, tossed from the nest and he nursed her back to health.

Now it was time for her to fly.

"Alone."

# 28

Fallon wanted to punch Amanda. Despite that it was obvious the woman took no pleasure in breaking David's heart. Again. How could someone deny going home with the man who spent weeks looking for her and who had to contend with his own attempted murder because of her mistakes?

*Bitch.*

After she'd dropped the bomb she was staying in Mexico, Fallon was eager to say, "That's that and let's go home," but David was too busy arguing his case. As was the other man with Amanda.

*Damn, she's influencing people and winning friends like a champ.*

Her phone buzzed again in her hand, but she ignored it. Her boss has been on her butt since before the sun came up in Nova Scotia to see when she'd be back from her unplanned vacation. As much as Fallon wanted to say as soon as they drove back into Texas, David wouldn't leave. Not without starting World War III to get Amanda to come with him. Judging by the way the woman sparred with both men, they were in for a long battle.

When Winslow called back a second time, it was serious.

"Weatherby," he said. "Where the hell are you?"

She covered the phone with her hair, hoping it would shield the shouting behind her and her conversation. "Well, sir, I'm still technically on vacation…"

"Do you see the criminals taking a vacation?" he barked. "Because I sure as hell don't."

Fallon wandered away from the threesome, not wanting them to hear the ass-chewing. "Look, sir, I'm almost done. I'll be back as soon as possible."

He took a deep breath and let out a long sigh, as if remembering some recent management training. "You never told me where you were."

She frowned into the phone. Fallon wasn't an overly private person, but she also didn't share every detail of her personal life with her colleagues. Details like which frozen dinner she fixed, or if she went with Chinese takeout or picked up tacos, or how her cat liked to chew on her bills if she left them on the counter for too long. Really personal stuff. "I'm in Mexico." She straightened her back.

Hopefully he'd accept her answer as one of the resort towns and not the border.

"Fallon, level with me." Winslow dropped his voice and used her first name, something he rarely did, except when he wanted to be seen more as a friend and colleague than a superior. "How many years have I known you? And how many vacations have you taken?"

She took another deep breath and looked at David.

His face was red and he was trying to reason with Amanda's back.

The woman faced Fallon's direction, but her gaze was focused on the ground. Red tinged her cheeks and neck, even her chest above her tank top was starting to turn pink. Why couldn't she just talk to David? Why was she putting up such a fight?

Winslow had a point. She'd never just taken time for herself. Instead she'd used her time off for David, to help him find someone he loved. If Amanda couldn't understand what he'd gone through for her, she didn't deserve him.

"Okay, you're right." Fallon glanced back at the group.

They were so engrossed in their own drama they didn't notice the small crowd gathering. Or, her standing off to the side.

She walked toward the fountain, standing near the water rushing from the top down to the pool below, hoping the splashing would cover her voice. "Like I said, I'm in Mexico, but it's not exactly a vacation. Do you remember that case in Chicago, the investment firm with the founder's son committing securities fraud?" She could hear her boss breathing, but he didn't answer her.

Either he was looking it up online or going through his mental filing cabinet.

"Vaguely, remind me."

"Pretty cut and dry, three employees indicted and all got away, but only because an angry investor shot the place up." She paused, waiting for Winslow to acknowledge he remembered the case. "I'm standing here staring at one of them, and she has a lead on where the other one is hiding."

Fallon could almost see her boss.

Winslow took a long, slow sip of coffee. Sitting in his office, the door closed but the blinds covering the large windows looking out were open, so he could watch without appearing to micro-manage.

"What kind of confirmation do you have it's really her, or she really knows where the other one is?"

She shrugged even though he couldn't see her. "I have a friend, former law enforcement, confirming the identity of Amanda Martin. And, she allegedly has a lead on Josh Williams."

The sound of a tapping keyboard answered her. "Martin was declared deceased earlier this summer."

She peeked around the spray of the fountain.

The argument appeared to be winding down.

All three of them looked down at their feet.

Amanda's face was wet.

David shifted between running his hands through his hair and rubbing his face.

The Mexican man, the one who'd served as Amanda's caretaker, pinched the bridge of his nose.

It was hard to tell who won.

Or, if there *was* a winner.

"Based on my friend's reaction, she'd gotten a little banged up, but it's her. The only confirmation I have on Williams is from her." Fallon looked over her shoulder, checking to see if anyone was in earshot. "Here's the other thing. Williams is being held by Rafael Vargas and—"

"The cartel leader?" Winslow cut her off.

"Yeah, allegedly. He's an American, remember? Perhaps we could get two birds with one stone."

She kept her eyes on the group. Their lips moved but no words made it to her ears. With the heat of the argument over, they were now acting like adults.

"You have no jurisdiction there."

She smirked. Winslow's tough exterior had a ding in it. "I'm on vacation. Remember?"

David jerked his head up, twisting it to look around the plaza before making eye contact with her.

Amanda and the other man were walking away, but the woman kept looking back at David.

"I've gotta go," she said, walking toward her friend. "A couple more days, I'll keep you posted." Fallon ended the call before Winslow could argue or agree. She'd just have to assume he was in agreement. "Hey, you doing okay?" she asked David. It was a weak thing to say to a man who'd just gotten his heart crushed.

A wry smile tried to crawl across his face, but it flat-lined before it reached the other side. "Wishing I hadn't given up drinking."

"That bad?"

He shrugged. "You could land a jumbo jet on her stubborn streak. Joaquin's going to try to talk some sense into her." David nodded toward the cafe where she'd found him and Amanda. "Want some breakfast?"

They reclaimed the same table he'd sat at earlier, their cups removed and menus in their place.

"Truthfully, I'm relieved to see she still has some fight in her, after everything she'd been through."

"Why won't she come home then?"

David took a deep breath and reclined, draping one arm over the back of the chair. "Mandy's loyal, to a fault, and if she believes someone she cares about needs her, she won't give up until she's helped." He looked across the plaza.

Fallon followed his gaze to where Amanda and Joaquin sat. The man was angled close, talking, but David's ex stared across the plaza at them, her brow knitted in a scowl.

"It's what I love about her," he continued. "But right now, it's what I hate about her."

# 29

They were sent to their corners. That was how Amanda felt. Like boxers at the end of a round sent back with their coaches.

Joaquin spoke soothing, encouraging words but they weren't making it to her ears, instead she watched David with Fallon.

Was he telling her this was typical Mandy? Irrational, stubborn, misplaced loyalty. At least she could blame it on a head injury now.

She didn't want to fight with David. She wanted to just be near his alive-ness. To hear his breath, to watch the muscles in his jaw move as he talked, to allow his deep Texas drawl wash over her. That was what mattered, not their argument over her going home with him. Or, not going home.

"Are you listening to me?" Joaquin's voice was sharper and he waved a hand in front of her.

"Would you believe me if I said yes?"

He shook his head and laughed, an infectious sound that forced a similar sound from her throat.

Once upon a time she'd laughed freely. Now it felt...foreign.

"You still love each other very much," Joaquin said. "But you're both stubborn."

"And that's why it'll never work, right?" She rested her elbows on the table. The low hum of pain grumbled at her movement. "That, and the fact a cartel boss is after us, and if I weren't declared dead by my family I'd be in jail for securities fraud. Oh, and let's not forget he was on his way to turn me in to the FBI when we got kidnapped."

"I've seen couples survive worse," her friend mumbled.

Amanda glanced over at David and the blonde woman again.

A waitress delivered plates to them both.

*Sure, he'll buy her breakfast and I only get coffee.*

She looked away, silently chastising the little bird of jealousy. "I'm starving. You hungry?"

Amanda flagged down a waitress and ignored Joaquin's stifled smile as she tried to order. The girl gave him a confused look and he translated her pathetic Spanish into something that sounded like food.

Silence settled in as she stalked her ex across the plaza. She couldn't figure out David and Fallon's relationship. Were they just friends? On the surface it seemed that way, but he also showed a little more tenderness toward her. Had they dated in the past?

David grinned at Amanda from his corner. A sweet, flirty look that covered her in warmth, soothing her sore muscles. Her sore heart.

Fallon lifted her head, whipping it over her shoulder in her direction.

David's smile took a dive.

Cold drained down her body, leaving in its wake heartbreaking realization. They hadn't dated in the past. But, they might in the future.

"You're missing the obvious," Joaquin said, forcing her to focus on her own table. "Teamed up, you and David would be quite formidable." He paused, studying her, waiting for his words to sink in. "Let him help us, *mija*, then you can go home with him. It's what you Americans call a win-win."

"No." Her voice was strong and loud. The conversations and clanging of silver around them stopped as the word echoed. She dropped her voice. "Have you forgotten about the number of body parts I've collected? I'm not letting *that* happen to David, too." The waitress arrived with her food, exactly what she'd wanted, but she was no longer hungry. "I'm sending him home."

Her friend chuckled and sipped his coffee.

"What?" Amanda asked through a mouthful of food.

"I want to be there when you tell him. That will be a great argument."

She studied him over the steam rising off her food.

Joaquin's jaw was set tight, but his eyes were full of humor. Full of challenge.

"I agreed to help to try to save Josh. I'm not going to ask David to put himself in danger for a man he hates."

"Of course not," he retorted. "Nor would he."

*Finally*, someone agreeing without her throwing a temper tantrum.

She picked up her fork and reclined in her chair, stabbing at the cooling food in hopes it'd revive her appetite.

"But he *would* put himself in danger for the woman he loves." Joaquin sat his cup down. "Can we talk about why you think you're going after Vargas alone?"

She'd been waiting for this. During the three-way argument Joaquin had only brought it up once, but it wasn't a shocker he hadn't forgotten her assertion she was going after Josh and Vargas, alone.

"It's something I have to do on my own." Not a lie, but not the complete truth. If she told him what the balloon man had said, he'd only push back harder.

"Explain how you're going to get a maimed man to safety." Joaquin's voice was steady, nonchalant, not much different than asking what her plans were for the day. "You're pushing yourself too much. You're still healing."

Amanda ignored his probing stare. Instead she went back to watching David and Fallon.

David pulled his wallet out, placing money on the table.

*Buying someone's breakfast doesn't mean they're dating.*

Unless they're just sleeping together. In that case, buying breakfast totally means *'thanks for last night, it was fun, let's do it again sometime,
I'll call you.'*

"Ahh." Joaquin drummed his fingers on the table. "We were
threatened, by Vargas' man. He told you to come alone, or else,
right?" He paused, tilting his head and pursing his lips. "Coming
back here today to remember the place, it was really to rendezvous
with the man."

"No." For the second time she shouted her response.

*Geesh, calm it down, Martin.*

"I mean, no, there was no rendezvous. I really did forget."

"But he did threaten us?" He arched a dark eyebrow.

She only nodded. Movement caught her attention.

David and Fallon were walking in their direction.

Joaquin gave her a *bless-your-heart* smile. "If I stopped the first
time I was threatened, you would have woken up in the hospital
alone, *mija.*" He grasped her hand and squeezed it, leaning in so
close she could feel his breath on her cheek. "His threats don't
frighten me, and they shouldn't frighten you. Not on my behalf.
You've been on your own far too long. Let yourself be part of a
team. Trust others." He looked up at the approaching Americans
and dropped her hand. "Allow David to help you."

"Um, we interrupting?" her ex asked, his gaze resting on her
now free hand rather than her face.

"No, join us," Joaquin said, pointing at the two open chairs.
"Amanda and I were just chatting about trust and teamwork."

David took the seat next to her.

Fallon hesitated, chewing on her lower lip before pulling out the
chair next to Joaquin.

"How're you doing?" David asked.

"You know I'd never intentionally hurt you, right?" Amanda
could almost hear the rip of the Band-Aid. "I thought I'd lost you.
Knowing that's not the case, I want to roll you in bubble wrap and
lock you away to protect you."

He smiled. "Thanks?" He glanced at Fallon. "Look, Fallon
pointed out this doesn't have to be an either-or situation."

"Funny, Joaquin and I were having that exact conversation." She gave David and Fallon the run-down of her encounter with the balloon man.

As she recounted the exchange, her nose tickled with the smell of warm rubber from the balloons, the sound of the trickling fountain filled her ears. She closed her eyes when she came to the hole in her memory, hoping that shutting out the people sitting there with her would call forth the forgotten words.

This time when she replayed the movie of the moment, it didn't come out garbled or fuzzy, like a TV channel covered in static. It came out strong. Clear.

"Prospera Pass. That's what I couldn't remember last night." She looked at Joaquin, but his face was blank. "Does that mean anything?"

"Not initially, but I'll research it." He pulled his phone out of pocket and began tapping.

"Do you want to stay with me at the hotel?" David asked.

"Not safe there," Joaquin answered for her. "We've got room for you both at the house. My guess is we won't be there long anyway."

Amanda and Joaquin stayed at the cafe while David and Fallon checked out of their hotel.

She contemplated her friend's words, about relying on others to help her.

Amanda, David and Josh needed each other to survive the desert. Needed each other, but also not fully trusting each other.

The same feeling now sunk into its familiar place in the pit of her stomach.

# 30

David followed Joaquin to a house on the outskirts of town. They didn't take the most direct route. More than once, they double-backed, forcing his gaze to stare into the rearview mirror longer than normal to ensure they weren't being followed.

Mandy sat beside him. Just a foot between them, but she felt a million miles away.

"Joaquin seems like a good guy," David said, because probing about what she was thinking would result in her clamming up.

"Hmmm," she said. "Yeah, he's been great. How long have you known Fallon?"

The car in front of them pulled into a garage in a burnt orange stucco house.

He parked in the driveway and killed the engine. "I've known her since college. Why?"

Mandy shrugged and opened the door. "You've never mentioned her before." She paused when he laid a hand on her arm.

"There's still a lot we have to learn about each other." David tried to make the words sound more promising, less judgmental.

He followed her into the house.

Mandy walked like someone decades older. She didn't lift her feet with confidence, instead they shuffled forward with short, shallow steps. Her face was pale, clammy. Her full lips were dry and cracked, more yellow than their natural pink.

All she'd mentioned was a hit to the head. What else had happened to her?

Joaquin stood in a large interior patio, holding Fallon's bag while she explore the first level. The tiled floor was the same ochre color of the house. Rooms branched off from the foyer. A combination living and dining room with a spacious kitchen filled the back, and an office jutted off to one side. Two flights of stairs rose up with more rooms encircling the courtyard.

Mandy stopped in the kitchen, filling a glass of water before silently disappearing up the stairs in slow, labored steps.

He started to follow her, but Joaquin called him.

"Thank you both for your help," he said. "We have plenty of bedrooms, but if you'd like to share with Amanda..." Joaquin trailed, leaving silent expectation to echo around the foyer.

David glanced up, toward her retreating figure. He wanted nothing more than to hold her all night, but he had to be patient. Pushing her would only drive her further away.

She had to come to him.

"There's a room open next to hers," Joaquin added, his voice low and nearly inaudible.

He nodded. "That might be best." David followed her path to the second floor. He approached the first room, the one Mandy had disappeared into.

She stood with her back to the door, gazing out the sheer curtains. One arm was wrapped across her abdomen, her other hand rubbing her temple.

There was something both familiar and completely alien about her. The woman he loved was still there, tucked away somewhere.

Was it Josh, or being on the run? Or, was it finding out *he* was alive?

Mandy dropped her arms and her shoulders rose and fell with a deep breath. She whirled, and jumped, as if startled to see him watching her.

"I'll be right next door." Heat crept up his face.

She crossed the room and reached for the door. "I'm wiped out. I'm going to lie down for a bit." The slightest hint of an apologetic smile touched her lips before she pushed the door shut.

His body urged him forward, to follow her and offer to hold her while she slept, but his mind whispered she needed time to process all this. Up until a few hours ago, she thought he was dead.

David dropped his bag in the next room and hurried back down the stairs, eager to find something to do other than read into Mandy's actions. Fallon and Joaquin were chatting in the combination living and dining room.

"I'm going to check in with the office," she said, slipping out the back door into a walled garden.

He glanced around the room. One wall was taken up with a giant stone fireplace and a comfy leather sectional faced it.

"Is this your home?" Small talk felt so...*small* considering they were now planning to rescue a man from a drug cartel.

Joaquin shook his head. "It belongs to my employer, Alfredo." The man pulled out his phone. "I've tried calling and texting, but haven't heard back. He'll be here soon, you'll meet him." He also looked around the living room, as if suffering the same small-talk deficiency. "Want a beer?"

"I don't drink, but I'll take some coffee if you've got it." David followed him into the kitchen.

A sarcastic laugh erupted from the man's throat. "I used to *not* drink, too." He took a long pull from an amber bottle before filling the coffeepot with grounds and water.

Who was this man? Why did he think having Mandy was so important to whatever mission he was on?

"Why'd you start?"

Joaquin shoved the carafe under the filter and pressed the 'on' button too hard. When he turned back, his eyes were hard, but only on the surface. The rest of his face was coated in sadness. "Helps with all the death. Even if you live, some part of you still dies."

Silence filled the room like smoke, swirling around them, infiltrating his lungs, making his eyes burn. He wasn't a stranger to how that felt, not just people dying, but relationships, careers. His life, the one he was so comfortable with, dying.

Seeing Mandy, broken; physically, emotionally, maybe even mentally. Would it have been better if she died? Was she like Joaquin? A part of her was now gone. If so, what part? Was it the part loved David?

"How is she? Really?" he asked before taking a sip of coffee.

The man studied him, as if trying to decide how much to share. "She was unconscious for a while. You've seen the scar; something hit her in the river. The other wounds are hidden, but she's strong. She'll overcome them."

The feeling that the guy was withholding information was so tangible he could almost see it watching them from the corner. "What are you *not* telling me?"

Joaquin shook his head. "What I'm telling you is don't push her. When she woke up this morning, you were dead. Now you're alive. Seeing you just ripped open a giant wound."

The heat from the coffee rose up from David's gut, igniting his desire to protect Mandy and hide her away from everyone. "That's why I need to take her home."

"No, that's exactly why she has to stay here."

"To help you."

"To help her heal. Vargas is poison. She'll never heal if the poison is still in her system."

An argument bubbled in his stomach, eager to spill out and ask him what made him such an authority on what Mandy needed, but the back door opening tamped it down.

Fallon entered, tucking her phone into her back pocket. She studied Joaquin, her gaze falling on the beer in his hands. "Got another one of those?" she asked. "Sorry." She mouthed to David.

"My sobriety shouldn't keep you from enjoying a beer. How's things at the office?"

She took a quick sip. "Fine, they can survive a few more days without me. So, what's the plan?" she asked Joaquin.

"First we need to figure out what Prospera Pass is."

The bottle popped as Fallon pulled it from her lips. "Or where? The mountains. Could the Pass be a mountain pass?"

Joaquin quirked an eyebrow. "Smart *and* pretty. Let's look. Follow me."

A quick blush tinted her cheeks, pulling her lips up into a grin before fading when she met David's eyes.

They followed Joaquin to an office off the living room.

He woke up a computer and pulled up an aerial map, moving it with the mouse.

The two of them mumbled in a mix of English and Spanish as Joaquin zoomed in and out on the map.

"Wait, go back," Fallon said.

He peered over Joaquin's other shoulder.

"There, zoom in." Fallon pointed at a dark spot on the map. "What does that look like to you?"

"Old buildings," David said, squinting to try to make out the fuzzy pictures on the screen.

"There's a ton of abandoned mines on the U.S. side," she said. "Would make sense there'd be some here, right?"

"Correct, and *prospera* means fortune," Joaquin said, opening another window on his browser and typing. "Ah, here, yes. An old mining camp, Prospera Pass, was decommissioned decades ago."

He backed away from the computer, trying to get away from the heavy feeling pulling him down. Every fiber in his body told him to throw Mandy over his shoulder and get her away from there, but his heart knew she wouldn't go.

Neither would he. Not with knowing the man who'd sacrificed himself to save her needed them. Not with knowing Vargas wasn't finished with them yet.

"Joaquin," David said. "I'll take that beer now."

# 31

Time was a fickle bitch.

She played games with Josh. Telling him an hour had passed, but then giggling and admitting, *'Surprise!'* it'd only been five minutes.

The sun had moved. It was now shining down through a window, illuminating his new cell. Musty straw tickled his nose. Thick spikes hung from the wall, as if once used to hold up bridles, saddles or other gear for horses.

An idea teased. If he could find a tack, or any other long strap, he could end it. Vargas couldn't draw Amanda to him if he was already dead.

He crawled around the floor, cradling his damaged arm to his chest. It was the only way to keep the pain at bay.

Josh searched the entire room, but came up empty. He sat back in the corner, out of the shaft of light and furthest from the door. The broken needle in his thigh itched. "Dammit, I can't even off myself."

He'd once scoffed at people who committed suicide. They were weak, unable to cope. Now, he not only understood them, but envied them.

He was going to die. Someday soon.

The number of days in his future were far fewer than the days in the past. He was willing to die, eager in some way, but he drew the line at asphyxiating himself on straw that previously served as a horse's toilet.

He was still vain enough to not want the rumors of his death to include 'choked on horse TP.'

Voices drew Josh from of his suicide fantasies. He pushed to his feet, and used the last of his strength to pull himself up and cling to the iron bars of the window to look out.

A couple of men flickered through the overgrown brush. They wandered between an old shed crumbling on one side, its yawning mouth looking like it'd suffered a stroke, and another opening, with train tracks leading into its dark, limitless maw.

Josh shivered at the infinity of that space, as if looking into a portal to hell.

He pulled himself to the other side of the window, trying to get a better view of the landscape. The sun faced him just above the treetops.

Mountaintop abandoned mine. West-facing barn stall.

None of this mattered, but he catalogued it anyway. If he did manage to get away, he was far too weak to make it to safety.

This was for Amanda. As long as she had most of her body parts, a sufficient amount of blood and had eaten or drank water in the last few days, she could survive. He could give her a chance.

Three other men joined the ones he watched.

The beige linen suit gave Vargas away, and the thick-limbed, broad backs of the others shouted that he came with reinforcement.

The crickets quieted. The few birds chirping their bedtime song hushed.

A message resonated throughout the camp.

Vargas was done talking.

Josh let go of the bars and dropped down to a crouch, trying to hide himself in plain sight.

Footsteps reverberated off the floor. Three pairs, two heavier, with a resounding thud of a boot heel, one softer, but no less determined.

They paused at the stall next to him.

With each step, he felt more and more like a scantily clad vixen in a cheesy horror movie. He glanced down at his naked body. He had it worse than those girls. They didn't have to worry about hay in inconvenient places.

The heavy wooden door pulled open with dramatic flair.

Vargas entered and somewhere in the back of Josh's mind, he could hear a live studio audience gasp. The goons entered next, and the audience booed.

At least he had the audience on his side.

One man carried a whip, the other had something metal, rusty in his hands.

Vargas wasn't empty-handed, he held a phone.

"How's the cell service up here?" Josh asked.

"Thinking of calling for help?" the drug lord's words were edgier than usual.

"Nah, was gonna order pizza. The food here sucks."

To his surprise, Vargas chuckled. "Oh how I'll miss you."

"None of your other prisoners are as witty as me?"

The cartel leader crossed the room and entered the shaft of waning light, lifting his face and smiling into it, as if the sun shone down on this whole planet just for him. "It didn't have to be this way."

"I've ended relationships with those exact same words. Does this mean you're breaking up with me?"

"It's always women," Vargas said to the outside world.

"For me, yes, but I don't judge if you want to bat for the other team." Josh shouldn't taunt the drug lord, but maybe he could antagonize him to the point Vargas would end it for him. It wouldn't be the most pleasant way to go, but he'd be gone and done with this shitty world.

"There's been a development in our plan." The man finally faced him. "It seems David has joined up with Amanda. My people tell me he wants to take her home, and they think she's capitulating." He closed the distance to Josh and knelt beside him. "Where some may see this as a cause for concern, I see it as an opportunity. The man I sent for David was unsuccessful. What's that saying? Two birds, one stone."

A shiver rocketed through his body.

*Go home with Stephens, Amanda. Go home, go far, far away.*

He'd never wanted ESP ability more than he did at that moment.

"Just leave her," Josh growled. Being locked up and tortured had brought out something primal, feral. "It's me you want. Give me a map, and I'll show you where I stashed your money. That's what this is all about, right?"

"I don't give a shit about the money," Vargas snarled back. "I've already made ten-fold what you stole from me." He took a deep breath and straightened his back.

Goon number one handed over the whip.

"Josh, what do you know about horses?" His voice returned to it's lyrical, deep hum. The anger and tension of moments ago gone.

*Bipolar, much?*

He took a step away, cradling his arm. "Rode a few growing up."

"Have you ever broken a horse, Josh?"

"They all seemed fine to me when I was done." He'd known what the man meant, but hoped humor would once again save his ass.

Vargas cracked the whip against the floor.

The tip of the leather nipped at Josh's feet.

"When you have an especially wild and stubborn horse, sometimes you have to show it who's the master." The drug lord cracked the whip again, this time it licked Josh's thigh, leaving a burning kiss in its wake. "I've let your mouth run unchecked for some time, mostly because it amused me. But you need to know your place." Vargas handed the whip back to the man and he held up the phone. "And, I need to give Amanda something that will override whatever Stephens is telling her."

He stared at his captor. What body part he was going to lose this time? The back of the phone blinked back at him.

The cartel leader looked over the top of the phone and grinned. "You're going to want to turn around. You don't want the whip messing up that pretty face, do you?"

The second goon grabbed Josh's shoulder and whirled him around.

The first lash struck him with the deafening crack of thunder. Saying his back *stung* was an understatement. There wasn't a word strong enough to capture the agony.

The second snap of the whip brought him to the floor. He tried to land on all fours, but forgot he was missing a hand and fell to the side.

Screams reverberated around the stall. For a minute, he thought someone was screaming for him, but his burning throat told him it came from him.

After that, Josh lost count of the hits. His body jerked and twisted, until he found himself face to face with the camera.

He swallowed big gulps of air, trying to power his lungs. It might be the last thing he ever said, but it would be the most important thing.

Vargas muttered a command in Spanish.

The beating halted.

Boots shuffled on the floor around him as one henchman handed over the reins to the next.

With the next man in place, before he could bring the whip down on his raw back, Josh found the camera, the lifeline to Amanda.

"Manda, no." The words were garbled. He spat blood.

"Go home."

Another hit.

"Please. Don't."

One more.

Darkness crept in from the side of his vision. Only one eye seemed to be working, the other was closed tight.

"Leave. Me."
A final hit closed the curtain on his consciousness.
The studio audience he'd heard earlier sat in stunned silence.
Mourning their fallen hero.

## 32

She should've invited David into her room. That was all Amanda could obsess over as she tossed and turned.

The words had been on the tip of her tongue, but when he'd said he would be in the room next to hers, they'd grown nervous and scurried back down her throat.

It was past midnight when she heard his boots climb the tile steps. They paused outside her room.

She sat up, wanting to call him, to ask him to hold her, but David's boots shuffled on to the next room, the gentle click of his door answered her unspoken request.

When she opened her eyes again, the window lightened with the approaching sun and Amanda could hear stirring echoing throughout the house. A door opened above her and footsteps padded down the tile stairs; deliberate, like those heralding Joaquin's visit at the hospital.

David's door remained firmly closed. She pressed one ear against the thick wood, willing him to call her name, but the only sound was his soft, rhythmic snore.

She found Joaquin in the kitchen.

He braced an arm on the counter, his face coated in two days of beard growth, dark circles stained under his eyes. His gaze was on the barren countertop, but she could tell his mind was miles away.

"If you would've told me a week ago that you're a journalist instead of a priest," Amanda said, walking into the kitchen. "And, not only was Josh alive, but so was David, I would've told you that *you* were the one with a head injury, not me." A light joke felt necessary, yet also inappropriate.

Her friend took a deep, long breath. "It's been a surprising few days, *mija*. How are you holding up?"

She echoed his inhale and perched against the counter next to him. "Physically, it feels good to move around. Mentally, I'm about seventy percent, and that's if I try. Emotionally…" As relieved as she was to know he was alive, a part of her wished David hadn't found her. That maybe she'd only seen him, but he'd looked past her. Like she was a ghost.

Amanda glanced at Joaquin. Although he'd asked, he didn't seem focused on her answer. "Hey, are *you* okay?"

He shook his head. "It's Alfredo, he's never been out of touch this long."

"What do you mean?"

"I've been trying to reach him since yesterday morning. Texts, calls, emails. And not just me, others are trying to track him down." He lifted his head to look at her. His eyes were wide with fear.

Her heart somersaulted. "Maybe he took a few days off, or had a business trip, or, or…" She couldn't come up with another suitable suggestion. "When was the last time you tried calling him?"

"Last night. You're right, it's probably nothing." Joaquin reached for his phone. The ringing from his end was echoed by a faint trill. His brows pinched together in a question as his gaze met hers. He jogged out of the kitchen, his head pinging from corner to corner to zero in on the source of the sound in the stillness of the early morning.

She heard the call go to voicemail.

He ended it and hit redial.

The sound started up again. "Front door," she mouthed, trying to jog as he did, but her body reminded her she had limits.

173

Joaquin pushed past her and flung open the door. His head was straight, as if expecting to see the man standing there, before dropping when confronted with empty space. A guttural cry escaped his throat as her friend fell to his knees.

Then she saw it. The body of a man, lying prone across the small front porch. The phone in his shirt pocket lit up with the incoming call from Joaquin. A call that would never be answered. Not only because the man was dead. Also because the man had no ear to hold it to, no mouth to speak from.

"Mandy?" David's voice was tight with concern.

Amanda couldn't tear her eyes off Alfredo's headless body. Vomit shot up her throat, but she swallowed it back, wincing at the burning acid. A tremor started in her jaw, chattering her teeth as if she were standing naked in a frozen tundra.

Joaquin lay across his boss, sobbing, apologizing in Spanish, cursing in English.

Two sets of footsteps approached.

"Get her out of here," David commanded.

Soft, but firm hands grasped her shoulders, pulled her away, but she fought them, trying to make her way to Joaquin.

"No," she shrugged them off. Collapsed on the floor, kneeling over Alfredo's body. "I'm so sorry, I'm so—this is *all* my fault. He warned me. It has to be me. Alone. Forgive me. I'm so sorry." The words tumbled over each other, fighting for dominance, shoving each other out of the way.

David was next to her, pulling Joaquin back from the body.

Fallon knelt on the other side of her. The woman's hair was pulled back in a low ponytail and she wore a T-shirt and pajama shorts. "Amanda, I need you to back up, this is a crime scene and if you contaminate it, we won't be able to catch who did it." She spoke calmly, non-patronizing, just two buddies having a conversation over a corpse.

"I can tell you who did it," Amanda snapped, her voice low, scratchy. "Vargas. It's not enough that he's torturing Josh." She paused, straightening, her gaze colliding with Fallon's green eyes. She lunged at the woman, gripping her upper arms. "Take him home. Today. Now. Far away from here. Please. Do that for me." A look passed the FBI agent's eyes.

One Amanda knew well. Love.

"Do it *for* him."

The woman used Amanda's grasp as an opportunity to make her stand, but her legs wouldn't comply. "Come inside. We can talk while the investigators do their work, okay?" Fallon whispered, heaving her under her shoulder to get her upright.

David had already coaxed Joaquin back inside.

Amanda looked down, punishing herself with one more look at the mutilated body. He'd only been trying to make his world a safer place. No one should die for that. No family should have to face the awful reality of losing someone the way Alfredo had died.

Her eyes wouldn't move past his torso, as if they knew better than to sear the image of his hacked neck into her brain. Instead, they focused on his chest, a chest that would never rise with another breath. Her gaze travel down his arms to his hand, a hand that would never touch a loved one's face.

Something small and metallic was cupped in his palm, peeking out from under his curled fingers.

"Wait," she said, pulling out of Fallon's grip.

"Amanda, don't."

She'd already pulled it out of his palm. A flash drive.

If they'd taken Alfredo's head, chances were they wouldn't have missed a flash drive in the man's hand.

Amanda held it up at the other woman. "What do you want to bet this is for us?"

Her face whitened. "You can't touch that. It's evidence."

"The rules are different here."

Fallon looked away, her lips pressed together in disapproval. When she looked back, she rolled her eyes.

Playing outside of the boundaries was going to be hard for Fallon. It'd been hard for Amanda at first, too, but she'd ultimately found it freeing.

She plucked it from Amanda's hand. "Let me see what's on it. If it's not for us, we hand it over. Understood?"

A quick nod was all it took for the woman to spin on her heel.

Amanda followed her inside the house, where Joaquin tried to speak with authorities, but grief kept overwhelming him.

Fallon pulled the phone from his hand and, in perfect Spanish, took over the conversation, allowing Joaquin to fall to the ground.

Amanda found David's gaze across the room.

In two quick steps, he embraced her, holding her so tight that her body protested slightly before settling in to the pressure.

"I was so scared something happened to you," he said into her hair.

"I know, that's why you have to go home."

He turned to stone beneath her arms. "Not without you."

"You've said it yourself. I'm dead. It's best to leave me that way."

David released her and held her at arm's length, bending to stare into her eyes. "Not to me, you've never been more alive than you are now. And sweetheart, if you think I'm going home without you, you don't know me very well at all."

The thing was, she *did* know him, better than he thought. What he didn't know was that she wasn't just trying to save Josh. She was trying to save David.

# 33

The police took longer to arrive than expected, and they stayed for less time than Amanda thought was appropriate for a murder investigation. Unless they, like her, already knew who did it, and their presence was merely for the survivors.

Instinct told her to hide, that the question of the crime would shift from Alfredo's death to Joaquin aiding and abetting a wanted criminal. She shouldn't have worried. The officers barely glanced in her direction.

After the police left, they gathered in the kitchen. Not that anyone was hungry, but it just seemed like the best place to be lost in their thoughts together.

"I don't understand how," Joaquin said, sipping on a full glass of whisky, his eyes blank and bloodshot. "How did they get into the neighborhood. It's gated. How did we not hear them come?" The lack of blood was an indicator Alfredo had been killed elsewhere.

Amanda studied her friend, silently answering his question. Someone had let Vargas' people in, which meant it would be just as easy for the cartel leader's people to get someone out.

Someone like her.

Or, someone like David.

Fallon entered the kitchen, a deep crevice between her pinched eyebrows. It hadn't taken long after the authorities had arrived for her to slide the flash drive into her pocket, hiding it away as she helped Joaquin answer their questions.

"Well?" Amanda asked.

The FBI agent perched against the counter across from David, ignoring Amanda and her question. "There's ways we can force her to come home. Arrest. Extradition."

It was only when her ex shifted and cleared his throat that it dawned on Amanda that Fallon was talking about *her*. "Don't you think it's already occurred to me?" he mumbled.

"What's on it?" Her voice came out as a hoarse whisper.

Fallon and David held eye contact for several more seconds, long enough for the kind of silent conversation that was shared only between people who were close. Intimate.

"But, I'm not doing that to her," he said.

She dug her fingernails into her palm, curious if she was actually in the room or really as invisible as they made her feel.

Fallon released a long, frustrated sigh and crossed her arms.

"How bad is it?" Joaquin asked.

She looked at him and shifted her gaze toward Amanda. "Come on."

They all followed her into the office, where Fallon woke the screen with a shake of the mouse. With the folder clicked open, she launched a video file and stepped back.

Josh stood there, naked, staring at them. He clung to a bandaged arm, hiding it from view of the camera. His ribs protruded and hip bones jutted out in painful angles. His head had been shaved, giving them a better view of the asymmetry courtesy of his missing ear.

The room he was in was mostly dark, except for a beam of light that sliced across his torso illuminating red scars; some round, others long and straight.

Two men circled, the same enforcers Amanda had last seen chasing them through the hospital.

Vargas' voice played through the speakers. Lyrical. Chilling.

One man slashed at him with a whip, the sound snapping like thunder. The other cheered and whooped like he was watching a sporting match.

When Josh fell, he tried to cover his head and protect his mangled arm.

The hits fell harder, faster, picking up steam like a raging storm.

Amanda's own body stung, as if absorbing his torture, and her left hand itched, showing it was happily still attached to her body.

Something warm trickled down her face. She wiped her cheeks and looked at her palm, expecting it to be stained red, but it was only tears.

The men paused, repositioning themselves to let the second man take over.

In between the hits, Josh looked at the camera. Bloody tears ran from one eye and scarlet saliva dribbled down his chin.

Her heart stumbled when he spoke to *her*, making this gruesome scene so much more real. Up until he'd said her name, acknowledged that he knew this was for her, and begged her to leave, she'd somehow told herself it was only a movie and her ex was an actor.

Another hit knocked him to the floor. He fought to get on his knees, but eventually he quit trying. Quit gasping.

Quit screaming.

Everything froze.

The men on the camera.

The people in the room with her.

Even Amanda's lungs paused, only remembering she was still alive when the ache for air grew intolerable.

"Is... Is he...?" she whispered.

Fallon shook her head. "Wait."

The camera flipped around, the room literally spinning.

Vargas came into focus. His cold, handsome face taking the full screen, his light green eyes glittering, his smile beatific. Torture was a religious experience for him. "Hello, Amanda. I'm happy to see you're out of the hospital. My people tell me you're healing nicely."

Logic told her he couldn't see her, that he'd planned this, knew she'd eventually bear witness to Josh's beating. Her logical mind couldn't stop the paralyzing fear slithering up her body, anchoring her to that spot on the floor and her eyes to the screen.

"And, *Señor* Stephens, greetings. I'm thrilled with the promise of getting the band back together."

David's hand found hers, squeezing to the point Amanda bit her tongue to keep from whimpering.

"You're probably wondering if Josh is still alive. Maybe. Parts of him, at least." The drug lord walked as he spoke. "I tried to play nicely, Amanda, really I did. But you were ignoring me, and I don't like to be ignored." The room behind him spun, as if he were walking in a tight circle. "The next message I send, you might wake up to find your beloved David's head in bed with you. The rest of him…somewhere else."

He stopped spinning and knelt next to Josh's prone body, bending over his face. "Good news, *mi amor*, he's still alive." Vargas handed the phone to one of the other men and grabbed her ex's chin, pulling his lower jaw down. "Save me, Amanda, please." He tried to mimic Josh's voice before breaking out into hysterics. Then grabbed the camera, his face once again filling the screen, hardening. "Ditch the blonde. Leave the journalist. Quit. Fucking. Around."

The video stopped, pausing on Vargas' face.

Joaquin cleared his throat, reminding Amanda she was in the safe house and not standing there with Josh. He closed the file, wiping away a scene of horror with a pastoral background photo.

"I think it's pretty obvious what we have to do," David said.

A heavy shroud of defeat settled on her shoulders, suffocating any argument she could make. Whatever words he said next would be logical, indisputable. They'd be spoken with her best interest at heart.

Amanda would come back to those words in the future, both condemning them and agreeing with them.

"We have to go get him." David turned to her. "We have to bring Josh home."

The shroud dropped to the floor, freeing her. *Exposing* her.

# 34

I t was clear by Mandy's gaping mouth and wide eyes that she hadn't expected those words from him. It'd been an impulsive move on David's part.

If he had his druthers, she would've agreed to go home with him the minute he'd seen her. If his druthers had any influence, she would've left Josh where he was to begin with, working for Vargas until the drug lord tired of him.

Then again, those druthers would've ended with him delivering Mandy to Fallon to be arrested.

Maybe he should be happy with the druthers he had.

"This is where you argue with me." He hoped a light joke would cut through the tension hanging in the room like thick curtains.

Mandy shook her head, her short hair whipping her face. "I couldn't live with myself if something happened to you."

"Yeah, I know. I feel the same way. That's why we're doing this together."

Her gaze bounced around the room, as if looking for an ally.

Joaquin sat in his chair, studying the last sip of his whisky.

Fallon was on her phone, working even when she was supposed to be on vacation.

She looked back at him, defeat etched on her face. She didn't have to say it; she was being tugged in two directions; to try to get Josh to safety and to keep him from getting hurt.

"Look," he said. "I'm not eager to do this. And, while I think Williams deserved a good ass kicking, he doesn't deserve that." He swallowed a lump that snuck its way into his throat. "He saved you. Probably more than just on the ridge."

Her eyes filled with tears and she nodded, chewing on her lower lip. If they were alone, he would've wiped the tears when they fell, or kissed her lips until they were swollen.

Having just watched her ex being tortured wasn't the time, and standing in a small office with Fallon and Joaquin wasn't the place.

Aside from holding hands and wrapping his arms around her after finding Alfredo, they'd shared no connection.

The intimacy of their last night in the desert hung between them, like an embarrassing one-night stand between friends.

"What do you think, Joaquin?" David needed the man on his side, not just for the extra assurance Mandy wouldn't back out, but he needed his network.

The man tossed down the last of his drink and stood, thrusting an outstretched hand in his direction. "I welcome the chance to avenge my friend's murder. I'll gather my colleagues." He pulled his phone from his pocket, dialing as he walked out of the room.

David felt Fallon's stare. Disapproval rolled off her like waves of steam. Of all people, she should be eager to go after Vargas.

"I'm going to see if I can help Joaquin," Mandy said.

David waited until he couldn't hear her footsteps. "You're going to tell me how stupid this is."

His old college friend let out a long, defeated sigh. "It wouldn't do any good. I'm just trying to think of how to keep you, or her, or hell, even me, from getting killed."

"Go home, Weatherby. This isn't your fight."

Fallon paced the room before stopping in front of him, hitching her hands on her hips. "Funny how everyone keeps telling everyone else to go home." She stared at the computer screen, the one that just minutes earlier had showed Williams being beaten. "We have no jurisdiction here. I could call my brother…"

"You know as well as I do bringing on the cavalry will result in Williams being killed."

"We don't even know if he's still alive. For all we know the video could have been made days ago, he could already be dead and we go skipping into a trap."

"So we ask for proof of life."

Fallon shook her head and pushed past him. "That only works in a world of order. You heard Amanda. In a world where the cartels rule, it's all chaos."

David collapsed into the desk chair. His gut told him this was the right move. Williams could've left him in the desert to die after his drunken dehydration. He hadn't, and he'd taken care of Mandy when David couldn't.

And that day…

*Was it just a couple of months earlier?*

It felt like a lifetime ago when they'd been running from Vargas. Sure, Josh had drugged him and tried to convince Mandy to run away with him, but that had been the desperate act of a man facing a prison sentence. He'd managed to redeem himself when they'd realized she wasn't behind them, that her intention had been to let them escape while she sacrificed herself.

The four walls of the office faded away.

Rain pelted his face, and the heavy hand of sleep threatened to pull him under.

*Later. You can sleep later.*

That had been his mantra as they'd been trying to get away from Vargas.

Josh grabbed his arm, stopping his sprint for the edge of the cliff, for freedom.

"What?" David felt the word slur from his mouth.

"Amanda." Josh looked over his shoulder.

He peered past him and saw her stand, hands up in the air. The classic surrender pose. "No," he growled. Seeing the woman he loved about to sacrifice herself for him was the shot of adrenaline he needed to shrug off the drowsiness.

"You have to swear to me you'll get her home," Josh said. "I mean it; don't fuck this up, Stephens."

Those were the last words Josh had said to him before sprinting back toward Mandy and tackling her, giving David a chance to get her home.

*That* was why he had to do this. Had to look Josh Williams in the eye and apologize, admit that he hadn't gotten her home.

Not yet. In Josh's words, he'd fucked up.

Joaquin strode back into the office, his back straighter, the idea of vengeance seeming to have reenergized him. His phone to his ear, he spoke in rapid Spanish.

David could barely catch any of the words before the man ended the call and looked at him.

"Tomorrow, we meet. We'll save your friend, and Vargas will pay for the death of mine."

## 35

The heat of the mid-afternoon licked at Fallon like flames, but she couldn't stay in the house any longer. Not after David had volunteered them for a suicide mission.

She sat on a flagstone in the corner of the courtyard garden. It was the only place with the most minuscule slice of shade, but it was also hidden away, tucked behind a larger planter with an unruly Bougainvillea stretching out in her direction. The flowering shrub teemed with life, between the explosion of bright pink flowers and a hive's worth of humming bees.

The half-written message on her phone stared back at her. She'd typed at least ten different emails to Winslow, to give him a heads up on what was happening with Josh Williams.

Would it be worth it to push to go after him, to try to bring him home? Or, was it better to let him face his fate at the hands of Rafael Vargas?

What would David do when she arrested Amanda as soon as they crossed the border? He'd brought it up himself, but it was as a way to protect her. To keep her from running head first into a stupid idea.

Fallon was bound by duty to uphold the law. She was also bound by the rules of friendship to not intentionally hurt someone she cared about. She sighed, hit the cancel button on the email and went back to her game of solitaire, letting the bees play the soundtrack to her buzzing thoughts.

Midway through her third game, soft footsteps approached, shuffling to a stop when they came around the dry fountain.

"Hi." Amanda glanced over her shoulder before darting her gaze back to the ground. "I've been looking for you. Mind if I join you?"

She shrugged and nodded down to the anemic shade next to her. "Pull up some dirt."

The woman gnawed on her bottom lip and tightened her face before slowly lowering herself. When her knees hit the ground, she winced, took a deep breath and braced herself with her arms.

Fallon's ninety-year-old grandmother could have gotten down faster than Amanda. "What happened?" she asked.

She smiled, a sincere just-two-girlfriends-gabbing grin. "As a kid, were you ever curious what it would be like to tumble around a dryer?"

"Can't say I did."

David's ex eased her legs around, stretching them out on the ground. A light grunt sounded deep in her throat. "That's probably for the best." Her voice was tight. She lifted herself up with her arms, repositioning her bottom. "You really only appreciate something when it's gone, or when it hurts like hell." Amanda wasn't looking at her when she spoke, instead staring straight in front, her eyes focused on the brick wall of the garden. "Hairline fracture in my pelvis, likely caused by flood debris in the Rio Grande." She took another deep breath, letting it out slowly. "Not that I remember. Got knocked out with something to the temple after I hit the water. Luckily I floated to the top, face up."

Fallon chewed on her cuticle. "You haven't told him yet, have you?"

The woman pursed her lips before a slight shake of her head. "And, give him even more of a reason to talk me out of it?"

Amanda needed to be in the hospital, not chasing after cartel leaders and trying to save ex-boyfriends. She was going to get herself killed.

Or, worse. Get David killed.

Fallon opened her mouth, but hesitated, unsure what to say that didn't start with *'WTF.'*

"How long have you been in love with him?" Amanda asked, filling the space in her indecisiveness.

She was so stunned by the bluntness, that she ripped a cuticle, cursing as she pulled her bleeding finger away. Fallon glanced at the woman.

Amanda stared back, her eyes sharp, steady, confident.

After several seconds, she broke eye contact and looked straight ahead, her choppy chin-length hair providing cover for whatever she didn't want her to see. "A while, right? Longer than I have, I'm sure." She nodded, as if Fallon's silence was an affirmation. "It's okay, I'm not angry. Or, jealous." Her voice was tight, as if she were holding in a sob. Or, the truth.

A bee landed on a nearby flower. The tiny creature crawled inside, dirtying itself with as much pollen as it could carry all in service of its queen.

Did Amanda think she was the queen? Expecting her, David, Joaquin and God knew how many more people to get dirty to serve her?

"What are you getting at?" Fallon asked.

When Amanda met her eyes again, her face was softer, smeared with sadness. "Sometimes we choose the lives we lead, and other times, they choose us." She paused, reaching forward to snap a bloom off a flower. "David was going to turn me in to you, before we were kidnapped."

Fallon opened her mouth to argue with her, to say something to defend her friend, but what could she say? Yes, David had told her he was bringing a suspect in to her, one he was adamant should be treated with respect.

"I had a pretty good life in Chicago; a great family, friends, a good job and an asshole boyfriend." Her mouth pulled up into a wry smirk. "Can't have it all, I guess. I know right from wrong. I also know the edges where they meet get fuzzy."

"No, the law is pretty black and white. You broke it. There's nothing fuzzy about that."

Amanda took a deep breath. There was a quiet determination about her.

Fallon felt a kindredness, despite the fact she enforced the law and the other woman broke it.

Was there a parallel universe where Amanda and Fallon were best friends?

"I agree. I broke the law, I deserve to be punished," she said. "But David's doesn't. Fallon, take him home. Convince him to leave me. Knock him out; tie him up, whatever it takes. I can't have what happened to Alfredo happen to him." She took longer to stand than sitting.

Fallon tried to come up with a snarky response, but she found herself speechless. And, that pissed her off.

Not because she couldn't come up with a suitable comeback, but because the Amanda Martin she thought she'd known was *nothing* like the woman shuffling away from her.

"He won't leave you," she called after her. "No matter what I say or do."

Amanda glanced over her shoulder, her brow pinched, eyes reddening. "If you love him as much as I think you do, you'll find a way."

She waited until she could no longer see David's ex moving slowly around the house before entering it herself. She paused in the kitchen, wiping tears that'd somehow leaked from her eyes.

"It's exhausting, isn't it? Holding on to your humanity amongst all the death."

Fallon jumped at Joaquin's voice.

He sat in the dim living room, nursing a steaming cup of coffee.

"More where that came from?" Fallon asked, nodding toward his cup.

"Fresh pot, help yourself."

With her own hot mug, she joined him, slipping off her shoes and tucking her feet under her on the soft leather couch.

There was something comfortable about sitting there with him, sipping coffee in a dimly lit room. She studied his profile. Wavy dark hair and a light dusting of stubble that was on the handsome side of unkempt.

She was surprised with his willing acceptance of her help in the face of Alfredo's murder. Most men, or at least the men *she* knew, would've waved her off, put on steel underwear and shut off the emotional spigot.

Not Joaquin. Not only was he openly distraught, when she'd shared that not only was she fluent in Spanish, but in law speak, he'd let her take the lead.

"How long have you been doing this?" she asked.

He took a long sip and sat the cup on the coffee table. "So long it's become my life. There's no separation between this and what else I do. You understand, right?"

Fallon laughed. "I haven't watched TV in years and my favorite pastime is trying new take-out menus or frozen dinners." She fingered a scratch on the leather, watching him stare into his cup from the corner of her eye. "We're doing exactly what he wants us to. You know that, right?"

Joaquin stood and crossed the room, studying the very garden she'd just escaped. "Maybe that's the unexpected."

"No, it's suicidal." The words flew out of her mouth before she could catch them.

Several emotions flashed across his face. Anger, betrayal, resentment, fear. Finally, sadness. "Faith means letting go of the wheel and trusting you won't crash."

"Carelessness is being in charge and throwing your hands up saying, *que sera, sera*."

"Control makes you stiff, hard, and it can break you when it doesn't go your way." His footsteps echoed down the hallway, cut off by a closing door.

"Making friends everywhere I go," she mumbled to herself. Her phone vibrated in her pocket.

A text message from Winslow. He didn't take too long pauses between responses.

*News?*

She hit reply, biting the inside of her cheek as she stared at the blank screen. It waited expectantly.

Her fingers pecked out a quick message. *Found Josh Williams. Rafael Vargas sent a torture video. Pretty bad. Organizing a team to go after him.*

It took less than ten seconds for Winslow's reply to come through. *Negative. You're coming home.*

Fallon stared at the screen, hoping lightning would strike her with the right words and tone to respectfully disagree, and end with Winslow relenting.

*That's an order.* He added, as if sensing her dissent.

She was out of words. Out of argument. Not to mention, out of her comfort zone.

Her thumb moved over to power button, holding it down until the screen went dark on her phone.

Fallon was also, most likely, out of a job.

# 36

O f all her new limitations, the one that frustrated the most Amanda was her inability for dramatic exits. She'd wanted to get away from Fallon before she lost her grip on the tears that'd been building since they found Alfredo had the nerve to fall.

That was when the balloon man's threats had sunk in. When his promise that someone was going to die punched her in the gut.

It was a painful climb up the flight of stairs to her room. It'd been several hours since her last pill. Or, pills. They were increasing in number.

Had to be all the stress. Alfredo, the video, David's decision to save Josh.

The strumming in her head drowned out the more upbeat tempo of the ache in her torso, radiating from the center of Amanda's body with the cadence of disco. It was beginning to feel like a never-ending dance party, to the point songs were being repeated.

The bottle was where she'd left it, tucked deep on a shelf in the armoire in her room. Before David had showed up, she'd left it sitting on the nightstand, unconcerned about who saw them. After all, it was Joaquin who'd given them to her, who thought she'd need them as part of her recovery.

So why was she acting like it was a dirty little secret?

Because if David stumbled into her room and saw what was on the label, he'd take them away from her. He'd be concerned about her becoming dependent, that she'd grow to rely on them too much instead of using pain as a way to keep from overtaxing her broken body. He'd have all the arguments *she* had with herself every time she took a pill.

*It takes an addict to know an addict.*

Amanda popped open the top and held the bottle under the light. Funny, the bottle had been more than half full when Joaquin had given it to her.

Wasn't it? Maybe Joaquin had taken some for himself.

She shook out two pills. Then two more, swallowing them down one at a time because nothing would be more embarrassing than choking to death on pills.

Amanda started to put the bottle back in its hiding place, but hesitated. Should she stick one more in her pocket just in case she needed it later and couldn't sneak off?

"No, you're fine. Four is plenty," she said, closing the door to the armoire after she tucked the bottle away.

She studied the wooden inlay door, light wood patterned with dark wood creating a beautiful motif that stood between her and her pills.

"Dammit." She reached back in, shook out two more pills and popped them in her jeans' pocket, hoping she'd forget they were there until the hurt became so excruciating she couldn't breathe.

Physical or emotional.

She'd figure out which pain later.

Amanda leaned against the armoire, tilting her head back and closing her eyes. Calming warmth spread throughout her body, loosening tight muscles, lulling the soreness to sleep.

If Fallon refused to convince David to go home, maybe Joaquin would. He'd understand, would probably even agree. Rescuing Josh didn't need an attention-grabbing army; it needed a team of two or three people capable of sneaking into Vargas' lair. Bonus points for individuals who had nothing to lose.

She wandered through the house, hoping to avoid Fallon and David in her search for Joaquin. A blonde head moved around the kitchen, Fallon's back to the rest of the house.

A quick peek out the back windows showed David sitting on a bench, his phone to his ear as he sat hunched over, his gaze stuck to the ground in front of him.

Joaquin was exactly where she'd expected to find him. In the study, watching the silent video of Josh's torture, his face just inches from the screen.

"Does it get better or worse?" Amanda asked from the doorway.

He paused the video and reclined in his chair. "Both. You become less shocked by what you see, which is just as alarming. How quickly we can become numb to violence." He tilted his head and his eyes roved her body. "How are you, *mija?*"

Amanda flashed a smile, but it had nothing to grab on to and quickly fell away. "Can we get out of here?"

He looked past her, as if expecting David to be lurking around the corner.

"I don't need his permission. I'm about to suffocate in this house."

Her friend nodded once and sprung from his chair, gripping her hand as he walked past her. They drove out of the gated community and he pulled over, shifting in his seat to face her. "Okay, where to."

She chewed on the inside of her cheek. Where did she want to go? Just down the block? To the Consulate? Did she just want him to drive as far away from Fallon and David as his little sedan could take them?

Did she want to go home? Wherever that was.

After several long seconds, she mustered an answer.

He stared, as if he couldn't understand. Or, didn't want to. "We're not going all the way."

"I just want to see what we're up against."

Joaquin let out a long, frustrated sigh and put the car in gear.

They drove in silence, only the air rushing through the vents sung to them. The road curved to the west, the dipping sun hovering in the middle of the windshield.

The buildings that'd dotted the desert landscape grew fewer and fewer, as if swallowed by the beige sand, eaten by the towering cactus.

At first, it looked like a cloud bank on the western horizon, but as they got closer, the distinct outline of a mountain range formed.

It wasn't an especially tall form, but rising up from the desert floor, the giant among the Lilliputian landscape towered with authority.

The road cut to the north.

This view of the mountain was vastly different than the gentle green slope of the eastern side. The north face was craggy, with long, straight rocks lined up like teeth, leering down at them.

Joaquin pulled off the road, parking on the desert floor.

Amanda joined him on the driver's side of the car, surveying her foe. Or, at least the lair of her foe. "Is all this Propsera Pass?"

He shook his head. "The mountain in the middle is Prospera, the Pass is on the western side. But they could have a road block set up over there. Or, worse. This is as far as we go today."

"Do we drive up it?"

"No roads." His voice was soft, flat. "Sorry, but we have to hike it." Joaquin glanced at her. "I'm not sure—"

"I'll be fine." If she said it enough, eventually she'd start to believe it. "I promise I won't slow you down."

He studied the mountain.

Amanda followed his gaze, narrowing her eyes, trying to make out anything moving in the trees, or any sort of structure that looked like where Josh could be held. "He asked me to run away with him," she said to the mountain.

"David? I thought he wanted—"

"Josh. The last day we were together, before the river. He wanted to leave, just the two of us. Promised it would be different." She took a deep breath and said the words that'd been racing through her head since the boy had given her Josh's ear, picking up speed with each new indication of the torture he endured. For *her*. "I wish…I wish I'd left with him."

"You're saying that out of guilt."

She looked at her friend. "Probably, but if I'd left with him…"

Would anything be different? Better?

Joaquin moved in front of her, cutting off her view of the mountain, and crossed his arms. "Whose name did you cry out in the hospital? It wasn't Josh. You don't love him. You pity him. So sure, you can wish you'd made a different decision based on where you both are today, but how you do you know you wouldn't be worse off?"

The regrets in her life were battling for domination.

Regret over hurting David clashed with Alfredo's death, only to have to fight all the other regrets lining up for their turn.

"Josh might still have his ear, and his hand, and probably a lot fewer scars and bruises. I wouldn't have this head injury, or feel like crying with every step I take."

"It could be worse."

"*What* could be worse?" Her shout reverberated around the empty desert.

"You would be living a lie."

Amanda pushed past him and half-jogged to the base of the mountain, stopping when the ground sloped up.

The base was thick with scrubby brush and cacti, but as the ground swelled up, trees crowded out the smaller plants.

Prospera loomed, filling her vision with its immense size, filling her heart with dread. How would she get up there? Climbing a few steps took her breath away. What would climbing a mountain do to her?

Joaquin joined her. He didn't speak; just laced his fingers with hers and squeezed.

This man had become one of her best friends in just a few days. He stood beside her even when she was unconscious, guarding over her, keeping her from harm. What could she do for him?

Not get him killed would be a start. Vargas. That was all he cared about now. If she was back in Vargas' study on his ranch, alone with him and Josh, and she had the gun again, could she do it this time? Could she pull the trigger? Not miss.

"Joaquin, I've been living a lie for so long I don't even know what the truth is anymore."

His only response was a squeeze of her hand.

"I lied to you in the hospital. I knew who I was; I just didn't want to *be* her. I lied to David when we met, because deep down, I wanted to be her. Mandy. The girl he loved. I lied for Josh, but that's because our entire relationship was a farce." She faced him, tucking her short hair behind her ear. "Maybe I'm really all of those things, or none of them. Or, maybe I'm completely *loco*." She let a laugh float out of her throat.

He looked down at her; a smile touched his eyes for the first time in several days. "*Sí, mija, tu loca.*"

They went back to studying the mountain.

Amanda tried to pick out a path through the thick copse of trees, to gauge the distance she'd have to climb.

Would they need to camp overnight? It didn't seem like they could get up there and Josh back down in one day. Even if she were in top physical form.

Her conversation with Fallon flashed across her mind.

David would definitely know what it would take to survive this terrain. He'd kept them alive through the desert. Then they'd been running *from* the madman, not toward him.

"I want to send David and Fallon home," she whispered, afraid to give the words more weight.

"Good luck with that," Joaquin said. "I don't think either of them are going to leave."

"Can you convince him, her, whoever? Can you try to send them home?"

Her friend looked down at her. "Why, Amanda? Why would you break his heart?"

She took a deep breath, chastising the lump that awakened in her throat. "Because it would destroy me if anything happened to him." She glanced at Joaquin and back up at the mountain. "It was so much easier when I had nothing to live for."

The sun had passed behind it; a dark gray-green shadow trundled down the slope.

A shiver rocketed through her body with the sudden temperature drop. "I can deal with anything but watching him die."

Joaquin reached an arm around her, pulling her in close for a side hug. His warmth seeped through her clothes, through her body. "Have you considered that *he* would be destroyed if anything happened to you?"

"It would be so much better if he just hated me."

"Once again, *buena suerte, mija.*"

She could almost hear the smirk in his voice.

"It's getting dark. Not safe for us to be out here. Let's go back." He broke the silence that had fallen over them like a shadow.

They walked back across the road, separating to go back to their sides of the car. When Amanda turned to get inside, she noticed Joaquin studying Propsera.

His head was tilted up, quick, soft Spanish words filled the silent desert. Then he bowed his head and made the sign of the cross.

They were going to need all the prayers they could get.

# 37

It was dark before Mandy and Joaquin returned.

When the garage door opened and his car pulled in, David's legs twitched to run out and meet them. Confront them.

Instead he took a deep, calming breath and sat in the dimly lit living room, tossing the bottle from one hand to the next, the pills sounding like maracas.

Her laughter struck his ear like a melody, but it felt out of tune. Just this morning they'd found a decapitated body on the front porch. What in the world could she be laughing at?

Unless...

There were many different scenarios playing out in his mind. All of them involved her and Joaquin in a relationship, and David punching a wall.

"You should've seen Alfredo's face when he realized it was a monkey stealing his food, not one of us." Joaquin's face was red with laughter. "After that, he said to hell with the jungle cartels, the monkeys can chase them."

Mandy wiped tears from her eyes, from the way her cheeks were pink and her eyes weren't puffy and red, but lively and crinkled, these were tears sprung from laughter.

David hadn't made her laugh like that, not in a while. Maybe not ever.

The tears she'd shed in his presence were from a darker place. Sadness.

Seeing that only brought one of the scenarios to the foreground.

Their footsteps stopped at the edge of the kitchen.

He wanted to whirl around and see if he'd caught them holding hands or in a lover's embrace, but he sat still, staring at the dark fireplace.

"Hey," Mandy said behind him, her voice strained, the lightness of laughter gone. "What's up?"

He didn't answer; instead he held up the pill bottle and gave it a good shake.

Mandy and Joaquin both cursed; his in Spanish, hers in English.

Several beats passed before she came into the living room, standing in front of him with her hands hitched to her hips. She tried to swipe the bottle out of his hand, but he yanked it back and closed his palm around it.

"Those are mine."

"These are narcotics." David was surprised at how calm the words came out.

She let out a long sigh and paced a few steps in front of him. Looping circles, like a trapped animal. "So you're snooping through my things now?"

"No, I was going to make a pallet on the floor in your room. To be closer to you tonight, but still giving you your space." His gaze stuck to the floor, the edge where the rug met the terra-cotta tile. It'd been a dumb idea, but he needed to break down the wall between them. The physical and emotional one.

Mandy stopped moving and everything in the room paused.

He lifted his gaze to look up at her through his lashes.

She tilted her head back, one hand massaging her temple.

It was never more obvious than at that moment.

Finding Mandy had been a mistake.

He'd assumed they'd pick up where they'd left off.

David couldn't help but feel anytime they'd tried to nurture a relationship, it shot up to the sky, strong and green, only to die quickly of neglect.

"Why wouldn't you just get in bed with me? Am I that repulsive?" Mandy's voice was hesitant, meek.

Before he could answer her, Joaquin rounded the couch, timid as well. "Maybe I should—"

"No, you should stay." The command came out in David's police voice. The one he rarely found much use for these days, but it still had enough sharp edges to bring Fallon into the room. "She got them somewhere."

His friend's eyes shifted between the threesome as she slowly moved to join the circle. "Is everything okay?" She paused, nodding down at the white cap peeking out of his palm. "What's that?"

He tossed the bottle in her direction.

She caught it with ease and read the label. "Some strong stuff, sure, but…"

Was she really making light of the fact that he found a large, nearly empty bottle of narcotic painkillers in Mandy's room?

"Strong enough to knock out a horse."

Fallon closed the distance between her and Mandy in just a few steps. "You have to tell him," she said, holding the bottle out.

His ex lowered her eyelids and shook her head.

His friend leaned close to the woman he loved. "I know what you *think* you want, but you're wrong. Talk to him." She'd lowered her voice, but in the stillness of the room, it carried as if she'd shouted.

The women stared at each other for a long minute.

Fallon's lips pursed in reprimand.

Mandy's face defensive at first, but softened into resignation. "Fine," she said in a soft sigh.

"Joaquin, let's go to the office and maybe do something productive." Fallon never took her eyes off Mandy as she spoke, sending her a silent…warning.

The living room felt cavernous when it was just the two of them.

Mandy stared down at the pills in her hands, her mouth pressed tight.

Once the red-hot flash of his anger had faded, she looked frail. Alone. Her hair fell across her face and she tucked it behind one ear, flashing the pink pucker of scar tissue at her temple.

Finding the pills was simply the catalyst for the confrontation. Ever since they'd reunited David had felt a long simmering anger bubbling between them, gradually upping the heat until one of them had to jump from the pot.

Or get burned.

He hadn't spent all that time searching for her, sacrificing for her to come away hurt.

"Sit with me," he said, his voice soft.

Mandy obliged, joining him on the couch, but keeping several inches of distance between them.

"It feels like a lifetime ago." He stared at his hands. "Back in Phoenix, when I was blissfully ignorant of your past." From the corner of his eye, he saw her wince. "Sorry, that came out... Look, what I'm trying to say is, life happens to people, and I understand we both have a history, that life happened after you left Phoenix. Hell, life even happened after we jumped into the river." David cleared his throat, trying to gather his thoughts. "You freeze up when you're near me. You sneak out of the house to be with him. I'm trying to understand what happened, but you won't talk to me, so I'm forced to draw my own conclusions."

She whipped her head in his direction, but he still couldn't meet her eyes.

He took a deep breath. "I hate what I'm coming up with."

"It's not what you think." Mandy started with the classic denial. "But I can understand why you think it."

David waited for her to continue. To say something else denouncing anything romantic between her and Joaquin, but she sat silently, staring at her hands.

"I started building that wall when I thought you were dead," she said. "I guess I used stronger mortar than I'd thought. I can't seem to knock a hole in it."

It was the most honest thing he'd ever heard her say.

He *felt* it. The cold spot that usually settled between them warmed.

She stood and offered a hand. "Come with me."

Her face was both determined and fearful. Mandy had made up her mind, but wasn't sure how he'd take it.

David tucked apprehension away. She was literally reaching out to him. It was what he'd wanted since he'd followed her into the church.

Her hand was cool in his. She quirked one side of her mouth into an uneasy smile and led him into her bedroom. "Sit," she commanded, closing the door behind her.

A single lamp illuminated the room, casting shadows in shades of gray and orange.

He eased himself onto the bed and she joined him, pulling her sneakers off before standing before him.

She nibbled on her lower lip, breaking eye contact for a split-second before her gaze found his again. Mandy took a deep, decisive breath and unbuttoned her jeans.

"Mandy." He laid his hand over hers as she started pulling them off her hips. "Baby, this has nothing to do with sex."

Her eyes glistened. "I know," she whispered. "This is what I'm hiding."

David couldn't tear his gaze from hers as the jeans fell to the floor and she pulled them off her feet. It was only broken when she pulled her tank top over her head and tossed it aside.

She stopped then, standing before him in a bra and panties. "Look."

He let his gaze drop, gliding past her chest, where a fading tan met skin that wasn't blistered by the angry desert sun, sliding down to her smooth, flat stomach. His eyes paused at her ribcage, where her porcelain flesh was met with ghastly green-yellow smear.

The further his eyes dipped down, the darker, uglier, the bruise got, to a point that at her hip bones, an angry red protruded from her panties. The bruise flamed out as it went down her legs, fading back to her normal skin tone mid-thigh.

His fingers lightly touched her abdomen, as if the discoloration were paint.

Mandy's skin broke out in goose pimples, and her breath hitched.

"I'm sorry," he breathed, pulling his hand back. "I didn't mean—"

"That didn't hurt." A throaty laugh erupted. "I'm on some pretty strong stuff, remember. It felt…good."

David lightly traced the bruises, turning her gently to see they went all the way around. "Who did this?"

"The Rio Grande. The farmers who found me thought I was dead, but apparently I screamed when they tried to move me. I faintly remember something hitting me in the head, leaving this souvenir." She paused, pulling her hair back to give him a good view of the scar at her temple. "It could've been a log or going through submerged boulders that fractured my pelvis. Not sure." Mandy stopped talking and cupped her hand to the side of his face. "I know it's stupid, but I couldn't stand the thought of you seeing me like this."

He cleared his throat. "Like what?"

"Ugly. Broken. Weak. You'd see this and treat me like a porcelain doll. That's why I have the pills. So I can keep going. To save Josh. To kill Vargas for what he did to you. To us."

"And Joaquin?" David hated having to ask, to taint the magic of the moment with his jealousy.

"A very good friend, who's seen me at my absolute worst." She tilted his face up, her mouth just inches from his. "Someone who sees my strengths instead of my weaknesses."

The knot that'd been slowly inching its way up his throat took a dive to his stomach. Since he'd met her, he'd seen nothing but her strengths. How she stubbornly solved a cold-case murder. How despite mistakes she'd made in the past, she'd doggedly set out to right her wrongs. How the desert was no match for Mandy Martin.

"Is that what you think?" he whispered.

She answered by looking away.

David stroked her face. "You're so much stronger than me. In every way possible. I'm no match for you. I'm just lucky you let me come along for the ride."

Big silent tears fell down her face.

He gently laid her on the bed, tucking her into the covers and getting in beside her.

She fell asleep quickly, deeply, but he stayed awake well into the night, cradling her.

Loving her.

# 38

The window glowed when Amanda woke the next morning. She stretched and rolled over, the aching burden in her torso grumbled at her but smacked its toothless gums and went back to sleep.

She hadn't slept this much, this fully, in a long time. Maybe not even when she'd been unconscious at the hospital. It was a different slumber, borne from her body's need to heal itself. Her heart's need as well.

It'd been stupid of her to want to hide her injuries from David. To think he wouldn't want her if she was a little banged up.

He'd been insulted, it'd been clear by the look that'd crawled across his face and the tightness in his voice. Next to Fallon; tall, blonde, athletic, unbroken, it would be no competition. The other woman was much better suited for…everything.

*When did I become such a jealous nag?*

His side of the bed was empty. Cold. He'd gotten up a while ago.

Amanda pulled her clothes on and padded down the stairs toward the smell of coffee. She found David and Joaquin in the kitchen.

David in profile, one arm braced on the counter, the other lifting a mug of coffee to his mouth.

Joaquin had his back to her and his head bowed down.

She knew him well enough to know this was his listening posture. The one he took to when being told something extremely important.

Something extremely important he didn't like.

David's lips moved, but whatever words he spoke were so quiet they didn't drift toward her ears. His head jerked in her direction and one corner of his mouth lifted up in a smile, a small gesture that managed to make her heart cartwheel.

He lifted his cup, half salute, half seduction. Coffee could make her do things that would make her mother blush. Especially first thing in the morning.

Between being seen and the lure of caffeine, Amanda had no choice but to join them in the kitchen.

David was already pouring her a cup by the time she got there, and handed it to her with a kiss to the top of her head. "How're you feeling?"

His question was very much pointed at what she'd revealed the night before. The answer was likely to determine if she was to get any pills that morning. A quick search of her room while dressing hadn't produced her white bottle of serenity.

"Rested." She took a long sip of coffee and eyed him over the rim.

His brow lifted, enough to tell her she hadn't quite answered his question. She already felt sorry for any kids they might have.

The coffee caught in her throat and she coughed, water rushing to her eyes in response to the burning hot acid going the wrong way.

One night of being just Mandy and David again, and the thought of kids had popped into her head. They had a better chance of winning the lottery —twice— than coming out of this alive.

Amanda couldn't let fantasy take hold in reality. It could be deadly. Physically and emotionally.

"On a scale of one to ten," she said once she was able to find her voice again. "I usually hover around a four when I wake up. Depending on how the day goes it could bump up to twenty."

He considered her answer, his eyes searching hers. Was he looking for a junky inside?

David sat his cup down and crossed his arms over his chest. "Joaquin and Fallon are running out this morning. They'll pick up some over-the-counter stuff for you. But let me know when you get to an eight." The conversation ended with another kiss to the top of her head.

*Well, that settles it. He has my pills.*

The desire to get mad and pout flared, but she quickly doused it with reason. He hadn't said she couldn't have them, nor did he give her an unreasonable pain level before she could ask for them.

She was usually an eight before noon. All she had to do was keep herself busy, but not too busy to awaken the need that lived deep insider her. The one that couldn't think without a pill. That couldn't move without a pill. That couldn't live...

The air in the kitchen shifted and Amanda jerked her head up, looking back and forth between the two men, who both stared expectantly at her.

"I'm sorry. What?" she asked. Clearly she'd missed a question directed at her in her narcotic-fueled daydream.

David glanced at Joaquin, who'd remained uncharacteristically quiet. "I said that while they're out, you and I need to do a little work. More specifically, I want to make sure you're comfortable using a gun."

Her hands went cold, the warm coffee mug practically scalding her. She'd never given guns more than a second thought before the attack on her office in Chicago.

Since then, just the thought of them stirred flashbacks of watching her colleagues being targeted like cans on a fence post.

Just a couple of months earlier, that fear had raged back at her when Vargas' men had kidnapped her and David. Even when she held one. The opportune moment to shoot the drug lord, she'd felt ill-equipped to wield the power in her hands.

She understood the mechanics of pointing and pulling the trigger. Amanda didn't have the emotional strength to live with taking someone's life.

As much as she wanted to kill Rafael Vargas for what he'd done to Josh, if she was in a room alone with him and had a clear shot could she do it?

"Can't you guys do that?" Her voice came out as a tight squeak. "I promise to stay with one of you. Just don't leave me behind."

"*Mija,* no one will leave you, but we all need to be armed," Joaquin's expression warring between sympathetic and stern.

If David wasn't standing there he would have likely given in to her fears.

"You saw how thick the forest is. Vargas will likely have people stationed throughout. Hiding. They could attack at any moment from any direction. We all need to be prepared," her friend continued.

Two against one. There was a strong chance Fallon would side with the guys.

"Do I have a choice?" she asked on the tail of a sigh.

David smirked down at her, obviously proud of himself for winning this battle with no visible scars. "Nope."

Amanda finished her coffee, mentally preparing herself for the shooting lesson.

Joaquin had a small handgun David felt would be perfect for her.

He talked through the type of gun, how to load it and other aspects of the firearm, but she mostly ignored him. Her mind was occupied by the cold sweat flushing her forehead, her body's attempt to cool the ember of ache.

Once she'd nodded enough to satisfy him some of the information had been absorbed, David led her outside, to an open lot behind the house.

She shivered at the heat. Her body was unsure how to respond to the sudden shift from air conditioning to the sweltering sun.

The landscape behind the house was a stark comparison to the lush, yet overgrown back garden. Beige sand collided with the buff-colored stone wall. A hill lazily rolled up ahead of them, steep enough to break a sweat, but nothing too strenuous to cause someone to gasp for air.

They stopped a hundred yards from the house. Nothing stirred outside. Nothing beside the wind, which whipped up clouds of sand.

"Okay, how about you aim at the cactus." David said nodded toward a spindly bush in front of them.

Amanda glanced at him, but couldn't read the expression behind his sunglasses. "Anywhere?" she asked, stalling as long as humanly possible.

"Point and shoot, then we'll figure out aiming." His voice was light, almost teasing. Like he was laughing at her.

Was he going to tell Fallon later the junky couldn't aim straight? That her shots went over the hill?

He held the gun up, offering it to her.

Her gaze darted from it to his face and back before she reluctantly took it.

This weapon was much lighter than the last one she'd held at the *hacienda*. Smaller, it fit her palm perfectly, as if it were made for her.

She held it out, one hand wrapped around the grip and the other cupping underneath it. Her biceps and shoulders burned, both from the heat of the sun and from the intensity in her muscles.

"Relax." David pulled one side of her earmuffs back and murmured, his voice soothing, but it didn't loosen her coiled nerves.

Amanda took a deep breath and on a slow exhale, squeezed the trigger. The gun fired and her arm jerked up, her taut muscles screeching at the recoil. A spit of dirt kicked up to the right of the cactus.

"Okay, so we have some work to do," he said, moving his ear protection down to his neck. "This time, I'll help you." He stood behind her and cupped his hands over hers, guiding her aim. "Now."

She more felt the vibration of his words from his chest through her back than heard them.

Amanda squeezed the trigger again and this time one of the pads exploded.

David stepped back, only touching her shoulders to help her adjust her aim as she fired on the remaining parts of the cactus.

Clammy sweat dripped down her brow and her neck, sliding down her chest. With each shot, nausea gnawed at her stomach, chewing its way up her throat, a tide of bile rising in its wake.

It was only a cactus, its green flesh there one second, gone the next. Her mind kept replacing it with her former colleagues, friends she'd worked with whose lives ended in a heartbeat.

The image of David, kneeling on a highway, the other possible outcome from their kidnapping, being killed.

The gun clicked as it spewed its final round, but her finger kept pulling at the trigger, as if it wanted to punish her for her sins. She tossed it to the ground and backed away from it, bumping into David, not looking up at him as she turned to run.

Amanda could hear him calling her name, muffled by both her rushing blood and the ear protection. She only made it a few feet before doubling over, spilling the meager contents of her stomach on the desert floor.

With each heave, the torment in her torso torqued, causing her to lose command of her legs. She dropped to her knees and caught herself before falling face down in the dirt.

David slid to a stop next to her, tugging the earmuffs off her head. "My God, Mandy." He clutched her upper arms, supporting her so she could relax. "What's wrong, baby?"

She opened her mouth to answer him, but her stomach twisted again. Several deep, slow breaths of air calmed the nausea, but the pain was fully awake. And, it was pissed. "Eight." The words burned over her sore throat. Amanda stared at the sand, hoping that by focusing on it she could stop the tilting world. "Eight."

"What do you mean?"

"You said." She swallowed back more acid. "You said to let you know when it's an eight. Eight." She glanced over her shoulder to look at him.

His lips were pressed tight and his forehead creased. "Baby, let's give something less powerful a try—"

Fire flickered in her midsection, threatening to burn her lower down to ash.

"Goddammit, no. Give me my pills." The words came out of her mouth on their own and she instantly regretted them.

He looked away, either to hide the look of disgust on his face or to not have to look at the monster she'd become.

# 39

Fallon could finally breath in Joaquin's compact sedan.

The wind whipped through the open window as they drove into town. Wisps of her curly blonde hair were sucked from her ponytail, sticking out in fuzzy tendrils from one side of her head, while her hair was smoothed back on the other.

She didn't mind her haphazard appearance. She had to get away from David and Amanda. David, because she knew it would break his heart when she arrested his girlfriend. Amanda, because her opinion of the woman shifted between pity to contempt to camaraderie and back again; sometimes in the space of a single conversation.

If Fallon had Amanda's injuries she wanted to assume she'd be able to function without the aid of painkillers, but if she had a head injury and cracked pelvis she'd likely have the luxury of resting comfortably. With her parents waiting on her. And, her brothers hovering nearby.

Away from the house, she felt confident enough to turn on her phone. It wasn't that she was afraid someone would see her text exchange with Winslow. It was more that she worried her boss would call in the cyber-investigators and have them hunt her down by the cell tower she'd pinged, and send her partner to come get her. Or worse, her brothers.

The phone buzzed in her hand once it found its lifeline to the outside world. Sure enough, she had voicemail, text messages and emails from Winslow.

From the tone of his written word she was in deep shit. Fallon could only imagine how much he'd screamed at her in a recorded message.

She started to press down on the power button to shut it down, but another message came in. This one from her sister-in-law, and when she opened the attached video, two tow-headed five-year-olds giggled at her.

"Aunt Fallon," shouted her niece Becca.

Her nephew Will took the phone from his sister and his mouth filled her screen. "I lost a tooth," he said, tugging his bottom lip down to show her the gaping maw.

"Hey, not fair." The phone was tugged out of his hand and Becca's little mouth came into view. "I think I have a loose tooth, too."

A chorus of nah-uh's and do-too's invaded the silence of the car before her sister-in-law took over the phone. "Hey Fal, we tried to call you, but your phone was off. The kids miss you. See you at Sunday supper? Bye now."

The ending of the video sucked her back into reality. Back into the stuffy car, speeding down the highway, driven by a man she'd just met.

Back into a world where they were going to walk into the den of a cartel leader with little more than hope and ambition.

Back into a world where her niece and nephew were a hundred miles and a world away.

Fallon wanted to crawl into the video. To hug them close to her and smell their baby-shampooed hair and listen to their rambling stories that led to more rambling stories which led to wanting her to play some new game or follow along a make-believe storyline.

She'd been away from her family before, but somehow the distance between them now felt greater, more infinite. More final.

One wrong move, and this could be the last time she'd see them.

She sniffed and shut down her phone, dropping it to her lap and letting the flying landscape out the window distract her.

"How old are they?"

She jumped at Joaquin's voice. Her mind was playing with the kids, laughing with her brothers, listening to her father's unsolicited advice. "Five and a half. In Becca's case, it's five and a half going on seventeen. Will, on the other hand, would be happy being forever five."

He grinned to the road in front of them. Traffic was thickening as more cars crammed on the narrow streets leading to the city center. "Don't you want to freeze them at that age?"

"I do, but I'm pretty sure my brother and sister-in-law would have something to say about that." Fallon shifted in her seat to study his profile. His hair was dark and curly, just days away from needing a haircut. His nose was straight and thin and one side of his cupid bow lips quirked up. "Do you have kids, Joaquin?" It felt like the safest way to pry.

He shook his head. "I don't exactly work in a field that's good for family life. You?"

"Same," she said, tilting her head back on the headrest. "But maybe someday..." She cleared her throat, chastising the lump that threatened to choke her. "How are you feeling about this plan? To get Williams and take out Vargas?"

"We're being forced to make decisions that I wouldn't normally make." His knuckles whitened on the steering wheel. It could've been because of the cars that cut him off, or shot out of random alleyways, but it was most likely because he wasn't confident in their success.

"I never asked, how did you and Amanda team up?" Fallon changed the subject.

Joaquin spared a glance in her direction before shifting his gaze back to the busy road. "There were rumors of a woman in the hospital. Someone who escaped Vargas, but she had amnesia. I posed as a priest and sat with her, to protect her, but also to see if she might remember." He blanched, as if he wasn't proud of his betrayal.

She could understand. Fallon was going to have the same reaction when she wrapped the handcuffs around Amanda's wrists. Guilt at doing her job, at using someone to get what she wanted. That niggling whisper, the one that told her life was more than black and white, even gray, life was as colorful as a cloud-smeared sunset, breathed in her ear. "Priest, huh?" She tried to make her voice light and teasing.

The car slowed in a thick mess of vehicles, people and bicycles.

Joaquin cursed under his breath. Obviously he didn't like not moving. Sitting there in the traffic, anyone could walk up, stick a gun to the window, shoot and be gone before they knew what happened. His edginess wafted off him, causing her hair to stand up.

"We need to move," Fallon mumbled.

An opening appeared and he swung the car around, slipping it in a narrow space and cutting off a delivery truck. Once they were moving again, he released a long exhale.

"Do you see your family often?" he asked, moving the conversation back to a subject that made her chest tighten.

"Most weeks, yeah. We do a big family dinner every Sunday at my parents' house."

His jaw tightened, as if chewing on her words. "That's tomorrow. You're going to miss it."

She sucked in a long breath. Sunday supper.

Something that seemed to always creep up on her, cut into her precious time off or poked at her when she was working on a case. Sunday suppers were for her family to pry into her private life, ask when she was going to find a nice man and settle down.

Sunday suppers were also for laughing with her brothers, hugging her dad and inhaling his warmth and love, for her mom to fuss over if Fallon was eating enough or getting enough sleep, for her sisters-in-law to offer to introduce her to the nice new guy at work.

It was where she forgot about a world full of abusers, criminals, women who trusted the wrong men and paid an inflated price. During those few hours with her family, the world was safe, fair, happy.

Joaquin steered the car into a parking spot and killed the engine.

Fallon turned her phone over in her hands. The rectangular lifeline to her family remained off.

What would it hurt? A quick call to her sister-in-law to chat with the kids, then a call to her parents, to let them know she was on a case and wouldn't be able to make dinner.

Telling them where she was and what kind of case she was on would only worry them, but coming from a family of law enforcement had its advantages. If she didn't volunteer any information, they wouldn't ask. "Mind if I meet you inside?" she asked when he popped open his door. "I need to make a couple of calls."

His smile caressed his eyes, lighting them with understanding and something else.

Envy, maybe? She'd spent so much time talking about her own family. Did he have an extended family somewhere far away from the violence of cartel country? Were they sitting down to a meal, leaving an empty seat for their son?

"Sure, *mija*, take all the time you need. I shouldn't be long."

She waited until he'd disappeared into a shop before turning her phone back on. While it booted up, she studied the busy sidewalk.

The first stop was a pharmacy, to stock up on first aid items and get Amanda something to help step her down from the prescription meds.

Fallon's phone dinged with a new voicemail once it came alive, but she ignored it and thumbed through her contacts looking for her sister-in-law's number.

Before she could hit her name, a call from her brother stole the screen.

"Hey Richard, I was—"

"Fallon," he cut her off. He breathed heavy into the phone, as if he were jogging. "Where are you?"

"I'm—" she hesitated. Something didn't feel right. Whatever

story she'd concocted to tell her family now felt wrong. "I'm in Mexico helping David. What's wrong?"

A siren screamed in the background of the call. A long piercing sound that normally didn't bother her, but goosebumps broke out at hearing it behind her brother.

"It's Dad." Huff, huff. The wailing grew louder. "He collapsed. I just got to the hospital. They have him stable, that's all I know."

Her numb fingers lost grip of the phone. When Fallon could finally grasp it, she brought it back to her ear, half listening as Richard gave a receptionist their father's name. She could hear him trying to control his emotions, trying to remain polite and tactful, but just under the surface he teetered close to panic.

"I'll be home as soon as I can, please keep me posted." An intercom spoke over her, its mechanical voice droning about something inconsequential. "Richard, please tell Dad I love him."

Fallon sat in the car for several minutes after ending the call. Her lungs took in the warm, stale air in uneven, jagged breaths. A bead of sweat tickled her cold forehead. A lead weight of worry thrashed around her stomach.

When the air in the car got too hot, her legs took over, heaving her out and into the store.

Joaquin stood at the counter, chatting and laughing with the clerk, as if they were old friends. He handed over a fistful of *pesos* and glanced in her direction. His wide grin hovered in place, but it fell like a duck shot out of the sky. "Fallon?" Her name was a tight whisper.

"*Mi papi está en el hospital.*" If she said the words in English, it would've made them real.

She didn't see him close the distance between them to wrap his arms around him. She didn't smell his woodsy, earthy scent, or feel his warmth seep through her T-shirt.

All Fallon could see was her dad, lying in a hospital bed with machines beeping around him. The antiseptic chemicals burned her nose.

She shivered at the coldness of not being there.

# 40

Amanda's self-loathing hit an all-time high when Fallon and Joaquin returned.

One look at David's friend told her something was wrong. Fallon's eyes were red-rimmed, her face a pale green and she clutched her stomach, hugging her arms tight around herself. Like a little girl trying to make herself small. Invisible.

David saw it too, and he quickly shot up from the dining table where he was cleaning the gun and pulled Fallon in for a hug.

"What happened?" Amanda asked Joaquin.

Her friend sat the bags on the counter and looked at the blonde woman. Concern knitted his brow together and he chewed on his lower lip. "Her father is in the hospital."

Amanda sucked in a gasp. Her own worst fear stared back at her. It'd been more than a year and a half since she'd seen her family, but it didn't mean she didn't think about them daily.

Hourly.

Every single second.

Fallon's phone rang and she stepped into the foyer to answer it. Her voice was soft, private.

"He collapsed," Joaquin said. "Her brother is at the hospital with him."

"She needs to go home. Be with her family." Amanda turned to David.

He'd barely looked at her since they came inside from target practice, since he'd relented and gave her *a* pill.

"David, you have to take her home."

His gaze darted down to her face, but only briefly. "Mandy." Her name came out as an exasperated sigh.

She understood. She felt that way about herself, too.

"Okay, thank you. Call me if there's any updates." Fallon headed toward them before hanging up the call. "He's stable, awake and giving them hell. They're keeping him overnight to run some tests, but it looks like severe dehydration." Relief loosened her face and shoulders, but Amanda could still hear the concern in her voice.

She could've just as easily have had the other conversation. The one that told her it was much worse than expected. That her life had changed and nothing would ever be the same again.

Amanda understood what it was like to get *that* call. She often thought back to the reporter, Roland Burrows, delivering her own life-changing message.

"Go home," she said, hoping they could put their animosity behind them long enough for Fallon to take her nudging. "You should be with your family."

The woman nodded down to her feet. "I will, as soon as this is done." She looked up at David and Joaquin, then settled her stare on Amanda. "Let's do this tomorrow." Fallon said it with such casualness. Instead of suggesting they trudge up a mountain and into the lair of a drug lord to rescue her maimed ex-boyfriend, it sounded as if she recommended pizza for dinner.

"Are we ready?" The real question Amanda wanted to ask was if *she* was ready, but the answer to that wasn't a shocker. No, she wasn't. They knew the answer to it as well. Especially David.

"My team is coming over tonight to map our route," Joaquin said. "Weather should be favorable. No reason to put it off."

Fallon and Joaquin slipped out of the kitchen, each with a phone to an ear.

Amanda and David worked overtime avoiding each other's eyes. Whatever steps they'd taken back to each other the previous night were now separated by the Grand Canyon.

She couldn't do this.

Not with David thinking she was weak, addicted.

Maybe it was all a terrible idea. Were the drugs clouding her judgment? Making her feel like she could fly when in reality she'd only fall.

The truth was, she was secretly envious of Josh. He was paying the price for his crimes.

Vargas had taken his ear as punishment for setting in place the events that'd resulted in her shooting off the cartel leader's own ear. He'd lost a hand for stealing from the same man.

What about *her* punishment? Sure, she was a little banged up from a wild river ride, but she'd spent the previous night lying in the arms of the man whose heart she'd broken. Not just once, but many times over. Where was the justice in that?

Her punishment would come in waves. The first wave was whatever would happen at Prospera Pass. They could get lucky. Vargas could go down quickly, easily. Maybe Josh was stronger than she thought and he'd survive.

She had to be tougher than whatever waited for them at the top of that mountain.

"Can we go back out?" Amanda asked.

David tilted his head in a question.

"I want to practice some more. Shooting."

"Mandy, if this is too much for you..." His Texas drawl coated his concern, even as his words dwindled.

She laid a hand on his arm, bracing herself for a flinch, but instead he relaxed under her touch.

*I'm not that revolting after all.*

"I feel much better now. I'm fine." She searched his face for any signs of disbelief. "Plus, if I can't handle target practice..." The seed of doubt was damned determined to grow. No matter how much poison she poured on it.

The midday sun was even hotter, but whether it was sheer determination or the drugs coursing through her veins, she didn't feel as if her body was on fire.

David ran through a quick refresher, and this time she found herself listening intently, the information soaking into her brain.

He hesitated only slightly before handing the gun back to her, his face pinched in concern.

She smiled. "I've got this."

For the first time in weeks, she actually believed it.

The gun didn't shake in her hands. Instead, it stared straight at her intended target. When the bullet exploded out of the chamber, she didn't recoil in fear or shock.

When it sliced through the cactus, at exactly the place she'd aimed, one side of her mouth quirked up into a self-satisfied, kick-butt-and-take-no-prisoners grin.

After emptying the magazine, she glanced over her shoulder.

David stood a couple feet behind her, his arms crossed over his chest and a grin as big as the Texas sky plastered on his face. "You're a bad ass, Mandy Martin." He closed the distance between them and kissed her, gently at first, as if her injuries included her lips.

Only when it deepened to the point where her lungs burned for air did he release her.

"I'm sorry," he said, resting his forehead against hers.

Her heart flipped. "For what?"

"Losing control." He released a long, deep breath. "Trust me, I want nothing more than to take you to bed, but that's probably not part of your recovery."

Amanda's core hummed, but not the angry gnashing of pain, instead it was the heavy warmth of desire. It felt...amazing. "Yeah, may not be a good idea." She ran her fingers through his hair. It was longer than she'd ever seen and starting to curl at the ends. "But I will heal, and I hope you'll lose control of yourself again."

He leaned in for another kiss.

She tried to focus on the feel of his lips against hers instead of the lump suffocating her.

David made her almost believe that she could do it.

"I'm serious, Mandy," he said as they walked back to the house, his hand squeezing hers. "You're a much better shot than me. I couldn't have hit some of the ones you did. You just have to be confident, baby."

Curly blonde hair caught her attention as they walked through the back garden. Fallon's back was to them, her head bent down.

"I'll meet you inside," Amanda said, slowing and pulling her hand from David's grasp.

He looked over her head in the woman's direction, smiling as he planted a kiss on her head.

Did he think they'd become best friends? Highly unlikely, especially given that a niggling suspicion in the back of her mind had grown into full-blown belief.

"How's your dad?"

Fallon's head jerked up, obviously startled by her appearance.

"Better. He seems to be more worried about his cattle than his own health," she said. "My brothers are threatening to handcuff him to the bed."

"I'm glad to hear that. I can only imagine how terrifying that call must've been." An alternate reality mocked her brain. One in which her own brother had a way to reach out to her, to call her with news of her father's, or maybe her mother's, sudden illness.

What had *she* missed in all these months? In the weeks following her escape from Chicago, the thoughts of her family had assaulted her daily, like a splinter stuck in her finger. Now it was less often, except when something irritated it.

Then it hurt like hell.

"How long has it been since you've talked to your family?" Fallon's voice lost its authoritative edge, instead it was gentle and sincere.

Amanda lowered herself on the bench, the sun-warmed concrete soothing, comforting. "I talked to my mom the night before, the…" All this time and she still had a hard time putting what happened into words. "I went to a baseball game with my dad a week before. My brother…"

When was the last time she'd talked to Kyle? He was in his final semester of college, preparing to go into medical school. Did he? Or, had Amanda's disappearance changed the trajectory of his life?

She glanced up at Fallon. "I don't remember when I talked to my brother last. Why don't I remember?"

Fallon sat next to her. The woman's arms flinched, as if she maybe wanted to reach out to hug her, but she gripped the back of the bench. "We live every day expecting tomorrow to be there."

"What about you? Do you expect tomorrow to be there? Or, the day after?"

A long sigh escaped her chest. "Are you asking if we're embarking on a fool's errand?" Fallon shrugged. "I've always had faith the good guys will win."

They sat in silence for several minutes. Amanda played with the words in her head. Flipping them over, testing them for strength, checking for holes. When she was confident in her assumption, her gaze found the other woman. "If there is a day after tomorrow, I want you to be the one who arrests me. Promise me you will. I won't resist."

"What about David?"

She relaxed a bit. "I'll handle him. It's the right thing to do. He'll understand."

"Why me?" The woman narrowed her eyes, surely thinking this was some trick.

"Because I trust you." It was the truth. That in a world where it seemed trust was made to be broken, Amanda sensed that David's friend would always do the right thing, whether it was getting him home, saving Josh or arresting her.

Fallon glanced away, her gaze surveying the wild, overgrown garden. Several seconds later, she bobbed her head in a quick nod. "Fine. But you have to make *me* a promise, too." She held out her cell phone. "Call your family."

# 41

Amanda stared at the phone in Fallon's outstretched hand as if it would shock her if she touched it.

"What are you afraid of?" Her eyes were full of challenge.

*Where should I start?*

Numb fingers picked up the phone. "What if they don't answer?" As many times as she'd wanted to call her parents, she'd talked herself out of it. The excuses were plentiful and creative, but it always boiled down to fear.

"Leave a message."

"What if they answer? What do I say?" Amanda looked up, expecting to see harshness in Fallon's face, but instead it was full of encouragement.

The woman pursed her lips into a soft smile. "You'll find the words. Maybe leave out the crazy-ass plan for tomorrow."

"What if I die?" Her lungs refused to take in the next breath. "Maybe it's better for them to keep thinking I'm dead."

Fallon glanced away, her gaze looking out over the rising hill behind the house. "Do you know how many people wish they had one more chance to tell someone they love them?" She retreated into the house.

Alone in the garden with Fallon's phone, Amanda's knees loosened. She fell back onto the bench hard, but the cranky ache was ignored over her speeding heart.

She could lie. Give herself a reasonable amount of time and say she talked with them. Then again, Fallon would know by the lack of an outgoing call. Maybe she could dial her old cell number, try to pass it off as her parents.

Why was she so afraid? Before any of this; before Josh and the stolen money, before the shooting and her running away, before they thought she'd drowned in the Rio Grande, she'd never had any qualms with calling her parents.

She'd never rebelled. Amanda had never been an angsty teenager who snuck out or broke into the liquor cabinet. She'd been a decent student, a good-enough cross country runner, stayed away from the party crowd. In college, Amanda always went to class, made her grades, worked her part-time job. It was only in her professional life that the dark side had lured her with money and a golden boy with a charming grin.

*That* was when conversations with her parents had become more difficult. For her at least. She always answered the 'how's work' and 'how's Josh' questions blandly enough, but only because Amanda had been afraid to voice her concerns. The ones that woke her up in the middle of the night, breathless, her heart-racing. Her parents would've reaffirmed her suspicions…something *wasn't* right.

Either with her career or her relationship.

They were a mirror she wasn't ready to look into.

"Okay, Martin, you've got this. Just press a few buttons."

Amanda dialed their home phone number quickly; holding her breath for fear her bravery would escape with an exhale. Her thumb hovered over the '*call*' button. She squeezed her eyes closed and pressed it.

It rang three times, then the noticeable void between the pick-up and first speech.

"Hello?" The voice was male, much like her dad's but still with a touch of youth.

"Kyle?" Her baby brother sounded less like the college co-ed and more like a man.

"Who is this?" His voice roughened, as if scratched with a pumice. It sounded so unlike her brother. He'd always been kind, offering a gentle teasing to his big sister, but willing to help anyone in need.

"It's Mandy. I—"

"You're disgusting, you know. Pretending to be her," Kyle spat into the phone.

Would it be better to let him slam down the phone in disgust? To go on thinking his sister was dead?

"You had a really severe case of the chicken pox." Her voice quivered with the almost-forgotten memory. "I played connect the dots all over your body with the spots."

The other end of the phone was silent for several beats. Long enough for Amanda to pull it back from her ear to make sure she hadn't already lost him.

"You used a Sharpie." Kyle softened, sounding more like her brother. "Mom and Dad were so mad at you."

A sob broke from her throat, but she tried to disguise it as a laugh. "But you stopped scratching, so it wasn't all bad."

Amanda listened to her brother breathe. Letting the connection to her family, albeit just a digital connection that stretched across two countries and bounced off cell towers, warm her heart.

"Mandy?" he whispered. "Where are—We thought you drowned. You died. We had your funeral."

"I'm sorry."

"You're sorry?" The soft edges from earlier were now sharp spikes laced with vitriol.

She cleared the lump that floated up. "I never meant to hurt you," Amanda paused, waiting for a response from Kyle. "How's Mom and Dad?"

"How do you think they're doing? Do you even realize the hell you'd put our parents through? Have you once in your little on-the-run adventure stopped to think about us?"

She opened her mouth to argue, but the words were like scared children, hiding in the darkness, afraid to come out and be confronted with her brother's anger. "So many times," she whispered through her tears. "I thought of you daily."

"Where *are* you?"

This was a huge mistake. They'd buried her. Or, the thought of her. Why had she let Fallon talk her into ripping open a healing wound?

"I'm sorry, I have to go, but I just wanted to make sure everyone's okay." Her stomach churned on the bad decision. She shouldn't have made this call. "Kyle, you can tell them I called if you want, or not. I trust you to make the right decision, but if you tell them, let them know I'm fine. I'm safe. And, I love them. You, too, baby brother. I love you." She ended the call before he could respond.

If she spent any more time on the phone, she'd abandon the plan to save Josh and instead run home to beg her family for forgiveness.

Her end of the bargain was held up. If Fallon wouldn't slap handcuffs on her wrist she'd do it herself.

As much as it soothed her to know they were okay, Amanda was rattled. Was this the most selfish thing she'd ever done?

Their healing had only just begun, and she cut it wide open again. Maybe even made the wound larger. Deeper.

How could they come back from knowing she'd intentionally stayed away from them? If she survived the mountain, if Fallon arrested her and she was sent back to Chicago, would they bother visiting her in jail?

She'd never doubted her parents' love.

Until now…

The mean-girl voice in the back of her mind whispered that perhaps this was all part of Fallon's plan. That she'd convince Amanda to cause irreparable damage to her family, knowing if she survived she'd be shunned. David would be disgusted by her selfishness. Ultimately, she'd get what she deserved.

*No, that wasn't it at all.* Amanda shook her head, admonishing her suspicions.

There'd been genuine concern in Fallon's expression. They'd had an understanding. A moment of realizing this strange little unit they've formed, this well-meaning, under-equipped, bitten-off-more-than-they-could-chew foursome wasn't the only thing in existence. While they'd isolated themselves, the world, their families, ticked on without them.

Movement inside the house drew her attention.

Joaquin's friends, the ones who'd help them trudge up the mountain to Prospera Pass, had arrived. As much as Amanda wanted to curl up into a ball and cry until she dehydrated herself, she couldn't wallow in the pain of hurting her family.

She raked her hands down her face once more, hoping to reset her features from sadness to restrained happiness from her moments with David. At best she hoped her face would fall into impassive attention and curiosity.

David and Fallon were shaking hands with four men. Three of the men were young, fit and trim, looking as if they ran up the side of a mountain as part of their warm-up routine. The other man looked to be north of fifty.

"Ah, there you are," Joaquin said, pulling Amanda into the room. "This is your team. Miguel, Diego and Sal are taking a few days from their military duty." The trio of soldiers nodded at her. "And Rodrigo here grew up on the mountain. He'll guide us, taking us off paths to give us the best chance of ascending undetected."

The older man gave her a wide grin, his missing front teeth somehow making the grin even more endearing, heartfelt.

She instantly liked him.

"*Mucho gusto.*" Amanda shook his hand.

Rodrigo pulled a topographical map of the mountain from a messenger bag and spread it over the kitchen table. He spoke in soft Spanish, his words looping together. A few words stuck in her mind, but without context to anchor themselves to, they quickly floated away.

Joaquin and the soldiers listened intently, asking questions. Her friend's face was serious, pensive. From time to time, he pointed at the map and interrupted the guide, as if questioning his logic, but the older man would provide a quick answer and Joaquin nodded in agreement.

Fallon tried to translate for her and David, but gave up trying to give a verbatim translation and began paraphrasing. "He's suggesting we make the steepest climb at the beginning, when we're fresh, rested. Then we start zig zagging." She paused to listen some more. "It could take us a full day to get to the top. They're discussing if it would be wise to find a safe place to camp overnight or if we go in as soon as we get there."

Amanda shivered, both at the thought of a windy, chilly overnight on top of a mountain and at the promised steep hike.

"The boys." The FBI agent inclined her head toward the soldiers, but kept her voice low. "Are wanting to attack at night."

"I'd rather rest up, strike before daybreak," David said. "We'll have to wait until sunrise to head back down anyway."

How could she make it to the top and be so close to Josh, and Vargas, and set up camp for the night? She had an ex, no, a *friend* to save.

There was no time for campfires and roasting marshmallows. Her life was scary enough; she didn't need any fireside ghost stories.

"We go straight in." Amanda sounded small and raspy in her own ears. "As soon as we get to the top, we get Josh."

David's pinched brow argued with her, even if his mouth was pressed tight. "Mandy, we'll be exhausted. *You'll* be exhausted."

"We can't afford the luxury of rest if Josh is near death." She folded her arms across her chest. "However long it takes us to get to the top, we catch our breath and go straight in."

There was another round of quick Spanish with Fallon arguing David's suggestion to rest.

At a lull in the conversation, one of the soldiers nodded slowly and pursed his lips.

"We'll aim to go straight in, but we will pack supplies in case we have to deviate and wait until night," Fallon said.

David gazed out the back windows, his jaw muscle tight.

Amanda tried to read his mood. Was he just mad he didn't get his way, or worried about the entire mission in general? Was he having second thoughts rewinding all the way back to when he asked her out on a date?

"Okay," the young soldier said.

Which one was he? She couldn't remember the line-up from Joaquin's introduction. "We start climbing at sunrise."

Amanda's breath hitched. The sun was just setting. By the time its light would shine back on this little part of northern Mexico, she'd be at the base of Prospera, starting her journey to save Josh.

It would be a painful trip through Hell, but after years of mistakes and hurting those she loved most, she was itching to repent.

# 42

The fly landed near his eye. Its tiny legs compelled a blink. It wasn't the first one that'd invaded his wounds.

They'd been hovering since Josh regained consciousness. If that was what this state could be called.

"I'm not dead yet, fucker." He lifted his head and gave it as much of a shake as he could summon.

It and several others scattered.

Why wasn't he dead yet? Was his life force so stubborn to refuse to part with his broken, maimed body? Was his soul afraid of what was ahead?

The sun cast its long yellow beam into his cell. Dust motes danced and dove, as if each were following its own beat.

Josh's good eye was blurry. Strange because he'd always had perfect vision. Had a hit caused his retina to detach?

His other eye was sealed. Blood or tears, or both, sewing it closed.

Movement at the door caught his attention.

Amanda walked in.

Not into the stable-turned-torture-chamber. Into his office.

Her red suit fit her perfectly; the pencil skirt hugged all the right places and was just on the right side of appropriate. The jacket was slim cut with sharp angles and the slightest hint of a black camisole underneath peeked out from above the top button. She showed enough skin to reveal her creamy complexion, but tasteful enough to take home to Mom.

Josh glanced down. Both of his hands were splayed on his wood desk. A quick run of his fingers through his hair revealed his ears were in place and his hair was back in its usual cut.

Amanda stopped at his desk and stood there, her hazel eyes studying his face, one side of her perfect mouth pulled into a confident smile. "Mr. Williams." It was a question without the question mark. "Amanda Martin." She stretched out her hand. "It's nice to meet you."

He stood and offered his hand. Shocked his body reacted when commanded. "Yes, nice to meet you." His voice came out like a pubescent boy, but she didn't seem to notice. "Please, call me Josh."

He studied her face when she sat. Was she really that young when he'd hired her?

Twenty-four, maybe twenty-five, but she'd carried herself with the daring confidence of someone decades older. That'd been what drew him in, but also scared the shit out of him. The totality of *her*.

Young, yet wise. Beautiful and smart. Caring, but not afraid to stand up for herself. Stubborn, but could be convinced with a compelling enough argument. She was so unlike the other girls he'd dated.

"What are you doing here?"

She tilted her head to the side. "I was called back for a second interview. I can go, if this isn't a good time." Amanda started to stand, slowly as if expecting him to deter her hasty exit.

"Wait, no, sorry, I, uh—" Josh stumbled to understand.

The Amanda standing in front of him was five years younger than the one he'd watched jump off a cliff in Mexico with another man.

This Amanda's hair was blonder, brushing her shoulders, not the light brown hair that reached the middle of her back. Her complexion was the flawless porcelain of a native Chicagoan.

Absent of the spattering of freckles she'd grown during her time in Texas.

This wasn't fully the past either.

He recalled exactly what would transpire. At that moment, he'd already found his dad's will and realized he wasn't a sole heir.

Within weeks he'd learn about a half-sister and would launch his plan to embezzle money from his father, from their investment firm's clients and commit securities fraud to cover it up. Six months from meeting Amanda they'd sleep together.

For three years they cohabited a relationship. That was the best way he could describe it. They'd been in a relationship together, but for very different reasons. His to keep her from asking too many questions, and hers because, well, maybe she really had loved him.

"Please, sit with me for a while," Josh said, finding his voice. "Tell me about yourself. Where did you go to school?"

Josh didn't really pay attention to her words. He luxuriated in her voice. A perfect pitch built on a foundation of huskiness with a layer of soft and sweet coated over it.

Her perfume wafted over him, pushing away the sour smell of his body odor and oozing wounds. What perfume did she wear?

He used to know this. Josh had surprised her with it back when she'd nearly caught him out with another woman.

A fly buzzed in his wounded ear. He shooed it away with an over-exaggerated gesture.

Amanda stopped talking and cocked an eyebrow. "Everything okay?"

"Sorry, I just…" He'd already apologized twice. "Why do you want to work here?"

She brightened, as if she'd practiced this question a dozen times in her bathroom mirror. "I'm glad you asked." The classic affirmation of his question. "While I certainly enjoy working at an agency, I'm ready for more. I'm ready to focus on one firm, one brand and dive in deep to deliver results that grow the business." Amanda reclined in her chair, crossing her legs and draping one arm over the back of the chair.

She was so self-assured. If there were a humidor on his desk, she would've stuck a cigar between her lips.

Josh remembered that move. He'd only been half paying attention to her until then. It was a challenge. A dare.

"Plus," she added, dropping her voice. "I'm incredibly loyal. Sure, I might want to cut your balls off if I find out you're cheating on me, or I might chase you halfway across the country to turn you in to the SEC, but when a drug lord has you sliced into a million pieces, you better believe I will come for you, Josh Williams."

*Wait. That's not how the interview went.*

He tugged at his tie, loosening it. His throat suddenly became thick, parched. "Excuse me?"

"I said I have a great relationship with media, but I'm fiercely loyal so you'd never have to worry about me crossing any lines." Her voice had brightened.

Was this his life flashing before his eyes?

Josh had never died before. Did the tape play back exactly as it had happened, or was it spliced in with some woulda-coulda-shoulda's and wishful-thinking?

Was he watching his greatest regret? The moment when he'd decided to bring Amanda into his world.

What would happen if he told her she wasn't a fit? Would she find another job?

Maybe marry a doctor or some corporate executive, have a suitable life in a Chicago suburb, she'd give birth to the perfect children; maybe quit her job to lead the PTA or something that would have bored her to a bottle-of-chardonnay-a-day habit.

No matter what he would've said that day, she would've still ended up in his life. Because sitting there, seeing her for the first time again, the ember of love sparked. Sure Josh had ignored it, exploited it. Hell, he'd doused it in water several times, but that stubborn fire smoldered.

It would never go out.

Not even when he'd lost her to another man. Someone much more deserving than him.

"Josh, are you okay?" Amanda's voice was strained, concern written across her youthful face.

"Sure, just…thinking. Why do you ask?"

She paled, flashed a bit green even. "You're, um, bleeding."

The fly buzzed again, but this time when he tried to swat it away his hand ignored the command. "Yeah, from where?"

His office stretched away from him, like a rubber band being pulled back. Amanda was three feet away. Then it was more like thirty feet.

Several years.

"Everywhere." Her voice was small.

Horrified.

Josh lifted his head. The sun shone softer now, it's light less vibrant, more muted. Nightfall was coming.

Only one thought stuck in his mind as his consciousness drained. That the drone of the flies feasting on his dying body sounded just like the hum of the fluorescent lights in his office.

# 43

Morning came early for David. He'd sat up with Joaquin and the trio of soldiers well past midnight, but sent Mandy to bed when her blinks became longer and longer.

She needed as much rest as possible. Her body was still healing. She was more fragile than he was prepared to admit.

Fallon retired not long after Mandy.

David had watched Joaquin's eyes follow his friend up the stairs, even following the path she'd take to her third floor bedroom. His mouth filled with words eager to come out. But which ones?

A gentle teasing? Encouragement? Yeah, that wouldn't go over well with his college friend.

*Sorry we didn't work out, but I found this nice guy here to hit on you.*

Yep, she'd ask him to hold the target for her at shooting practice.

They were at the base of the mountain before the eastern horizon had lightened. At best, he'd gotten two hours of sleep, but a combination of nerves and adrenalin was better than any shot of espresso.

Whether by exhaustion or apprehension, everyone was quiet,

standing shoulder to shoulder. Without the daylight, the mountain felt like an apparition.

David knew it was there. Could feel its presence even if he couldn't see it. When he stared straight ahead, all he saw was a giant maw.

"*Vamanos.*" Rodrigo's quiet voice felt like a shout in the pre-dawn silence.

The guide set off, the copse of trees swallowing him whole.

One of the soldiers set off after him.

Joaquin motioned for Fallon to go in front of him, then the second soldier followed after he fell in behind her.

Mandy took a step, but David grabbed her arm.

"Are you sure you can do this?" His gaze roved over her face. Only light circles cushioned her eyes. Her cheeks were flushed in the brisk morning air. The sun they'd gotten during their time in the desert brought out a constellation of freckles across the bridge of her nose.

She glanced up at the mountain then back to him, determination cemented her normally soft face. "I didn't come this far to turn back now." She took a deep breath and started her climb. "I've survived three days in a scorching desert. A tree-lined mountain with cool breezes sounds like Heaven."

Only the sound of branches cracking under her feet told him she hadn't disappeared completely.

As Rodrigo had said, the first half-mile was the steepest. The ground rose at an incline so steep that at various points, David had to pitch forward, his hands scraping the ground.

They were all gasping for breath.

The soldier behind him huffed and Mandy's panting was softer, quicker. No one spoke, not that they could have, but they'd all agreed to stay absolutely silent.

Voices carried on the wind in a remote mountain. They couldn't risk a word floating up to Vargas and giving them away.

Once the sun broke over the horizon, their guide led them to a leveled clearing. Protected from the face of the mountain by a large boulder and the thick trunk of a pine tree, it was the perfect spot to rest.

Sweat glistened on the foreheads of the three soldiers, but they seemed to have recovered their breath the fastest.

Joaquin chugged water.

David would've admonished him, told him to slow down, but he didn't have the lung capacity for it.

Fallon clasped her hands behind her head, her face tilted to the sky as she took deep, long inhales.

Mandy leaned against the boulder, her chest heaving and her eyes closed. She tried to take a deep breath, too, but winced.

"Want me to get your water out of your pack?" he asked.

She'd insisted on carrying something up as well, so he'd fitted her with the lightest pack and put the little gun in her waistband.

"Yeah, thanks," she gasped and pivoted so he could pull it out the side pocket.

"Pain level?"

He watched the muscles in her throat as they welcomed the water.

Mandy looked out over the edge, as if trying to figure out the answer. "My brain says it's only a four, but my body thinks it's a seven."

He'd given her two pills when they woke up. The bottle was tucked away in his pack. David should've let her have control, show that he trusted her to make the right decision about her own body, but he was afraid she'd overreact and take too many. They'd made a deal. At noon, if she needed another, he'd give it to her.

He sipped his own water. The day was already warm and the air was thick, clouds raced north, sailing in from the Gulf, bringing stifling humidity in their wake.

They'd already ascended a considerable height, at least a thousand feet, maybe more. The hazy desert floor stretched out in front of them.

Was that Texas there on the horizon? He could almost see the void in the landscape where the Rio Grande flowed, separating two countries.

Two worlds.

He looked above them. The next segment was short, but with a series of switchbacks along a vertigo-inducing cliff wall. The path was shale, the same slate gray as the tall rock jutting out of the side of the mountain. What was worse about this part of their journey; one wrong step and someone would literally slide off the face of the earth, or they'd be totally exposed?

Joaquin and Rodrigo stood at the place where the path picked up again, their heads close together.

The guide pointed up the trail ahead of them.

Joaquin followed the man's gesture, nodded and glanced over his shoulder in their direction. His gaze met David's and he joined them.

"*Mija,* how do you feel?" The man directed his question at Mandy, but he glanced between both of them, as if expecting each to have their own response.

"Good," Mandy said. "I feel fine."

He pursed his lips and narrowed his eyes. "Is she lying?" he asked David.

"She's doing great." Was that for her reassurance or his?

"This next section is going to be difficult," Joaquin said. "We must be careful, but we also have to move quickly. Are you ready?"

Mandy nodded. "Let's go."

They followed the same line-up as before.

The first leg of the switchback rose steeply, the shale and scree crunched under their feet. With each step, the trees lining the path shrunk.

By the time they reached the turn, they were higher than the treetops.

David glanced up. He counted six more of those climbs. Each one looked steeper than the last. They could easily ascend nearly another thousand feet by the time they reached the plateau at the end.

The second switchback was much like the first, except they were more exposed without the cover of trees both to hide them and the rising sun.

They all slowed for the third one, even the guide seemed to take this one at a more deliberate pace.

Mandy hugged the uphill side of the trail. Her fingers tracing the craggy rock, as if she could grab something should she lose her footing. There was nothing to grab, just the smooth facade of rock.

He couldn't blame her for putting as much distance between herself and the edge of the narrow trail. The path swam in front of David. Gray on gray on gray. That was all he saw in front of him before the trail dropped off into the blue sky.

Mandy's voice flowed over the high-pitched sound of the wind. At first he thought she was talking to him, but he didn't want to ask her to repeat herself for fear she'd look back and lose her footing.

Only when she hesitated on a step and he nearly collided with her was he able to make out her words.

"Ten, nine, eight..." Her countdown tick. A calming mechanism. Something she'd let him see when he broke up with her in Phoenix, and again when they narrowly escaped being killed at Hank Snare's office in El Paso.

He understood. Pressure squeezed his head. His vision felt unreliable, as if it lied to him about what was the edge of the trail and what lay ahead of them.

Like Mandy, David hugged the right side, unable to trust his ability to stay on the trail and not tumble off the edge.

They rounded the final switchback.

Only one more climb and they'd be at their second plateau. Safer ground.

David wanted to glance up, to see what the trail held for them, but they walked straight into the rising sun. "Mandy, you okay?"

She only nodded her answer.

He waited until the group started moving, like cars untangling from a traffic jam. Nausea washed up his throat, but he swallowed it back. His body felt even more unstable. Vertigo squeezed his head.

David focused on Mandy's shoes. One step, a pause, then the next. She moved slowly, not pressing her sneakers into the path until she seemed sure the ground wouldn't give way under her. After a few steps, she pitched forward. Her hands landed on the rock and

David gripped her waist, holding on to her for dear life. Hers. And, his. "Crawl if you need to, baby," he whispered in her ear.

She nodded again, and half-walked, half-crawled.

David looked up over her and saw Rodrigo cut in far to the right.

They were almost there.

The soldier behind him grunted, cursing in both English and Spanish. During a pause in Mandy's forward motion, he spared a glance over his shoulder. The man was a pale green, sweat pouring from his face. His footsteps were uneven, stumbling, as he weaved from one side of the trail to the next, like a drunk coming out of a bar.

"Hey, man, you okay?"

Only a groan answered him.

"Look, stay right there, let me get her to the top and I'll come back for you."

This time, the man retched. "Yes," he answered, his voice hoarse.

Fallon rounded the corner.

Only the second soldier and Mandy to go.

No more footsteps crunched behind him. David hoped it was because the man, boy really—he had to be in his early twenties—had taken his advice and waited for him.

At the next glance up, the soldier in front of Mandy offered her a hand, pulling her to the wide flat mountaintop meadow.

David guided her from behind, his hands clinging loosely to her hips.

Once she stood and took several steps from the edge, he exhaled. The fuzzy stars that'd been clouding the edge of his vision disappeared.

"I'm going to help him up," David said to the group.

The trail going downhill was more harrowing than climbing it. The shadows of the sun made it even more difficult to discern between the trail and the side of the cliff.

The soldier was frozen in his spot, standing stiffly over a puddle of vomit.

"You're Diego, right?" David asked, taking a few steps down the trail. At best it was only two feet wide. There'd be no way he could safely get behind the man to guide him up; he'd have to talk him through it from in front of him.

The man nodded.

"Are you married? Got a girlfriend?"

Diego retched again, his hand trying to hold it back, but it only spilled through his fingers.

David took another three steps, his boots sliding in the shale. "Listen to me, Diego. We're going to make it to the top. I'll be with you every step of the way. Put your hand on my shoulder if you'd like, or watch my shoes. Just focus, one step at a time, one breath at a time."

The guy gripped his shoulder hard. They took small steps, the soldier shuffling behind him. Diego panted, and a whimper fell out between heavy breaths.

The end of the trail was just two feet in front of him. The faces of the others peeked around the sharp corner.

David waved them back, wanting to give Diego as much room as possible once he got to the top. That was when he saw it. Getting off the final switchback included a short scramble up a smooth boulder.

*Shit.*

The only way to get the soldier up would be to pull him, but that meant David would have to leave him alone on the trail to get himself in position.

"Diego." He whirled enough to see the man from his peripheral vision. "Last few steps. Follow me to the base of that boulder and wait for me, I'll pull you up. *Entiendes?*"

Terror wrenched his face, but he closed his eyes and nodded.

David found a foothold in the edge of the boulder and boosted himself up, one of the soldiers, Miguel, gripped under his armpit to help guide him.

Once he was up, he spared a glance at the group.

Fallon and Mandy were as far from the edge or the trail as possible, both of them dripping in sweat, their faces pale.

242

He dropped down to his knees, hoping that by staying low he could give Diego all of his strength to pull him up. David reached down. "Okay, Diego, take a step and grab my hand."

The boy's gaze shot up from the ground and found his face. The air around him trembled with his shivering. He lifted a tentative foot, held it aloft but put it back in its place.

"Come on, one step."

The same foot lifted again, but this time landed several inches forward.

"Good, one more."

Diego was still just out of his grasp.

He lifted his other foot. This time, he placed it more firmly on the edge of the rock. A large exhale fled his body, as if all the air he'd ever breathed was being held in his lungs. He lurched forward, his right arm outstretched to reach for David, but the flat shale rock shifted.

Diego panicked and yanked his arm back, throwing his body weight backward, tipping the shale all the way down. Like a teeter totter, it went down and the edge closest to David flew up, nearly colliding with his chin.

Diego yelped. His eyes widened, as if fully understanding the direness of the situation.

David and Miguel both lunged to catch him, but it was too late.

Diego disappeared, swallowed by the blue sky behind him. He didn't scream when he fell. No cry, no curse filled the void.

Only the horrific sound of crunching bones.

# 44

Amanda had never seen David so upset.

"I had him, I swear, I had him." His body shivered violently, erratically. He raked his fingers down his pale face. "I should've stood on the other end of the rock, to balance it."

It took Joaquin and the other two soldiers to pull him from the edge after Diego had fallen.

He'd started to scramble down the boulder, as if he were going to dive after him. David probably would've jumped in hopes of saving the boy if not for six strong hands holding him back.

"You didn't know it was going to happen," Amanda said, pushing a lock of sweaty hair off his forehead. She knelt in front of him, ignoring the tightness in her legs. "We all made it just fine. Including you. It was the angle he hit it."

"I should've realized we'd loosened it." His eyes didn't meet hers, instead they twitched, shifting back and forth on the ground between them, but he didn't see the ground. He saw Diego falling. "If I'd stood on it, maybe I could have grabbed him before he fell."

"Or, he could have pulled you down with him." She gripped the sides of his face, his gaze finally meeting hers. She'd never seen so much guilt in his eyes. "You're *not* leaving me. You got that."

Desperation and fear fueled her words. "If you have to choose between saving someone else and saving yourself, you better choose *you* every damn time. You hear me?"

He held her gaze for several seconds. "All right." David's hand trembled as he took a swig of water.

They sat in the shade of a tree.

The landscape on the mountain-top prairie practically schiz-ophrenic from what they'd just climbed up. Thick grass swayed in the wind. The breeze was cool and it quickly dried the sweat that drenched her shirt.

Rodrigo, Miguel and Sal made their way down the mountain to where Diego had fallen. They said it was to see if he needed help, but from the quick glance she stole over the edge and the way his broken body had landed in unnatural angles, they were most likely just going down to confirm he'd died in the fall.

Fallon and Joaquin approached from the top of the trail where'd they had been watching the others backtrack.

"They're starting their way back up." Her voice shook.

"Is he?" Amanda didn't want to finish the question, she didn't want to say the word in front of David.

"Yeah," Fallon said, looking down at the ground, sniffing.

Joaquin crouched beside them. He lifted up his black baseball cap and wiped sweat from his forehead.

"How far behind did I set us?" David asked.

"This wasn't your fault." Her friend's voice was sharp. "You tried to help him. It was all a tragic accident."

Amanda was shocked she made it up that climb. Each step had felt as if the ground rolled and pitched, like she wasn't walking on craggy earth, but angry waves. Every time she'd tried to look up ahead, to see how much further they had to go, her vision narrowed. Nothing but gray rock. Ahead of her, beside her, below and behind her. Enveloping her.

The seed of a panic attack had taken root at her first step up the treacherous switchbacks, and each step had nourished it. The only way to keep it at bay had been to focus on the feet in front of her.

Her heart sank for the young man. When he'd signed up to help Joaquin, and her, he hadn't expected to die a terrifying death.

What plans had he had for tomorrow? Next week? The rest of his life? Who went about their day thinking Diego still walked this earth? That they'd soon see his boyish grin and bright eyes walk through their door.

Amanda had no plans for tomorrow.

Or next week, or even the rest of her life.

Until yesterday, the only people who'd expected her to walk back through the door were sitting on that mountain with her, either as part of the rescue party or being held captive up above. Did she have the responsibility of living through this now that her brother knew she was alive?

Rodrigo and the remaining two soldiers appeared at the top of the trail.

Miguel and Sal walked with their heads down, their shoulders rounded.

Miguel's eyes were red, his face wet.

Rodrigo was stoic, but rather than join the group he stood to the side and pulled a cross from the chain around his neck and held it tightly while his lips moved in quick prayer.

David looked up as they approached.

Sal cupped his shoulder. "Thank you."

"I didn't save him." His voice was a thick whisper.

"You tried. He knew that. In his final moments he knew someone cared."

David ducked his head, his fingers clumsily finding Amanda's.

She didn't have to look at him to know tears ran down his face.

Joaquin cleared his throat. "Should we take a few minutes? Regroup, go back over the plan?" He paused to join Amanda and David on the ground.

Fallon stood behind him, and the two soldiers paced behind her, their fingers on their guns and eyes scouting the tree line around them.

"We can still make it to the top, as much as I hate to say it, losing Diego doesn't mean we have to abort." Joaquin looked at each of them, holding their gazes before moving on to the next person. "But, what it does mean is we have to be extremely careful. And, if we need help, we have to ask for it."

"What're you going to do about…Diego?" Fallon asked. They were only ascending on this side of the mountain. The plan, the hope, was to steal a vehicle from Vargas and drive down the other side.

"We've done our best to secure him from scavengers," Sal said. "We'll come back for him."

The FBI agent blanched.

Amanda felt the same way. She appreciated their commitment, but at the same time, hoped their friend would be spared becoming some animal's dinner.

"Okay, from here, it's fairly flat," Joaquin said, drawing the conversation back to cheery topics, like how the rest of them could face death on the mountain. "We're going to be exposed in this field for a few hundred yards, but then we enter the woods again."

"Not that it's any better." Fallon crossed her arms over her chest. "Plenty of places for someone to hide."

"But more cover for us," David said. "We're just going to have to keep our eyes open."

Amanda was relieved to have him participate in the conversation.

"Yes. The forest is much more gentle, *mija*." Joaquin nodded in her direction.

Her cheeks burned. It wasn't a secret *she* was the lame one of the group, she'd just rather it not be thrown in her face every second.

"As we get closer to the top, we should start seeing some structures used for the mine," Joaquin said. "That's when we let the soldiers take the lead."

They all nodded.

She glanced around the silent group. Rodrigo was still praying. She hoped that in addition to praying for Diego, he prayed for their safety.

Fallon and Joaquin huddled close together. The blonde woman's gaze kept lingering on her friend's face.

*Maybe if we all survive...*

Sal and Miguel stood steel-faced, holding their rifles close to their chest. They were both as young as Diego. Boys.

When her gaze met David's, she found him studying her face. Sadness pinched his eyebrows together. His jaw muscles were so tight he could've been a statue. His brown eyes intense, as if he were trying to learn everything about her by sight alone. Everything that would come with a lifetime of knowing someone. He was trying to siphon it from her.

Amanda opened her mouth to speak, but instead his lips collided with hers. A desperate, painful kiss. He wasn't merely kissing her. He was committing her to memory.

Maybe even imprinting his own mouth on hers, scarring it so if ever touched by another man, there'd always be the memory of David there. Lingering.

"We're going to make it through this." She felt him nod against her face.

Joaquin roused them from their break.

They took their places in line again, only this time, David pulled up the rear.

The thigh-high prairie grass made shushing sounds as they traipsed through it. The path veered to the right and the opening of the forest welcomed them with shade, and also, foreboding.

It had grown quiet behind her.

Amanda glanced over her shoulder.

David lingered several feet behind, his back to her. He stared out over the prairie. Over the boulder that stood sentry over a treacherous path.

Over the spot where a young man, gripped by paralyzing fear, had fallen to his death.

# 45

It wasn't the first time Fallon saw someone die. Death was an occupational hazard.

It was seeing what the young man's death did to the mood of the group, and worst of all, David; that was a sucker punch to the gut.

The faster they made their way to the top, the faster they found Josh Williams, captured Rafael Vargas and safely made it back down the mountain, the better.

Leaves crunched under their feet. They marched on, in a straight line, like cattle heading to slaughter.

She wiped the sweat off her face, also hoping to wipe away negative thoughts.

The sun filtered through the leaves of the massive oaks. The air was significantly cooler with the higher altitude and shade, but sweat dripped down her stomach under her body armor.

The right side of the trail was a wall of shale, and the left was a tree-filled slope down to a stomach-churning drop-off. Wind rustled the leaves high overhead, but none of it wafted down to them. The air was still, thick. A canyon-locked doldrums.

Rodrigo pulled off the trail and wiped the sweat off his forehead with a red handkerchief. The soldier in front of her paused and the entire contingent gathered in a tight circle, catching their breath and wiping off sweat.

"It's past noon," Joaquin said. "Should we break for lunch?"

At the mere mention of food, Fallon's stomach grumbled. It felt wrong to eat, as if her brain was telling her to starve herself out of respect for the dead, but her body was saying screw that, it'd just made a thousand-plus foot ascent. Give it food.

"Sure, but just a quick one," she said. "We still have a lot of mountain to cover."

He flashed a smile. On the surface it seemed friendly enough. To the unaware eye, it'd said hey-we're-two-people-heading-the-same-direction. But the added wink said if-we-were-alone-I'd-kiss-you-six-ways-to-Sunday.

At least that was what she hoped it said.

"*Bomboncita*, this is a marathon," he said. "Sprinting it will only get someone hurt."

She scowled. Not for the chastising and the forced break, but for calling her '*sweetie.*' The only person alive who called her that was her mom, and it was usually wrapped in a sentence inquiring when she'd find a nice guy and settle down.

Joaquin's smirk proved he knew *she* knew what he'd said. He just didn't give a damn what she thought.

Everyone nibbled their sandwiches silently. Maybe it was exhaustion setting in. Or the rule to keep conversations to a minimum.

This was a solemn silence. Even Joaquin's teasing grin faded as quickly as a cloud moving across the sun.

David looked grimly at his food, as if he might be sick if he took a bite.

Amanda leaned in close, her mouth moving, but whatever words she said to him didn't cut through the silence of the forest.

The soldiers studied the map with Rodrigo. Their heads bent over the paper, the guide traced a path with his fingers.

The younger men looked up, their eyes scouting the trail and faces pinched, bleak.

She'd felt the same concern since they'd entered this part of the climb. If attacked, they could only run forward or backward.

As long as they were on this path, they were trapped.

"So this is your idea of a vacation, huh?" Joaquin reclined against the rock, his shoulder bumping into hers.

"Beaches are boring," Fallon said, taking a bite of her sandwich to hide her schoolgirl beam.

"Yeah, who wants to sit on white sand watch the ocean roll in." He flashed his own schoolboy smile.

*Maybe...*

"And cabana boys bringing me drinks..."

"Cabana boys?" He laughed. "Why would you need cabana boys when *I* would be more than willing to bring you drinks?" As soon as the last sentence dropped from his mouth, he pushed off the rock and joined the guide and soldiers.

She stared at his back. Was he flirting? With her?

*Not the time or the place, Weatherby.*

Fallon closed her eyes and listened to the forest, tuning her ears to what her eyes couldn't see. The leaves above them rustled with a breeze that wouldn't fall into the narrow canyon. Predator birds high overhead screeched.

More songbirds tweeted. Their songs happy, carefree, inappropriate. Like the person who tells a joke at a funeral.

A branch snapped above her.

She opened her eyes and took a few steps back from the rock. It towered over the trail by at least twenty feet, and more trees grew on top of it. Her breath held in her lungs, waiting to see if another sound followed. The birds paused their singing, but picked it right back up.

Fallon stepped off the trail, moving as far as she could before the ground pitched steeply down, but still couldn't see more than a foot or two into the top of the rock.

"Fal, what is it?" David asked.

"I heard something. Above me." She pushed up on her toes and craned her neck, but it only gave her another half inch of view.

"Could be a bear or a mountain lion," Joaquin said. "Maybe even a deer. This mountain range has a lot of wildlife."

Growing up near the big national park in south Texas, she'd spent plenty of weekends camping out in its mountains and wasn't scared off with a brief bear sighting.

Mountain lions were a different story. They were hunters. Stalking their prey, waiting until they had nowhere to run to attack.

Was it better to be stalked by an animal instead of a drug lord?

"We need to get moving," she said. "We've been in one place too long."

The soldiers nodded and everyone packed up their gear and got back in line.

If Fallon could've walked with her eyes closed, she would have. She didn't trust that whatever she'd heard was an innocuous forest sound. It felt intentional. Then with the absence of any further sounds, it felt accidental.

"What type of drinks would you like me to bring you, *bomboncita*?" Joaquin spoke behind her.

"What?" she whispered over her shoulder.

"While you're lounging on the beach. Piña Colada, *cerveza*, margarita…"

As he rattled off drinks, Fallon could almost feel the cool ocean breeze mingled with the warmth of the sun. The roar of the waves hummed.

He'd been right. It'd been way too long since she'd had a honest vacation. Considering that, unless she handed over Rafael Vargas on a silver platter she was most likely out of a job, she'd have plenty of time for a beach vacation.

With Joaquin.

*What the hell.*

The path ahead was straight, flat. Just a little bit further and they'd have to begin the next climb, another series of switchbacks, but these less steep and the trail would be lined with trees, less vertigo-inducing, less exposed.

She spun and walked backwards. "*Cerveza.*"

His eyes brightened and his mouth quirked up. "Good, I don't want to spend all my time mixing drinks."

"But you can't get off that easy, you'll have to do something else."

Was she really flirting?

An eyebrow shot up. "Oh, like what?"

"Adjust the umbrella, fan me if the breeze dies down."

Joaquin licked his lips. "Sunscreen? I could help with that as well."

A snarky retort sat on her lips, but a whizzing sound by her ear stole it.

He grunted and stumbled to a stop. His shoulder jerked back. Joaquin paused, as if disbelieving he'd really been shot before red seeped from the wound. One leg stepped forward, but it buckled and he hit the ground.

Amanda's wide eyes stared back, her hand clasped against her mouth, but the scream escaped anyway.

More bullets pinged around the forest, coming down from above.

She grabbed Joaquin around his chest and pulled him against the rock wall. The two soldiers leapt out from the trail, returning fire to the tree line above them.

David pushed Amanda against the wall and joined the soldiers. "Fal, you stay back, cover us."

Her eyes jumped over the landscape behind them. Everything looked sinister. The trees, the shadows. She glanced on the trail behind them. Thankfully it was empty, as was the path ahead.

The men ducked behind trees, bark flying as bullets struck.

She crouched to check on the fallen man. Blood streamed down his chest in a small, rivulet. His forehead was flush with sweat and he took deep breaths. Fallon pulled him forward and felt his back. Dry. There was no exit wound. The lack of gushing blood meant it either missed his artery or was lodged against it.

"Amanda," she said.

The woman was frozen to the rock. Her head turned, eyes closed.

"Amanda, come here, I need you to put pressure on his wound." Fallon pulled a long-sleeved shirt from her backpack and pressed it on Joaquin's shoulder.

Like a newborn calf, Amanda took a few stiff steps toward them and crouched down next to her friend, taking Fallon's place.

A branch broke above her in the pause of the gunfire, leaves fluttered down softly.

Gunfire erupted from the ground before her as David and the soldiers took advantage of the sniper's mistake.

A man's scream echoed and then, nothing.

Fallon shivered in the sudden silence. The songbirds took their music somewhere less violent. The predator birds flew on, giving up the fight to the bigger predator.

The men waited a minute before moving, checking to make sure there was only one shooter and not another waiting to take his place.

After several seconds passed, they joined them in the shadow of the rock.

"The good news is we got him," David said, popping the magazine from his gun. "The bad news is they know we're coming."

## 46

Amanda stared at her hands. The blood had congealed to a syrupy consistency. She tried to wipe it on her pants, but it only smeared, changing from a deep red to a salmon pink.

Joaquin rested against the rock while Fallon dressed his gunshot wound. "This is good for my street cred, no?" he joked, but a flash of pain across his face told her he'd rather keep his not-quite-a-bad-ass reputation.

"Shush," Fallon said, her lips pressed tight. "Your jokes aren't funny enough to waste your energy."

The soldiers and David approached.

It was all Amanda could do to not throw her arms around his neck and drag him back down the mountain.

"From what we can tell only one shooter," he said to the group. His gaze found hers and fell to her hands. "Here." He poured some of his water on her fingers and rubbed them, the pink fading away. "You okay?"

She could only nod. Her throat was raw from screaming during the brief gunfight. It'd lasted for less than a minute, but it felt like hours.

"Think he works for Vargas?" Fallon asked.

"Most likely," Sal said. "He might've just been out on patrol. Looks like he tracked us once we entered the forest."

Amanda shivered. "Do you think he alerted them?"

Miguel pulled a radio off his belt. "He had this on him, but it was off. So we wouldn't hear him. He might've radioed first, or not."

"But we can use it to hear them." Joaquin winced as he stood. "We might be able to hear where they are as we approach."

Her stomach dropped. They were at the point of no return. It was now late afternoon. The sun had started its descent, casting long gray shadows. The rock that served as their cover now felt like a monster, reaching over them, threatening to devour them all.

The dusk squeezed her lungs. One man had died. Another was hurt, at risk of dying if he lost any more blood.

Who was next? One of the other soldiers? Rodrigo, a man who grew up on the mountain and offered to lead them to Vargas?

Or, Fallon, someone who was only there to help her friend.

*Or, David. Please God, keep him safe.*

"We scouted the trail ahead a bit," David said. "Clear as far as we can tell. Another couple of miles and we should find a place where we can rest a few hours until it's time."

"How much more daylight do we have?" Amanda asked.

"This side of the mountain? Another hour or so," Joaquin said. "Don't worry, I won't slow us down. And if I do, leave me." He was pale and sweaty, a couple of wayward curls plastered to his fore-head. A pinprick of red poked through the bandage wrapped around his shoulder.

Fallon had guessed the bullet was keeping the bleeding from being worse, but what happened if it shifted. Would her friend bleed to death right in front of her?

"Does it hurt?" she asked.

"I've had heartbreaks that hurt worse." The truth was written in the grimace at the end of his sentence.

She turned to David, her hand outstretched. "Just one. For him."

He hesitated a second before pulling his backpack off his shoulder. "What about you?"

The pain was there, growling louder with each step. It would only be a matter of time before it morphed into withdrawal, shifting from aching muscles and bones to the dizzying, stomach-twisting need for a hit.

She'd needed a pill, or several, since Diego had fallen. Amanda had to be strong. Stronger than the pain. Stronger than her addiction. Stronger than her fear of facing the dark.

She needed to show David she could do this. Hike up a mountain, rescue Josh, capture Vargas. All the while dealing with a little discomfort from a cracked pelvis and an aching heart.

He shook two pills from the bottle. "Here, I'd feel better knowing you're not suffering."

Amanda frowned at the medicine in his outstretched hand. Was she an old dog that needed to be put down?

"Well, *salud*," Joaquin said, tipping his water bottle in her direction before tossing the pill down his throat.

They were quiet as they walked.

The soldiers, David and Fallon all had their guns at-the-ready.

A flock of birds squawked and cried as they settled into the trees for the night. The cacophony covered the sounds of their own footsteps. And, anyone who might be following them.

Each step toward the mine, toward Vargas, toward Josh filled her with heaviness, even though the narcotic rushing through her veins gave Amanda strength, courage.

What would she find when she got there? Was Josh even still alive?

There was no way of knowing that he hadn't died in the final frame of the video. A scene deleted for the sake of giving her what she so desperately needed.

Hope. Hope Josh was alive.

Hope she could save him.

Hope she could finally rest. Finally stop running from something and run *toward* something.

Hope she could finally go home.

Hug her parents.

Be happy with David.

The forest had deepened to ash gray by the time they finally reached the spot where they'd rest. Night seeped in as the sun fell to the west side of Prospera.

The ground was caved in, like someone had come in with an ice cream scoop and spooned out a chunk of the earth. Skinny trees grew in a haphazard circle, and scrubby brush jutted out from the base of boulders nearly as tall as Amanda.

It was the perfect place for them to hide out. Private, protected, yet they could have the element of surprise if anyone approached.

Fallon helped Joaquin to the ground.

His color was better, but the bandage was smeared with red.

"We're going to hike in a little closer and have a look." David pulled binoculars from his bag.

"Okay," Amanda said, shrugging her pack on her shoulders. "Let's go."

He stared at her for a second, then his gaze darted over her head before dropping his voice. "Mandy, baby, you stay here. I'm going with Sal and Miguel."

"No, I'm going with you, or you stay behind."

David glanced at the group, before gently pulling her away. "Look, I don't know what we're going to walk into—"

"Exactly, even more reason we're not splitting up." She took another step closer to him. The smell of his sweat tickled her nose. The sexy, athletic smell that took her back to their evening runs.

Back before she'd found Josh. Before she'd pissed off a drug lord. Before Josh had sacrificed himself for her.

Before her ex was tortured. Because of her.

"You wouldn't let me go without you," she added.

David's jaw flexed, then relaxed. "You're sure you don't want to rest?" He nodded to the remaining soldiers. "Let's go before it gets too dark."

Sal and Miguel took off in the lead.

"Thank you," Amanda whispered.

David squeezed her hand.

The temperature took a nosedive between the elevation and the approaching nighttime. Goosebumps erupted on her skin and her teeth chattered, but once they got back into their hiking rhythm her body warmed.

After a half hour, an orange light glowed on the horizon.

Miguel held up a hand and the group slowed. A sharp rock jutted from the ground.

David pointed at it and they crouch-walked to it. He pulled the binoculars from his pack and held them to his face.

Amanda narrowed her eyes, trying to see what was cloaked in dusk. The glow seemed to emanate from three areas.

The mountain rose up sharply to the right, as ominous as a black hole. The abandoned mine was built into this peak.

A generation ago, man rooted around the mountain's insides, violating it, excavating it for minerals. Now it was depleted, exploited. Tossed aside.

Amanda felt a pang of sympathy for the mountain.

David handed the binoculars to one of the soldiers. "There's a building with several lights on inside. Looks like a cabin. Adjacent to that is an old pen, probably where they kept animals. Right next to it is—"

"A barn." *Josh.*

He nodded. "How many men do you see?"

Miguel handed the binoculars to Sal. "Five. Three patrolling the main building, saw one walking around inside and another sitting outside the barn."

"Can I look?" Amanda needed to see for herself that this was all real. Somewhere inside the barn was Josh.

Somewhere inside the house was Vargas.

The binoculars were passed to her. It took a moment for everything to come into focus, but as David said, a long cabin sat on a plateau to the left.

They looked at the back side, there were only windows, no door leading inside.

She swung them to her right, to the barn sitting next to the mouth of the mine. It looked old, yet well-built. Rough tree trunks served as the exterior and a large stable door led inside.

The man who sat outside it looked bored; a forgotten cigarette in his mouth, he tossed a pocketknife into the dirt next to him, bent over to retrieve it and flicked his wrist again, sending it back to the ground.

Suddenly he jumped. He grabbed the knife and tossed his cigarette to the ground, stomping it out as he stood.

Amanda shifted to get a view of what'd startled him.

Three men walked around the side of the building. The first two she recognized right away from the hospital; the tall man with the greasy ponytail, his pockmarked skin visible through the distance. The shorter, heavier man followed.

They walked over to the door of the stable, talking to the guard.

A third man broke from them and walked toward her, David and the soldiers' hiding place.

His beige linen suit radiated in the glow of the rising moon. He lit a cigarette, his cheek hollowed as he inhaled.

A breeze blew behind her, barreling toward Vargas, lifting his hair. The skin puckered and pink where his ear had been. Vargas' eyes scanned the mountaintop darkness.

Up, down. Right, left.

He exhaled a cloud of smoke, momentarily obscuring her view of the cartel leader. When it dissipated, his light green eyes were staring straight.

His face impassive for a split second before it cracked into a wide, jackal sneer.

## 47

"Mandy, baby. Wake up, it's time."

Amanda jolted upright.

David crouched in front of her, half his face obscured in the shadow of the moonlight.

Miguel and Sal were behind him, their faces smudged with black tint.

Fallon was tucking blonde hair under her black baseball cap.

Joaquin shoved the magazine into the butt of his gun with his right hand, his injured left arm huddled close to his body.

Only Rodrigo stood to the side, the guide ordered to stay behind until someone came for him.

She hadn't expected to fall asleep when they'd made it back. Not after seeing the layout of the mine site, or the men guarding the grounds.

Especially not after seeing Vargas.

Or, him seeing her.

Could he really *see* her? They'd been hiding a good half mile from where he'd stood. There was no way he could see her peering out from behind a boulder in the dusk.

But…that look.

It hadn't been wasted on the night. It was meant for someone. For her.

"Are you ready for this?" David asked, rubbing her upper arms.

"Yeah. You?"

His Adam's apple bobbed as he swallowed. "I'm ready for it to be over." He pressed his lips tight. There were more words fighting to escape. David dropped his voice to a whisper. "I love you. You know that, right? Even when I wanted to hate you, I loved you."

She rested a hand against his face. Amanda deserved his hate so much more than his love. Why did Fate put her through so much turmoil just to get her in David's path? Was their relationship doomed from the beginning? Or, was all this, all the hurt, death, betrayal, simply to cement their love in something indestructible?

Amanda pushed on her toes and pressed her lips against his, wishing that they weren't about to go running into a drug lord's mountaintop lair, wishing they weren't trying to save her dying ex-boyfriend. Wishing that she wasn't going to jail when all this was over. "I love you," she said on the tail of their kiss.

She stepped away from him. If she didn't, there was a good chance she'd abandon this foolish notion they could save Josh and capture Vargas. Out of David's orbit, she focused on her wounded friend.

Joaquin pulled his cap on with his good arm. Sweat shone on his forehead. He looked even paler in the moonlight. A fresh bandage covered his gunshot wound, but a circle of red already marred it.

"I wish you'd stay behind," Amanda said. "We've got this."

"And, let you have all the fun? No way, *mija*."

The night was completely still. All the sounds of the forest were in deep sleep. Only the nocturnal predators prowled. Is that what they were now?

Amanda didn't feel like a predator. Seeing Vargas made her feel more like prey than ever before.

A fly buzzing straight into a spider's web.

"This shouldn't take long," Fallon said. "Miguel and I will go after Vargas. Joaquin and Sal stand guard at the mine, Amanda and David get Josh. Five men, four, five good shots is all we need." She paused to look around the group. Full of confidence, so sure of how this would all happen. As if the world would bend to her command. Her eyes rested on Amanda. "You've got this." Like a coach preparing them for a game, instead of a raid.

They followed the same path back to the mine site. Single file, in the same order. Joaquin's labored breathing interrupted by the whistling mountaintop wind.

When they reached the boulder, they ducked behind it.

The orange flood lights were still on outside the buildings, but the inside was dark.

David pulled out the binoculars again. He held them to his face for what felt like several long minutes. "Let's go."

Amanda's breath hitched. Two simple words that would begin the end of a very long journey.

*This* was the moment she'd waited for since Josh had left her in Chicago, since she'd chased him to Mexico, found him and lost him again.

Since her goal had changed from punishing Josh to saving him.

The soldiers and Fallon took the lead. They moved faster, covering the half mile of rocky, rutted terrain in what felt like seconds.

Time moved strangely. It passed too slow as they ascended, but suddenly they were there. Like waiting to graduate college. Years slogged by with a snail's pace, but the moment of walking across the stage was over in a blink of an eye. Much too fast for the effort put into getting *to* that moment.

They paused behind an abandoned piece of equipment.

Miguel and Fallon paired up, readying for the assault on Vargas.

Sal and Joaquin disappeared into the shadows outside the light pool, slinking to their outpost near the mouth of the mine, where they'd have the best view of the barn and the cabin.

David grabbed Amanda's hand. His face was stoic, somber. Scared.

She tried to pull up her mouth into a reassuring grin, but it came out as a grimace.

He nodded to Fallon and they left the protection of the shadows.

Another gust of wind covered any sounds their steps might've made, but it also kicked up a plume of dirt.

Amanda hesitated, afraid someone would emerge from the darkness once the dust fell, but it was still just them when they made it to the stable.

David waited at the door, pushing it open an inch, pausing to make sure it was safe before opening it wide enough for them to slip in.

Her nose tingled at the earthy smell of hay. The barn was pitch black. Her eyes had adjusted to the outside darkness, but they'd moonlight guiding them.

David clicked on a dull flashlight, keeping it low to the ground.

She closed her eyes and called up the video in her mind. The light that'd filtered in was sharp and bright with the late afternoon harshness of an angry sun, not the gentle glow of the morning star. If she was right, they'd only need to search the stalls on the left-hand side.

They walked down the hallway.

Tacks and saddle gear cast long shadows on the wall. No animals resided in the stable, but the warm smell of horse sweat lingered in the air.

She reached the second to last stall and peeked in.

A figure lay prone on the floor, huddled under the window.

Amanda pushed the door open. A mound of flesh. That was what she saw. If it was Josh, she couldn't tell.

She moved closer, but had to step back.

The smell of rot attacked her, making her gag. She licked her lips and opened her mouth, determined to make it all the way across the room without getting sick.

Like in the video, Josh was naked. Stubble covered his head, growing between cuts and abrasions. He laid in the fetal position, his maimed hand tucked against his body.

At a foot away, she saw his back rising. Shallow breaths, not enough to disturb the flies attacking his flesh.

"Shoo," she waved them away.

She knelt beside his head.

His eyes jerked wildly beneath his lids. Sweat dripped down his sallow skin, although it was cold enough to see her breath. She rested a hand on his forehead and recoiled. He was so feverish it nearly scalded her.

How much of this was her doing? Sure, he'd been stealing from the very man who'd tortured him, but Josh was clever. He would've gotten away with it.

"Oh Josh, what have they done to you?" There would be no way he could walk out of there. Carried maybe, once Vargas was in custody.

He stirred at the sound of her voice. His gaze bounced around the room, confused, as if he woke into a nightmare. When his eyes finally met hers, his lids fluttered closed. "Amanda," his voice was weak. "No. No. You're not here."

"I am, David, too." She glanced behind her. "We're going to get you home, but you have to stand, walk."

Josh rolled into her, wrapping his maimed arm around her, tucking his face in her lap. A child hiding from monsters.

His body shook. Big, deep quakes. The kind that could only come with sobs. "I want to go home," he cried.

A shudder rocketed through her body. The Josh she knew was gone. The man lying there was a hallowed out shell. Shattered to the point that none of the charm and cocky self-confidence was there. Vargas' men had managed to break him down to something that only resembled a man on the outside, but inside he was a raw nerve.

"I know, honey, that's why we're here. I need you to stand." Amanda swallowed, banishing the knot in her throat. She'd cry for him later, but now she had to be strong.

For him. For her.

Footsteps shook the floor under her.

David knelt across from her. Lines crossed his forehead. He sniffed and cleared his throat. "Hey man, we're going to get you out of here."

He shook his head. "Too late."

Amanda's exes eyed each other. "I didn't get her home," David said. "All this for nothing. I'm sorry."

Josh closed his eyes in a long, slow blink. "Your job's not done."

He rolled over, his head still cradled in her lap. His sobs had stopped, his breathing slowed, but his body still twitched in feverish shivers.

She studied his eyes while she rocked him like a newborn. His green irises were gone, dilated pupils taking over. He looked up, but his gaze missed her, instead staring at the ceiling before it fluttered down and found her.

Their entire relationship flashed through her mind. The first kiss, the fights, the makeups, the suspicion, the flirtatious glances. The betrayal. His sacrifice to save her.

A filthy, scabbed hand reached up and caressed her cheek. "You know, right?" A tear trailed down his face.

Amanda opened her mouth, but her voice refused to work. She gripped his hand. "Know what?" Her voice came out a watery whisper.

He rubbed her knuckles with his thumb and smiled. That handsome grin, the self-assured one that could manipulate the devil. Josh was still in there, packed away where the final crack of Vargas' whip couldn't touch him. "You know I love you." He closed his eyes. His tongue darted out and licked his parched lips. "And, I don't deserve you to love me back." His head lolled to one side.

She waited for his next inhale, but his lungs took too long. Amanda shook him. "You asshole, no you don't get to do this."

His eyelids closed and his lips parted. Those gorgeous full lips that used to sneak kisses from her in his office when no one was looking.

"It's a trap." Josh's eyes closed. "He knows you're here." The words floated out on his last breath and his shivering stopped.

She waited several long seconds for his next inhale, but it never came. She put her hand on his chest, but nothing beat beneath it.

He slipped out of this world so quietly.

A heartbeat.

That's all it took for Josh to leave her world.

A breath.

A breath stood between his being alive and dying.

He'd been a huge part of her life for nearly five years.

What was it going to feel like to not have him there? Like a house empty of furniture? Would she feel a gaping hole where Josh once was?

Would it ever heal?

It was only when the first shots rang out that his final words sunk it.

*It's a trap. He knows you're here.*

# 48

Josh's head hit the floor when David pulled her away.

Her ex-boyfriend's death grip on her hand was tight. Their entwined fingers slowly pulled apart.

Was Josh trying to cling to her even in the afterlife? Or, was she afraid to let him go?

Shouts, whistles, gunfire. Flashes of light. A fuse that'd been lit slowly burned down and then...*boom*. Chaos detonated in an instant.

They jogged down the stable, light from the flashlight bouncing on the floor. The door pulled open and the man who'd been sitting outside earlier entered the doorframe.

David flashed the light in the man's face and fired his weapon.

They hurdled over his body and entered a battlefield. Flashes flared from various sides, gunfire popping from all directions.

Smoke filled the air. People shouted, ran in various directions.

If David hadn't been holding her hand, Amanda wouldn't have known which was him.

He pulled her to the mouth of the mine. "Joaquin," he half-whispered, half-shouted, but her friend didn't emerge.

They ducked into the shadow and David gripped her shoulders, his face close to hers. "Mandy, listen to me, I want you to stay right here. Don't move for anyone but me. I'll come back for you when it's safe."

He let go of her, started to run back into the fray, but she clung to him so tightly his shirt ripped when he tried to pull away. She just lost Josh, she couldn't lose him, too.

"No, no, no."

"Baby, I'll be fine. You've got your gun?" She nodded. "Use it."

Amanda backed into the mine. The darkness devoured her. There was no difference between having her eyes open or closed. She shuffled along the wall, sharp stones jabbing her back, slimy rocks beneath her fingertips. Stale air, dust, rot, even something with a faint chemical tang assaulted her nose, forcing tears to her eyes.

Water dripped somewhere far away, the pings echoing, the sound like concentric circles, growing, bouncing off the various surfaces.

She stopped when her shoulder bumped into a crooked wooden support beam. She was still close enough to the mouth to see people running and the flashes of gunfire, but hidden away to satisfy David's request.

Her legs gave out, the sharp edges cutting into her back as she slid to the ground.

She'd been so close. A day earlier and she could've saved him. Hell, hours earlier.

They should've rushed right in. Shot Vargas as he sucked on his cigarette. Gone after the others. They wouldn't have expected it. That was why Vargas had smiled. Like the ultimate predator, he'd sniffed them on the wind.

Shouts outside the mine grew louder. One of Vargas' goons ran by, something flaming in his hand. He tossed it onto the roof of the stable, the orange glow disappearing for a moment before spreading.

"Josh." His name came out on a choked cry.

He was gone. His body was growing cold.

The flies were finally getting their meal. What did it matter if he burned?

Her legs twitched, yearning to go in there and pull out his body, to at least give his mother something to mourn, but long shadows approached her. Running.

*David?*

Amanda almost popped up from her hiding spot, but Vargas' profile flew past her, followed by the tall, long-haired man.

Her heart skidded to a stop before taking off racing in the other direction pumping freezing dread throughout her body. Her lungs tightened, refusing to take in the stagnant air.

The men hid in the shadows across from her. Two sets of labored breathing. Did they know she was there?

Could she slip back outside? Find David?

Every sound was magnified in the antechamber of the mine. Something scratched in the dirt next to her. It could've been ten feet away, but it felt like she could reach out and touch it.

The men murmured in Spanish, their disembodied words enveloping her.

A whimper bubbled up her throat, but she swallowed it back. Hysteria stirred in her ribcage, stretching its wings, threatening to escape.

She had to get out there. David would understand.

Amanda took a deep, trembling breath and slowly pulled herself to standing, using the rock wall to do what her broken body couldn't. She reached up and a sharp rock sliced into her palm, sending searing bolt down her arm. A muffled mewl escaped her throat before she could stop it.

A sharp intake of breath inside the abyss answered her.

She'd given herself away.

She held her breath. Her fingers traveled along her waistband, finding the cold metal barrel clinging to her hip.

The gunfire had paused, but the crackling sound of fire grew louder. If she stayed silent, maybe they'd think she was further inside.

Approaching footsteps crunched. Fallon entered the mine. Wisps of her blonde hair fell from her cap. Her chest heaved as she stood in the glow of the outside light.

Had David sent her? Was it over?

The woman opened her mouth as if she were about to speak when the goon shuffled from his hiding place.

He rushed the FBI agent, his big body barreling toward her. Like a graceful matador, Fallon stepped out of his way, but the shoulder of the bull clipped her and she stumbled back, her gun hit the dirt in a thud.

She jumped into a martial arts ready pose, readying for the man to come back from more.

He righted himself, and tried the same move. This time she jabbed her elbow between his shoulder blades. He stumbled, landing on his hands and knees.

Fallon kicked his backside, shoving him face first into the dirt. She jumped back into ready position, hands up, feet light.

The man lay there for several seconds. In one quick move, he sat up, twisted and threw a handful of dirt into her face.

She screamed and cursed, rubbing her face into her shoulder.

The man used her distraction to hit her in the stomach.

Air whooshed from her lungs in a grunt. She took a blind step back, trying to right herself, but her feet got tangled up and Fallon fell backwards.

A dark object jutted from the ground. In slow motion, Amanda watched as the woman's head fell right on it. Fallon's body went limp.

The goon laughed and straddled her body. The orange glow from outside glinted off his gun.

*No.*

Her legs twitched, eager to help the downed woman, but David's command echoed in her mind. Stay hidden. Don't move unless it's for him. He'll come for her.

She could stay there. Out of sight. Let Vargas and his goon think that Fallon was the only one in the dark cave. Amanda could hide from the drug lord, but she could never hide from herself. A person was only as good as her actions.

She couldn't save Josh, but she'd do her damnedest to save Fallon.

Amanda jumped up from her hiding spot and took aim. She exhaled and squeezed the trigger.

His head jerked as the bullet struck. He stumbled back, sideways. Like a drunk unable to find his footing.

She fired again, not hitting him, but the sound echoed again and again and again.

The goon fell to his knees and tumbled to the side.

Amanda started to run over to check on Fallon, but the ground shook beneath her feet. A piercing screech overtook the echoing gunfire.

At first it was far away, but it grew louder, closer.

Air rushed up like a surging geyser. Cold, stale, a bit sour. A deeper darkness emerged from inside the earth. This darkness was different. It wasn't the empty gaping void. It was teeming with life.

Black on black on black.

The cries grew louder.

Amanda had no choice but to throw her body against the floor.

The colony of bats flowed over her. Their wings, claws catching her shirt, pulling her cap off.

The silence in their wake was painful. She leaned up, Fallon lay next to her. The woman's chest rising in slow breaths.

Vargas emerged from the shadows.

"Hello, Amanda."

# 49

Dirt rained down between them.

Even in the weak glow from the fire, she could see his hair was matted with dirt. Vargas' normally pristine beige suit was filthy. A large tear cut down the side of his shirt, the bottom of one leg of his pants was torn away, revealing fine leather shoes that were completely inappropriate for hiding out in an abandoned mine.

The drug lord stepped over a pool of dark blood encircling his henchman's head.

Had she really killed him? It'd felt like a video game when she shot him. As if the game would end, someone would hit reset and they'd start back over.

"It took you long enough." Vargas pulled a pack of cigarettes from his pocket. His hand trembled as he lit it with a match.

"Wait, you don't know what gases—" Amanda waited for an explosion.

What kind of mine was this? What noxious fumes were poisoning them?

"Who the hell cares," he spat. "You fired twice and all you did was piss off a colony of bats."

She scooted back, feeling behind her for her gun. She'd lost track of the weapon ducking the bats. The ground rumbled beneath her again, like a hungry giant. She closed her eyes against the second storm of falling dirt.

"What did you think of my gifts?" Vargas asked. His voice lost the edge, was soft, congenial.

Anger flashed through Amanda's body, heating her from within. She scooted back again, still no gun. "My thank you notes must have gotten lost in the mail." She had to keep him talking. To give Fallon time to wake up, or for David to find them.

His face lit up with the drag of his cigarette. "Brutal, but effective, I admit." He stepped over Fallon. Vargas was now just two feet in front of her. "Did you make it in time? To Josh?" He exhaled, a long, jagged breath. "You know, I couldn't decide if it would be better for him to die before you got there, or if he died in your arms. Both seemed equally...damaging. Shame only one scenario could play out with him. But maybe with David... Tell, me Amanda, which was it? I can test the other with David. You can tell me which hurt worse."

Something deep within her sprung to life. Something primal, protective. Love, when tilted on its axis, turned into a spear, ready to pierce anyone who threatened David.

It was too late for Josh, but the love she'd felt for him was still there. Barbed, ready to protect his memory.

Amanda lurched forward, like an attacking animal. She threw her body into the drug lord's torso, knocking him backwards, out of the pool of light and back into total darkness.

Stunned, Vargas didn't move, and she pummeled him with her fists, shrieking with the furor of a toddler's temper tantrum.

She was ill-positioned. None of her punches hit above his chest.

The cartel leader shoved her off him.

She fell back. Could feel him shuffling around in the darkness. Was he searching for his own weapon?

Amanda had to get back into the light, back to Fallon, to where David could see her if he came for her.

She flipped over and crawled forward on her elbows, but Vargas grabbed her ankles and pulled her back to him.

Amanda twirled, kicking and twisting, but he tightened his grip, his fingernails digging into her skin through her pants.

She screamed, summoning her strength from her broken pelvis, fueling it with all the hurt, physical and emotional, that she'd felt since she'd first laid eyes on this man.

He knelt over her, his legs pressing on the outside of hers. His hands flailed, trying to keep up with her thrashing. One ankle came out of his grasp and it landed in the softness of his torso.

She spun and pushed up into a crouching run back toward Fallon. Then she saw it.

Fallon's weapon. A hair's breadth from where the woman fell.

Amanda skidded to a stop next to her, palming the firearm.

The woman stirred and moaned.

"Shhhh," she breathed. "Don't move."

Fire ripped through her head as Vargas grabbed a handful of her hair, dragging her back into the darkness.

"You think you're so smart?" he growled.

"I've beaten you twice." Amanda gritted out. Tears rushed her eyes. "Third time shouldn't be too hard."

Rocks and stones clawed at her as he dragged her over the rough mine floor.

Her feet tried to gain purchase on the ground, but they slipped. One hand fought his, trying to disentangle it from her hair while the other held tight to the gun.

Finally, one heel caught a rock, giving her enough leverage to twist and fire in his direction.

Vargas dropped her. The bullet missed its intended target and instead pinged into the mineshaft.

The blast reverberated. An auditory avalanche that picked up momentum as it sped deep into the hole.

The ground shook.

More severely this time.

Enough that seismologists might think an earthquake was imminent.

Amanda stood, holding her arms out for balance.

Beams of light crisscrossed the shaft. Momentarily illuminating the drug lord's cruel face.

Her ears rang, fighting the rumbling rising up from deep inside the earth.

She heard someone call her name, but it felt distant. Miles away. A lifetime away.

Amanda held the gun out, preparing to squeeze the trigger once more when Vargas tackled her again.

Her right arm pulled free and she held it against his stomach, but the ground shifted. Not a gentle roll, but a shocking lurch that pulled them apart.

The gun went off and someone moaned.

She didn't wait to see if it hit him or not.

The ground bucked like an angry bronco. This time throwing her up, helping her to her feet.

She ignored the agony flying through her body and sprinted toward Fallon.

It was coming again. The same push of air rising up from the deep, but this one was different from the bat colony.

This one was like an angry god.

It wouldn't be appeased until it had a sacrifice.

The woman stirred. She'd rolled to one side, trying to push herself up.

Amanda came behind her, cupping her hands under her armpits, pulling with all of her strength. "We have to go, it's going to collapse."

The roar was all encompassing.

Support beams groaned and cracked. The shift of air sucked them in and expelled them at the same time.

Fallon ran beside her, loose, wobbly steps.

The mouth of the mine was just a few feet away.

Figures stood in the courtyard. Friends or foes, it didn't matter. They had to get out.

The tidal wave of debris nipped at their backs. Pushing them forward.

"Jump," Fallon said, her eyes focused and alert. "We won't make it."

They launched forward at the same time, and when they did, they picked up a current of air. Amanda felt like a bird being blown into a hurricane.

She hit the hard ground, knocking all the breath from her lungs. The blast of air blew past her. Hot, stale. Full of dirt and debris that'd never seen the light of day.

The cloud passed and she looked up.

Fallon coughed beside her.

A tall figured limped toward her, backlit by the rising sun, his body outlined in the lingering dust.

Pain sliced through her as she stood, but Amanda ignored it. Nothing would ever hurt again.

She jogged toward him, falling into David when he was close enough to catch her.

# 50

The machines beeped with the rhythm of a metronome. How did this sound not drive Amanda crazy when she was in the hospital?

Maybe it did. Or, perhaps her body was so focused on healing it'd become numb to the incessant beep.

It was the same hospital, but a different room. It had the same whitewashed, cinderblock walls. Same threadbare blanket covering the bed. Same warped, dirty mirror over the sink. The only distinction was the orientation, the window faced the east.

The soft glow of the rising sun kissed Joaquin's sleeping face.

The sheets were tucked under his arms. His chest was mostly bare, except for the bandages covering the area where the surgeons had removed the bullet lodged in his shoulder.

"Anything?" Fallon appeared in the doorway. The steam from two cups of coffee wafting around her face.

Amanda took one of the cups from her. "He stirred a couple of hours ago."

The woman pulled the chair up on the other side of his bed. She took Joaquin's hand, stroking it.

In the battle, the bullet wound had worsened. His breathing had been shallow and his face white when they'd found him. Luckily, the drive down the mountain in one Vargas' cars took much less time than the climb.

Amanda thought they'd lost him by the time they rushed him into the hospital, but the doctors had assured her they could save him.

She planned to hold them to it.

David's deep voice came into earshot outside the door, speaking a halting Spanish.

Fallon laughed softly. "He's so butchering that poor language."

"Okay, *muchas gracias.*" He entered the room, dropping Joaquin's phone on the nightstand. His gaze collided with Amanda's; a deep green-gray shiner cushioned one of his eyes.

Her heart somersaulted. It'd done that every time she saw or heard him since she'd come out of the mine. She'd prepared herself to find him dead. To spend the rest of her life alone, both David and Josh gone. When he'd held her, when he'd murmured her name over and over...

It was over.

It was just beginning.

"That was Miguel and Sal's commander. They found Rodrigo hiding, he's fine."

"And Diego?" It'd felt like years ago when Amanda had watched the young man fall to his death.

"They got him," David said, the tightness in his voice told her it would bother him for a long time, if not forever. "What they don't know about is Vargas. They don't want to declare him dead until they find a body." He stood behind her, massaging the back of her neck. "How're you doing?"

"Fine," Amanda said, leaning into him.

The real answer was complicated.

David was alive. Joaquin and Fallon safe.

Amanda had even managed to come out with only minor injuries. She wasn't really fine, but she was better than so many alternative scenarios.

In the twenty-four hours since they'd come off the mountain, her pain hummed at a three, mostly from the adrenalin. Now that was waning, Amanda could feel it crawling up the scale, but she refused to acknowledge it.

She was coming off the pills, effective immediately.

"Talk, talk, talk," Joaquin murmured. "How can I sleep with all this noise?" His eyes fluttered open and he shifted in the bed, trying to sit up.

"Hang on." Fallon leapt up and adjusted his pillows. "Better?"

He nodded and settled back in. "So, did we get the bad guy?"

"Mandy shot him." Pride lifted David's words. "Again."

"And his top enforcer," Fallon interjected, smiling at her from across the bed. "She saved me. Twice."

"*Mija,* I always believed in you."

Amanda bowed her head. Heat crept across her face and flowed down her neck. Somehow killing two men didn't feel like anything to be proud of.

She kept telling herself their deaths were simply a side effect of saving her friends. It helped. Some. It was also why she'd volunteered to sit the overnight shift with Joaquin. Every time she closed her eyes, she replayed the fight in the mine. Could feel Vargas' grip burning into her.

"Injury report?" Joaquin asked.

"Miguel was grazed on the thigh, Sal and Rodrigo are fine," Fallon said. "I've got a concussion."

"Tweaked my bad knee, but I'll be fine," David said. "Not sure if you remember, but the bullet in your shoulder shifted, we got you here just in time."

Amanda looked at the scabs on her palms. The scrapes and cuts had been thoroughly cleaned by the nurses she'd gotten to know during her stay. They were none too happy to see her again, especially with injuries that indicated she'd done more than sit and heal. Luckily, nothing was deep enough to need stitches. "I'm just a little banged up," she said.

"And, Josh?"

The air froze in the room at Joaquin's question.

David cupped her shoulders.

She stared at the blanket. Josh was the second reason she couldn't close her eyes. If it wasn't Vargas, she'd see her ex dying. Broken. Body and spirit. He'd given up. He'd lost the vibrancy for life, and that sliced through her heart.

What if it wasn't giving up? What if he'd held on?

For her.

Would it have mattered if they'd arrived two days earlier or two days later? Was his will to live tied directly to Amanda? To warn her it wasn't going to be a simple in and out mission. Maybe he hadn't given up.

Maybe he'd fulfilled his destiny.

Joaquin's hand found hers and he squeezed. "I'm sorry, Amanda." Tears glistened in his dark eyes.

She shook her head. "He didn't die alone. That's all that matters."

The doctor and nurse rounded the corner, shooing the three Americans out the door.

Amanda stood to leave, but her friend held tighter. "What's next?" he asked, his voice laced with concern and his brow wound tight.

She glanced across the bed at Fallon. Silently reminding her of their agreement, holding her to it. "I should probably go home, but I promise to call and check on you."

Joaquin's eyes called her a liar, but he nodded and let her go.

"I'll be right there," David's friend said.

Amanda glanced over her shoulder, just long enough to see Fallon lower her face to Joaquin's.

Maybe they could have the happily ever after she couldn't.

# 51

The landscaped whirred by. Beige sand smeared by a handful of green trees, interrupted by the occasional billboard advertising a variety of legal services.

Unfortunately for Amanda, none of the personal injury or immigration attorneys could help her. Was there someone who specialized in white collar criminals dodging authorities? Probably, but she wouldn't see *that* on a billboard.

David squeezed her hand, as if he knew what she was thinking.

He'd had the option to sit in the front with Fallon, but he'd chosen the backseat. It was such a simple gesture, but she'd held her breath to see which door handle he reached for.

El Paso came into view. The final miles of a journey that'd started early one spring morning more than a year ago.

Like a long race, Amanda yearned to sprint to the finish line, but she also wanted to hold back, to start over, even knowing the hurt along the way. Would she have taken a different route? Or, was the path she'd chosen the only logical one?

She felt someone looking at her and glanced in David's direction, but he studied the landscape out his window.

Her gaze met Fallon's in the rearview mirror.

Amanda smiled. Could she call her a friend?

That might be too…familiar. But what else do you call someone whose life you saved?

There had never been a question about doing it, but after witnessing the stolen kiss between Fallon and Joaquin, she was even happier she got the woman out of the mine.

Joaquin. The more miles racked up between them, the more she missed her friend. It was amazing how much someone could become a substantial part of one's life in such a short period of time.

That was what this journey had been about. Short, intense connections with people she would've never met if she hadn't taken the job at JWI or dated Josh.

Friendships formed over bonds tighter than shared employment or similar hobbies. After just a few days, she'd trusted them with her life. With her secrets. Amanda protected those bonds with the ferocity of a mother protecting her nest. They may not thrive or exist after she went back to Chicago, but she still held tight.

The car slowed and they exited the highway.

She didn't pay attention to what was passing by outside. Instead, she studied her and David's hands. How his tanned skin enveloped her bandaged palm. The cuts on his knuckles covered by scabs. The warmth growing between them.

Amanda could almost feel their jointly beating pulses, synced after too much time apart.

They were alive. Together.

"This isn't the way to your office."

His words drew her to the outside world. Instead of heading toward the FBI office in downtown El Paso, they were pulling into a bus terminal's parking lot.

"What are you doing?" Amanda scooted to the edge of her seat.

Fallon shoved the car into park and spoke into the rearview mirror. "I'll say you died in the mine collapse and it was too dangerous to recover your bodies."

The words hovered in the car before they collided with Amanda's brain.

"No."

"What do you mean 'no'?" That line appeared between the FBI agent's eyes, the one that made her look as if she'd lived many more lifetimes than her age.

"We had a deal. You're supposed to arrest me."

Fallon sighed and twisted in her seat. "Amanda, I'm giving you an out."

"I'm tired of running. That's all I've been doing for these last two years. It's time to go home."

David squeezed her hand. "I'll be right there with you."

She took a deep breath. "You won't. You can't. You'll be there until they take me away, and then you'll be at the trial. You'll stay in Chicago to come see me every opportunity. You'll find a way to make a life in a place that is foreign to you, for me. I'll love you for it. And, hate you for it. Because my punishment shouldn't become your prison sentence."

Fallon pressed her lips into a tight white line. "You're missing the point. We don't know for sure Vargas is dead. If he's not, someone else from his organization will step in, and they'll want to make an example out of you. We can't keep you safe, not for the long haul." She nodded in David's direction without breaking eye contact. "Neither of you. One day, maybe years from now, when the memory of this doesn't wake you up gasping for air is when they come after you, or after him."

What had been a roomy sedan a few moments ago collapsed into a claustrophobic coffin. Amanda pushed open the car door and the smell of bus exhaust and rotting trash assaulted her nose with the rising heat. The world twisted and trembled, and just when she felt her knees loosen, David was there to catch her.

"Mandy?"

"I'm fine. Just stood up too quickly." Her head pounded, but was it detoxing or because Fallon was right?

She'd lost Josh. She won David.

She'd lost Vargas. She won her life back. Her family back.

Hadn't she? What life would they have if they were constantly waiting for one of Vargas' people to appear from a dark corner?

Most of the drug lord's mountaintop crew had perished. One man had lived long enough to say he thought the mine had a back entrance, but the cave-in might have rendered it useless. Just because Vargas died didn't mean his empire went with him. There'd always be someone willing to step up and lead. Old grudges didn't die; they just became someone else's priority. The next leader's opportunity to show he was stronger than the last. The best way to do that would be to settle old scores.

A *tabula rasa*.

"You know I'm right," Fallon said.

"I'm not running," Amanda said through gritted teeth, begging the rising acid to stay put. "That's not our deal."

"That was before." Her voice was sharp, tired, but her face was gentle.

A bus rolled by, a cloud of dust and fumes followed in its wake.

David's jaw flexed and loosened as his gaze followed the lumbering bus departing for its journey. After several seconds, he pulled her into a tight embrace.

His scent taking over the odors of the parking lot. Warm and safe pushing out the hot and pungent.

"She's right," he whispered into her ear. "He'll come after us."

She pulled back, but he wouldn't let her go. "I have to do this."

"It was always about Josh. He's dead, Mandy. You don't have to keep paying for his crimes."

Amanda looked at the buses lined up. Mandy Jackson had been born in one, on a long journey from Chicago to Texas. She'd grown into Mandy Martin in south Texas.

Who would she be when she emerged at the end of the next journey? Would she like that person? Would David love her?

"I can't run away again." The words barely made it out of her throat.

He rested his forehead on hers. "There's a difference between running from something and running *to* something." He squeezed her hands. "Run toward *us*."

She nodded and took a deep breath.

Would they have to spend the rest of their lives looking over their shoulders?

"How will it work?"

"You know how to disappear, you've done it before. Don't tell me where you're going. The report will list you both as dead, which I'm sure will get back to Vargas' people. If he's alive, hopefully he'll be satisfied. If he's not, that should knock you down the priority list for whoever takes over." Fallon pulled a thick wad of cash from her purse. "I don't know how far this will get you, but it's all the cash I have."

Amanda broke from David's embrace and stood toe to toe with Fallon.

Could she ever be as unselfish as her? A woman willing to give up her career to save them. A woman who risked her life to help Amanda, the person David loved instead of her.

"Why?" she whispered.

Fallon looked away, sighing. "Not every crime deserves prison." She met her eyes again. "Love him, harder than he loves you. Promise me, okay?"

Amanda nodded before pulling the woman into a tight embrace. Fallon tensed for a moment, as if she weren't sure what to do with the hug, but then relaxed and gripped her back.

"Take care of Joaquin for me," she said. "Be happy with him."

The woman pulled back and smiled. Her eyes glistened, but she quickly blinked back the tears. "Get out of here. Go wherever you want, maybe stay away from the border."

They watched her retreating car until it merged into traffic and was lost in the sea of vehicles.

David reached for her hand. "Where do you want to go?"

"It doesn't matter, as long as it's *us*."

The automatic doors opened.

They paused, the air conditioning washing over them, welcoming them to their new life.

A loudspeaker announced a departing bus.

Last call.

## The End

# NOTE TO MY READERS

Thank you for joining Amanda on her journey. I'll admit, I'm going to really miss her, David, Josh, Shiloh, Joaquin and Fallon. I feel so honored to get to know them all.

If you have a moment to spare, please share your thoughts on Prospera Pass on the site where you purchased it, or Goodreads and BookBub (writing it in fireworks would be cool, too! Be sure to snap pictures!). Reviews help readers discover new stories to fall in love with.

While Amanda's story ends, there's so many new characters whose stories I can't wait to share. You can sign up for my newsletter to learn more about new releases, book signings and giveaways.

Until next time!

Kim

# ACKNOWLEDGMENTS

Thank you to so many of you who helped push me along as I finished Amanda's story. To my husband Colby, for his unwavering support. Thank you to my wonderful parents, my sister Angie and brother-in-law Mike for always cheering me on.

To Carol Barreyre for naming this baby. To my girls C.A. Szarek, Susan Sheehey and Sarah Hamilton for being there for probably the hardest chapter I've ever had to write - and for having the hugs and wine waiting. Thank you to Christine Broderson for being my guinea pig - I hope the weird glowing goes away soon. My eternal gratitude to my friend and fellow writer Jeff Bacot. It's our loss for the stories you've left untold.

And, finally, thank you! The relationship between readers and authors is one built on trust. Thank you for trusting me with your time.

# ABOUT THE AUTHOR

Kimberly Packard is an award-winning author of women's fiction. She began visiting her spot on the shelves at libraries and bookstores at a young age, gazing between the Os and the Qs.

When she isn't writing, she can be found running, doing a poor imitation of yoga or curled up with a book. She resides in Texas with her husband Colby, a clever cat named Oliver and a yellow lab named Charlie.

Her debut novel, *Phoenix*, was awarded as Best General Fiction of 2013 by the Texas Association of Authors.

*For more information:*
www.kimberlypackard.com
kimberly@kimberlypackard.com

# ALSO BY KIMBERLY PACKARD

The Phoenix Series

Phoenix | Phoenix Book 1

Pardon Falls | Phoenix Book 2

Standalone Titles

This Time Around

Dire's Club

Vortex

The Crazy Yates | A Christmas Novella